The Red Hollow

Also by Natalie Marlow

Needless Alley

THE RED HOLLOW

NATALIE MARLOW

BASKERVILLE
An imprint of JOHN MURRAY

First published in Great Britain in 2024 by Baskerville
An imprint of John Murray (Publishers)

1

Copyright © Natalie Marlow 2024

A CIP catalogue record for this title is available from the British Library

Hardback ISBN 9781399801843
Trade Paperback ISBN 9781399801850
ebook ISBN 9781399801874

Typeset in Bembo by Hewer Text UK Ltd, Edinburgh
Printed and bound in Great Britain by Clays Ltd, Elcograf S.p.A.

John Murray policy is to use papers that are natural, renewable and
recyclable products and made from wood grown in sustainable forests.
The logging and manufacturing processes are expected to conform
to the environmental regulations of the country of origin.

Carmelite House
50 Victoria Embankment
London EC4Y 0DZ

www.johnmurraypress.co.uk

John Murray Press, part of Hodder & Stoughton Limited
An Hachette UK company

To the dancing men.

The Eternal Female groan'd; it was heard all over the Earth:
Albion's coast is sick silent; the American meadows faint.

William Blake, *A Song of Liberty*

Day One

I

Thursday, 1 February 1934

William stood near the office window, tea tray in hand, and stared out onto Needless Alley. It was not quite eight o'clock, and Birmingham was bathed in a mucky morning light. February was a short but cruel month: a time of itching, preparatory greyness, with the whole world poised for something to bloom. It was only twenty-eight days until March, and yet burgeoning spring, with its daffodils in Cannon Hill Park and city dawn chorus of sparrows and pigeons, seemed far away.

Outside, two women teetered along a pavement slick with ice. The brims of their hats pulled fashionably over their eyes, and the collars of their coats drawn up against the chill air, William only recognised them as the shopgirls from the neighbouring Maison Chapeaux when the plump one craned her neck and flashed him a pretty smile. William balanced the tea tray on the corner of his desk, managed a tentative wave, and noticed how his shoulders ached from lack of sleep.

William had read through the night. A foolish act at his age, but he'd borrowed a book from Boots Library and was due to return it. The book, an account of German fascism, was full of chill, dispassionate detail on rising militarism, and university departments dedicated to creating poison gas, and rampant anti-Semitism fuelled by the popular press. William had woken, gritty-eyed, after a few hours' sleep to the dark of a winter morning, knowing his fresh understanding of world politics had done nothing but sour his stomach.

He turned away from the window and cleared some of the detritus from his desk, so the tea things were no longer precariously balanced. And there he sat, waiting for Phyll and the start of their daily routine, a comforting, if unprofitable, round of tea drinking, smoking, trawling through the daily papers, and hoping the telephone might ring.

William didn't have to wait long. Soon, he heard the familiar click of the Yale lock, the sound of Phyll's soft, quick tread on the staircase, and the clatter of his office door. There she stood, in the doorway, smart in dark overcoat and trilby. Ruddy-cheeked, she was laden with both the newspapers and breakfast – bacon rolls from the café near her digs. 'This place stinks like a navvy's armpit.' She wrinkled her nose and moved towards the desk. 'Open the window and let in some air before we choke to death.'

'I suppose it is a bit ripe in here.' William tipped the contents of the overflowing ashtrays, and the greasy remnants of the previous night's supper, into the wastepaper basket, but his shame-fuelled attempt at tidying up only served to disturb, and intensify, the stench. And so he did as he was told, opening the window a crack, propping the sash with a ratted copy of the *News of the World*. He sniffed decorously at his shirt. Clean on yesterday, he would pass muster, just. 'We've done nothing but smoke like chimneys and eat chips since the New Year. If we don't get a bit of honest toil soon, we'll fall into ruin.' He returned to his desk, and then lifted the lid

4

from the teapot, inspecting the state of the brew. 'Shall I be mother?'

'Have you heard nothing from Mr Shirley?' Phyll glanced at the silent telephone, placed the newspapers and rolls on William's newly cleared, if not clean, desk, and took a seat. 'I do prefer to take my tea with lemon, Billy.'

'You'll be demanding petits fours next.' William handed her a cup of black tea. 'Shifty's still got the hump over the Morton business, but he'll come round. Holding grudges is bad for business. We must give him time, though. I did hurt him in a very tender spot.'

'His wallet?' she asked.

'Indeed.'

Since he and Phyll began their partnership, they had worked the sum of two cases. An errant husband found in the tender embrace of a buxom neighbour, and a lady bookkeeper, who had absconded with charity funds, discovered living in Bournemouth with a retired games mistress. Business was slow, and would continue to be so until Shifty Shirley, Birmingham's most pragmatic man of law, was back on side.

William reached for his bacon roll, peered beneath the bread, took a bite, and flicked through a copy of the *Birmingham Post*. 'Still up for the pictures tonight?' he asked. '*King Kong* is on at the Select.'

'No, thank you. I can't seem to get behind this giant marauding ape you're so wild for.' Phyll opened *Picturegoer Magazine* and ignored her bacon roll. 'You know what I like. German Expressionism, light comedy with plenty of dancing girls, gangster flicks, or pictures starring Fredric March. I find everything else is unbearable.'

'What about *Flying Down to Rio*?' William licked bacon grease from his fingertips. 'They strap the dancers to the wings of an aeroplane and none of the girls are wearing brassieres.'

'You seem terribly well-informed.'

'I made a study of the poster when I was hanging around the lobby of the Odeon last Friday. I had nothing better to do since you'd ditched me.' Immediately, William regretted the dig. Phyll had already apologised for standing him up. He picked at his friendships like a child worrying a scab. It was a bad habit, and it had thrown Phyll into a cool silence. William broke it. 'I'm sorry,' he said. 'Having no work is getting on my nerves. Christ, if things don't pick up, I might have to go back to clerking, and I'm too old for all that adding-machine bullshit.'

'Thirty-six is hardly geriatric.'

'No one wants a middle-aged office boy. It's embarrassing.'

'What else can you do?' she asked. 'I mean, what other work experience do you have?' There was something of the schoolmistress about her tone, but William chose to ignore it.

'I was a decent soldier, I suppose.' William added an extra sugar lump to his tea and watched it dissolve into the brew. 'But there's no way I can go back into the army. I've got flat feet, and I'm too knackered to fight another war. I might write a stern letter to Herr Hitler and tell him to fuck off out of it.' He glanced at Phyll's uneaten breakfast – a waste. 'Besides, there's the baby to consider. Queenie might be the richest unwed mother in Ladywood, but I want to stay alive and be a proper dad.'

In truth, William and Queenie had never talked about how they would care for their child. William associated his fatherhood with the terrible events of the previous summer and had, until now, let Queenie rule. However, he also knew that if he didn't assert himself soon, his relationship with his son would devolve into that of indulgent, if infrequent, visits where he would behave like some nervous bachelor uncle. Tomorrow, at his son's christening, William knew he would play little to no part, but he abhorred the idea of being on the sidelines of his own child's life. His every instinct raged against it.

'Look, Billy, I've found just the tonic to make you feel young again. The divine Marlene, double spread.' Phyll placed the open magazine flat on William's desk and prodded Dietrich's creamy décolletage with such force William thought the star might bruise. 'Isn't she splendid? So very stylish. She has *it* in buckets. I don't believe I shall ever get over seeing her in *Morocco*. What a film.'

'I wish she'd come to Birmingham and lead me astray. That would take my mind off war. Me and Marlene indulging in a bit of *Entente Cordiale*.'

'Ladies first, Billy. Ladies first.'

Outside, the distant hoot of factory sirens called the day shift into work. The draught from the open window caught the back of his neck. William wanted it shut, preferring a cosy fug, but Phyll was a fresh-air fiend. 'Here's a story just for you.' He rattled the newspaper in Phyll's direction. 'Your lot are at it again.'

'Sapphists?' She didn't look up from her *Picturegoer*. 'Have we formed a political party? If we're marching, I do hope our shirts are a nice lavender stripe.'

'No, nudists.'

'I'm not a nudist. I simply appear naked in the cause of art.'

Phyll had recently taken up life modelling at the art school. The bohemian milieu suited her personality, and baring all to a bunch of budding commercial artists paid the rent.

'Listen to this.' William began to read aloud, grinning. '*The cult of nudism is spreading to the Midlands.*'

'Spreading? How vulgar.' Phyll returned his smile, happy to play the game. 'It's a wonder such filth got past the copy editor.'

'It gets better.' William continued. '*The cult of nudism*—'

'Did you say *cult*?'

'I did indeed.' He shot Phyll a music-hall wink. '*The cult of nudism, firmly established in Germany and other Continental countries, is rapidly gaining followers in England with at least ten thousand believers in this country. There has been a practising colony near Coventry for some time. Plans are well advanced for the establishment of a camp at Four Oaks, Sutton Coldfield, next season.*' William took another bite of his bacon roll and shivered at the blast of February air hitting the back of his neck. 'It's not natural. Not even in Coventry. What are the people of Sutton Coldfield thinking? I'd rather get rickets.'

'You are quite bandy-legged.'

'No, I'm not.' He flipped over the page, making small, greasy smudges on the newsprint with his fingers. 'That northern bank job has gone from bad to worse.'

'Is Stoke-on-Trent in the north?' she asked.

'Stoke-on-Trent is like Camelot; no one truly knows where it is.'

'Staffordshire.' Phyll yawned. 'And that's a Midlands county.'

'The coppers finally found the lady bank clerk. Dead in a ditch outside of Lichfield. Christ.' William placed his copy of the *Birmingham Post* on top of Marlene Dietrich, covering her louche, Teutonic glamour with a grainy photograph of an English rose, all mousy brown and respectably pretty. 'Poor kid had been there for months. I feel for the parents. It was a frozen drainage ditch, you know, in a farmer's field. She was under the ice. The coppers had to use a pickaxe to get her out.

The ice must've preserved her body, though. They say she was raped and then beaten to death.'

'These newspaper reports, they seem so prurient. I wonder how many copies this poor woman's death has sold. She looks so kind and happy. The sort of girl who'd befriend the outcasts at school.' Phyll reached for the newspaper, peered at the photograph, and let out a great sigh of exhaustion. 'A woman goes to work in the morning, safe, boring, conventional work, and by the end of the day, she is raped and murdered. For all our talk of equality of the sexes, modernity, rationalism . . . Oh God, it's horrific. It's the twentieth century, and we're still not safe.' Phyll looked up at him, her honest eyes wide under her thick, unfashionable brows. 'Why do men do it?'

'Because they want to, and because they like it, and because other men let them.' This was the truth, plain and simple. A pause came, akin to a two-minutes' silence, and William used it to think about his dead.

Phyll placed her hand on his shoulder and squeezed, in a brief, but comforting, contact. William's aching muscles relaxed at her touch. 'Did you see this about the necklace?' She pointed to a line of newsprint further down the page, and then handed the *Birmingham Post* back to William, whistling through her teeth.

William shook his head, and began, once more, to read aloud. '*Police now believe the gang are not professional jewel thieves and intended to steal five hundred guineas kept in the safe deposit box. Our Northern Correspondent . . .*' He nodded to Phyll. 'Stoke is north, then. *Our Northern Correspondent,*' William repeated, '*can confirm the necklace of sixty flawless blue-pink pearls and thirty rubies which was stolen in the heist is worth twenty thousand pounds. The anonymous owner of the safe deposit box has offered one thousand pounds as reward for the return of the necklace.*'

The return of the necklace. Bringing the murderers to justice was immaterial to the man who offered the reward. William wondered why women didn't go on the rampage at each outrage their sex suffered. He smiled, thinking of Queenie. She once abducted a notorious pimp and left him naked and trussed up like a loin of pork, rope cutting into his flabby, pale skin, outside a police station on the Coventry Road. If Queenie was the future of womanhood, every misbehaving fucker with a pair of bollocks ought to watch his back.

However, one thousand pounds would see him and Phyll right for a year, giving them breathing space to establish themselves as respectable private detectives. Then, of course, there would be the publicity. Perhaps he should get his arse up to Stoke-on-Trent and have a sniff about. William shook the thought from his head. This wasn't the pictures. Who did he think he was, Bulldog Drummond? He had no connections in Stoke. Besides, he was fated to be universally hated by all coppers and most journalists – the men he would need on side if he was even to begin solving the case.

The shrill, insistent call of the telephone interrupted William's hesitant dreams of wealth and fame. He stared at the machine, frowning, as if momentarily unsure how to deal with the thing. It was Phyll who answered, her manner formal, professional. 'Garrett and Hall, private enquiry agents.' Her slim body tensed at the male voice, an inaudible hum to William, at the other end of the line, and then she nodded sharply, twice. 'Yes, speaking. Yes, I understand. Yes, of course.' Perching on the edge of the desk, handset cradled between her shoulder and chin, she scribbled flowers on the blotting pad in thick, deep pencil marks. 'What do you mean by an incident? . . . Has Freddy regressed in his treatment? . . . What exactly happened and when?' With each question came another flower. Soon there would be a garden. 'You don't want to give details over the telephone. I understand, yes. We'll come right away. Right away, Dr Moon.' Phyll dropped her pencil and glanced at her watch. 'Yes, we'll be with you within the hour.' William heard the decisive click of the call ringing off. Phyll replaced the handset on its cradle, her once ruddy cheeks now pale. 'That was the psychiatrist who runs the residential home where my brother lives.' She ran her finger over the blotting-paper garden and bit her lip. 'There's been some kind of problem, an intruder. The doctor wants us to investigate.'

'Is he rich?' asked William. 'Can he afford us?'

'Oh yes, Billy.' Phyll seemed suddenly closed off to him, as if she were protecting some vulnerable core of herself. 'He's quite wealthy. I believe all our family money has gone in paying his fees.'

2

Before them, Watling Street, a flat strip of near traffic-free road, glittered like polished pewter in the morning light. Phyll drove in silence, and her lightly vibrating nerves filled the air of the Austin with a tetchy, headache-inducing thrum. She sped them past ugly country. Strange, pinkish ploughland, iron-hard with hoar frost, bordered by horse chestnut trees stark in winter black, flanked each side of the road. William watched the circling crows gather above their high, tangled nests. Then, just ahead, he saw a road sign. 'Red Hollow,' he said, pointing. 'We're nearly there.'

'I know where I'm going, William.'

She was testy with him, and schoolmarmish. William's hackles rose. '*Billy*, for fuck's sake,' he said. 'You know I go by Billy. You're not my mother.' He glanced over at her small frame, stiff with tension, and was ashamed of both his temper and his language. 'I'm sorry,' he said. 'That wasn't very friendly of me.'

Phyll flicked the indicator and turned another right. The Austin bumped along a narrow country lane rutted with age. He sensed her considering their spat, and of how far to take umbrage. 'I accept your apology, dearest,' she said finally. 'Maybe we should go to the pictures tonight. After we've finished here, of course. I could do with a bit of glamour.'

At first, Red Hollow appeared to be just a few brick cottages hugging the roadside, their bow fronts leaning slightly forward, as if poised to make a run for it. Then, the country opened out into a patchwork of meadow, scarred with centuries of work, and edged with ribbon-like drainage ditches, blackly frozen. And beyond the pasture, a river, no more than a brook, its sinuous meander partly outlined by willow and spindling beech, led to ill-managed woodland that hunkered dark in a distant dip in the land.

Suddenly, Phyll swung the car a sharp left. She slowed down, and they followed a muddy trackway – splashing, almost immediately, through a wide, shallow ford – until they reached the entrance to Red Hollow Hall. It was flanked by open wrought-iron gates so mournfully elaborate that William was reminded of those of a municipal cemetery. Then they drove down a twisting avenue, bordered, not with the usual country-house limes, but with oaks. Thickly ancient, their curved, low-slung branches skimmed the frosted grass of the parkland, and sheep, fat in lamb, gathered in threes and fives under their bare canopies.

Red Hollow Hall was not the kind of house a child would draw. A brick-built confusion of gables, doors, small leaded windows, not one architectural feature was symmetrical to the other. One corner of the manor house was fortified with stone the colour of rusted iron and crenellated like a castle. A huge bare wisteria clung, parasitical, to the frontage, like the skeleton of some hideous foreign spider.

To the left of the hall, a church squatted so low in a hollow that William only saw two-thirds of the tower. Built of soft red stone undulating with age, it was topped with an incongruous weathervane, in the form of a mermaid, which swung and clattered in the uncertain breeze.

Phyll parked the Austin hard against the porch. She sat, not moving, deeply breathing and reluctant, as if readying herself for the day. William got out first and opened the driver's door like a gentleman. Still she held on to the steering wheel, her knuckles tight white with the grip. 'Come on, Phyll,' he said. 'It's colder than a witch's tit out here, and we need to make a start.' Phyll nodded, stepping out of the motor car in accepting silence.

William took a few steps towards the main door. To the left of the porch hung a painted black and white sign. He read out loud, his finger hovering over a brass electric doorbell. '*Red Hollow Hall. Residential Treatment for Alcoholism, Drug Addiction and Depressive Neurosis. Resident Medical Superintendent Dr. H. E. Moon. MA, MD, DPM, MRCPsych.*' William laughed and turned to Phyll. 'Half of Birmingham could do with a bit of residential treatment.' She did not laugh but stood craning her neck, peering about the corner of the hall as if expecting someone. William lit a cigarette, and as he did so, a sickly feeling of déjà vu shivered through his veins. He inhaled deeply, letting the tobacco work its magic, and gathered himself. 'I know where I am,' he said. 'I remember this place.'

'What?' Phyll was shrill. 'Have you been here before?'

He sensed her thinly stretched nerves tauten further. 'Only when I was a kid. The Coventry Canal runs through the grounds.' William mustered a breezy reassurance. 'Me and Queenie hauled coal along here. The house is much smaller than I remember. She always said it looked like a picture-book castle.' He flinched at the half-truth, and at his own self-deception, for it was not only Queenie's fantasy, but Ronnie's too. A survival instinct, he thought. Erase Ronnie out of history or flounder under the weight of gut-churning betrayal. William gathered himself by assessing the topography. Soon, he found his bearings.

Beyond the ancient copse of woodland, and to the south, loomed a slag heap. Like a large black burial mound, it hung threatening and powerful against the white winter sky. Flanking it were the cast-iron workings of the pithead, and the distant factory chimneys which coughed out clouds of dark smoke. 'Look,' he pointed. 'Quarrying, coal, brickworks, I remember this town well. Small but rich. Rich in the stuff.'

'What stuff?'

William scuffed the toe of his shoe against the gravel drive and unearthed the natural red soil. 'Clay and coal. They call it the Warwickshire Thick.'

The Warwickshire Thick. Edward Morton had once owned a good chunk of it. William couldn't shake off his hatred for the Blackshirted bastard, just as he couldn't stop loving Clara, Morton's wife. She must have spent her childhood in some village, or nearby town, built to house the men who unearthed it. William knew he would never make the pilgrimage to his former lover's birthplace, because she had never named it in the short, wondrous time they had spent together. His mouth became acidic, metallic. He felt it in his body – the sad, strange suffering of grief. This, at least, he understood.

Phyll squinted at the slag heap. 'I've always thought it rather spoils the view.'

William was holding his breath. He exhaled, letting it go, and watched the smoke trail from his mouth. 'Capitalism does that,' he said.

'Promptness is a wonderful virtue, Phyll Hall.' William heard him before he saw him. He had the voice of a great actor, educated but not without character, and William thought he detected something of a Cornish burr. William turned to see a tall redheaded man in his late forties limp towards them. His face was so deeply tanned it spoke of

15

decades of outdoor work in warmer country than the middle of England. He wore an army greatcoat, darkened with age, and carried, quite casually in his right hand, a pistol.

'Dr Moon,' said Phyll. 'How terribly stealthy you are.' She tilted her pale face upwards and at an angle, and the doctor bent to kiss the proffered cheek. William raised his eyebrows at Phyll's unusual display of girlishness.

'It's good of you both to come.' The doctor turned to William and held out a gloveless hand in formal greeting. 'Mr Garrett, I presume.' William accepted the handshake. 'Dr Henry Moon. This is my place, which sounds very grand, I know. However, it's a small operation, as I'm sure Phyll has already told you.' Phyll had spoken little of Dr Moon, but William nonetheless nodded, and then glanced pointedly at the doctor's revolver. Dr Moon smiled. 'Rather handy for country living, Mr Garrett. May we talk as I work?' He waved the handgun towards the patch of woodland, and William feared for the lives of its circling crows. 'There is a great deal to do today, and we have limited staff at the moment.'

'Yes, do let's talk and walk. I need to stretch my legs.' Phyll pulled the brim of her trilby down hard against her forehead and set off with Dr Moon.

William paused for a moment before joining them. The church weathervane to his left clattered once more, and a sharp easterly wind pricked his skin like a terrible foreboding. He shivered at the exposure and ran across iron-hard ground, white with rime, to join Phyll and the doctor.

Together, they walked towards what looked to William like a jungle of bare branches, smack in the middle of the pasture. As if he had read William's thoughts, Dr Moon turned to him, saying, 'It's part of the ancient Forest of Arden, Mr Garrett.

Wonderful to have it on one's land. I use it as an imaginative resource for my patients. One must always be amazed at the healing qualities of our native woodland.'

'*Here shall he see no enemy but winter and rough weather.*' William spoke and then winced. Why must he display his knowledge like a peacock unfurling his tail feathers?

Dr Moon laughed. 'You quote Shakespeare, Mr Garrett. You'll do. You'll do very well indeed.'

They crossed a muddy boundary ditch and into the wood, walking a thin path of fallen leaves, single file, through holly thick with red berries, their leaves softly curled, and ancient clusters of alders, their dark, fissured bark wet with moss.

'How's Freddy?' Phyll spoke, finally.

'Oh, recovering, and quite well, considering,' said Dr Moon. 'Can you hear the robin?'

The little bird trilled a big-voiced, territorial call.

'Very pretty,' said Phyll. 'Is Freddy sedated?'

'My dear Phyll, there was really no need. Freddy is quite well, considering.'

'Dr Moon, what exactly happened last night?' Her voice was thin and nervy over the music of the birdsong. 'You were so vague over the telephone.'

'Poor Freddy had a frightening experience, that's all.' He turned towards her, pausing as if gathering his thoughts. 'He's quite alright, but nonetheless, I can't help but think someone is out to terrify my men.'

'Your men?' asked William. It was a curious phrase, rooted in army life and all its strange, paternalistic benevolence.

'The men under my care.' Dr Moon ran his fingers through his faded red hair. 'I want you to know I'm a man of science. I consider matters of the supernatural to be human experience we cannot yet explain through scientific process. We

17

have only just begun to explore the power of the human mind—'

'Supernatural,' Phyll interrupted. 'My God. Dr Moon, you told me you had an intruder.' Her lips were a hard, pink line.

Communication between an enquiry agent and client was often coy. A fan dance of meaning with each pertinent fact revealed in frustrating slowness. Most people endured endless embarrassments and self-recriminations at their situation before finally, in desperation, calling in a detective. William, an old hand, knew direct questioning was in order. It saved time and was kind.

'Do you believe there is a strange, or uncanny, element to the nature of your intruder?' he asked.

The doctor nodded, but then said, 'I do not believe in the supernatural.'

'But your patients do.' William reached for his cigarettes, lit one, took a drag.

'Yes, Mr Garrett, yes.' The doctor's voice held a note of panicked relief. 'And after Freddy's unfortunate experience, I think it's time this nonsense stopped. That's why I telephoned through to Phyll. It's not a matter for the police, because I don't believe what's happening is strictly illegal. Although if the intruder is an outsider, it is, of course, against the law ...' The doctor's voice trailed off. 'The police would consider it breaking and entering, I suppose.'

'But what exactly has the intruder been up to, Dr Moon?' Phyll retrieved a notebook and pencil from the pocket of her overcoat. In their short time as partners, she had become the organised one, the notetaker, the bill payer, the diary keeper. She had once told William she was ashamed of her skill at shorthand, because it spoke of an unhappy stint at a London secretarial school. 'Please start from the beginning and do try to be clear. More scientific, if you will.'

Dr Moon focused his eyes on Phyll's pencil and began. 'It all started in early November. There were strange noises in the night, pattering footsteps, banging doors in the attics, unearthly moans, that sort of thing. I'm afraid I put the men's complaints down to our Victorian plumbing; it whines and clatters in the most dreadful way.' The doctor closed his pale blue eyes, in an act of concentrated recall, William supposed. 'But then the intruder became destructive and quite sinister. We have a fine old library in the hall, and I woke one morning to find it in complete disarray. Books off the shelves, valuable, ancient books, spines bent, pages torn, all on the floor.' William winced at the violence. 'It seemed such a vindictive and pointless act. We made good the best we could, and I sat vigil for a few nights but nothing else occurred. Then, I found a strange carving in the panelling of the patients' sitting room. That's the old drawing room of the manor. It was pretty, like a flower, and puzzling rather than threatening, but the patterns kept appearing, and a few were surrounded by burn marks, as if our intruder had been careless with their cigarette.'

William threw his fag into the mulched leaves of the wood-land path.

'And then came the phalluses.'

'Did you say *phalluses*?' William coughed out a guffaw.

'Childish, I know. I was angry about them. Again, they were carved into the wood panelling, and the lintels and doors. Freddy had to chisel them out and make good. One of our daily women found one, you see. The poor woman was disgusted and handed in her notice. This left us short-handed.' The doctor shook his head, rueful. 'We are always short-handed, I fear.'

Dr Moon turned away from them, resuming his woodland trek, so that William and Phyll had no choice but to follow.

'Finally, there was poor Mr Trent.'

Dr Moon stopped once more, and so suddenly William trod on the back of the man's heels.

'What happened to Mr Trent?' asked Phyll.

'Didn't Freddy tell you?' Dr Moon faced her, blinking, as if only now remembering her presence. 'Trent was a patient, and he died. He'd been in a bad way. Delirium tremens, don't you know, and he had a weak heart. It's not unusual for alcoholics to die from heart attacks. Well, that's what happened. The poor fellow's heart went when he was in the bath, and he drowned. This happened on New Year's Eve. The coroner ruled death by natural causes in January, but by that time, the men had become obsessed and frightened. We need three days' written notice, but a man is free to leave Red Hollow any time he wishes, even if he has been committed. No one here is criminal or dangerous in any way. Ten men have left since Trent's death, and I'm finding it difficult to keep staff. There are only three patients left at the hall, and since Freddy's incident, I fear I may lose the rest. To put it bluntly, the intruder threatens to destroy everything I've worked for, and ruin a place of respite and care for men who so sorely need help.'

William repressed a twitch of irritation. Help. Respite and care. Dr Moon talked as if mollycoddling a few rich nerve cases were tantamount to curing leprosy. 'What exactly are these men so obsessed with?'

'They've got it into their heads that the intruder comes every time it rains. There was a terrible downpour on the night of Trent's death. Our orderly, Mr Brooke, noticed a connection between the visits and the weather and did the unforgivable. He kicked up a fuss about it and blabbed to the men. He'd got the wind up, and I had to be firm with him, reminding him of his duty to the patients. By then, I think, the damage had been done.'

'And is there a connection?' asked William. 'Is this Mr Brooke correct?'

'No. I'm sure the library was ransacked on a dry day. However, we are in a wetland. The very watershed of England. People associate stories of ill omen with strange landscapes and places. It's part of human nature.'

'Dr Moon, you still haven't told me what happened to Freddy,' said Phyll.

'I think Freddy should tell his own story. It will be good for him, and I think good for you, too.' He smiled at them both, a host once more. 'Our destination. The hamlet was named after this place. This is the Red Hollow.'

They stood on the edge of a large and near-perfectly round pond. Water, frozen to a smooth black mirror, reflected the fronds of winter willows bordering its far banks. In the surrounding woodland, bracket fungus, as large and dark as an undertaker's umbrella, hung on the trunks of leggy oaks, and the once green ferns were now stunted dark with frostbite.

'It doesn't look red,' said William. 'The whole place looks black.'

'Look into the pool,' said Dr Moon. 'You'll soon see. It's quite remarkable.'

William did as he was ordered, taking a few tentative steps down the bank, and leaning as far as he dared over the water's surface. At first, he saw only his own pale reflection as a distorted flicker. But yes, Dr Moon was right. Beneath the thick shell of ice, William glimpsed a red clay quivering at the heart of the pond. Suddenly, there came a swift and shadowy surge of muscle. A fish, as slick and heavy as a jungle snake, rising from the muddy depths. William watched the creature's sinuous path until it disappeared into the shadows at the far edge of the pool. How would it feel to be entombed under the ice with such an animal? Unable to escape; the black water filling your lungs; the roots of willows feeling for your flesh in the darkness; the deep, nibbling unknown. 'Christ almighty.' His voice was gruff, oddly dampened in the still, wet air. 'Look at the size of the thing.'

'Are you alright?' Phyll grabbed his right arm, steadying him as he rose from the muddy banks. 'You looked as if you were about to fall.'

'Jesus Christ, there's something funny in the water.' William took a few faltering steps until he faced Dr Moon, who held out a rough hand and dragged him onto the woodland path. 'Some great big bloody fish.'

'Water disturbs you, Mr Garrett?' Dr Moon gave him a curious interrogative look.

William shrugged.

'Billy has a fear of water,' said Phyll. 'He was a canal boatman as a child.'

'I'm alright.' William shrugged once more. 'Phyll's making too much of it. It's no mystery. I can't swim, that's all, and the pond looks deep.'

'Yes, few people can bottom the Red Hollow, and that is, quite naturally, a disturbing thought. However, it makes an excellent bathing place for the men in summer. You must come in summer, Mr Garrett. We'll soon have you swimming, and cure that fear of yours.' Dr Moon's voice had that reassuring tone of dispassionate professionalism adopted by all medical men. William found it irksome. 'The winter makes nature sinister,' he continued. 'I believe it is our atavistic fears and instincts made manifest. Winter is both death and representative of death. In the summer, this place is quite an idyll.'

William said nothing. Death in the Red Hollow seemed absolute. He couldn't imagine its rebirth, a germ of green, spring, or the full flourish of a glorious English summer, and he had no intention of accepting the doctor's invitation for a future, and probably stark-naked, splash about.

'That's what I want, you see. I want this place to remain an absolute idyll.'

And with that, Dr Moon stepped forward, and, aiming his pistol at the Red Hollow, he shot a full round of bullets into the mirror-like ice.

3

Gunfire echoed, and the circling crows cawed in flurried panic, retreating into their nests. The cordite hovered in the winter air, and bile rose to William's throat. There came a slow, eerie creak, as the ice fractured into jagged fissures. He glanced at Phyll, who stood wide-eyed and with her hands at her ears. 'Christ almighty, man, what the bloody hell are you playing at?' William's voice was a shameful, boyish squeak.

Dr Moon smiled, insensitive to their fear and mistrust. 'Shooting at the ice is one of my more amusing winter chores. It saves all that bashing about with rakes and whatnot, and it does one good to let off steam.' His reply was almost jovial. 'We can't have the fish drown, you see. It's just a precaution, but the Red Hollow contains some absolute monsters. We're proud of our coarse fishing. Mr Brooke is a son of the estate and a skilled fisherman. He's teaching our residents the sport.' The doctor turned, and waving his pistol in the air, as a London tour guide might an umbrella, called to them. 'Come, come, let us find Freddy. Come to the church, and then perhaps we'll have coffee.'

They trudged after him, Phyll panting in her attempt to keep up with the doctor's long, uneven strides, and William nursing his fractured nerves. As they neared the church, Dr Moon increased his pace to open a wrought-iron gate, the entrance way to the small graveyard. Then he stepped aside in an act of good manners, allowing both Phyll and William through first.

Here, the grass had not yet thawed, and the fallen berries of a thick-trunked yew seemed like garnets strewn on the white frost. In the distance, he heard the tinny rattle and scrape of the pithead. It seemed so high above him, and remote. William turned to Dr Moon and said, 'We're in another hollow. Isn't it unusual for a church to be built on low ground?'

'I suppose it is,' said Dr Moon. 'But I'm no expert on things ecclesiastical. You should ask Freddy.' He then paused and glanced about him, as if noticing the listing gravestones for the first time. 'Everything about the manor is eccentric. Nothing seems to have been planned with order or purpose in mind. It's all rather organic, I fear.'

'It's anarchy.' Phyll shuddered. 'It's as if they've been buried where they dropped.' She wrinkled her nose at the ancient, uneven ground. 'Why do I always want to wipe my feet after I've been in a graveyard?'

'All flesh is grass,' said William. 'It says so in the Bible, but I don't know if it was meant literally or metaphorically.'

Phyll grimaced at his answer and strode ahead with Dr Moon, while William lingered to read inscriptions. The older graves were of the same stone as the church, their Jacobean carvings of skulls and fat cherubs a baroque memento mori. Nearby, a stark, white marble grave memorialised a Captain Sir Redvers Pike, Bart, of the Royal Warwickshire Regiment. Died in 1921. And beyond the dead soldier were the poignant hummocks of the unmarked paupers' burials.

'Come, Mr Garrett.' Dr Moon beckoned, and then glanced up at the undulating clouds. 'We shall soon be in for snow.'

'No, it's a mackerel sky,' said William. 'It means rain.'

'Oh good God, I hope not.'

The red stone of the church seemed paler, almost pink, in the grey light. Lichen burst in fresh, rubbery roundels on the pointed arches above the porch.

Phyll gazed upward. 'Perpendicular Gothic,' she said. 'A nice survival.'

'You are most definitely Freddy's sister,' said Dr Moon.

'A shared childhood spent in draughty vicarages surrounded by mouldering books,' she said. 'I believe father taught Freddy to read from Pugin's *The True Principles*.'

They stepped into a musty stone porch. Two wooden benches, smoothed with the seats of ages, stood either side of the door. A yellowing notice pinned to the blistered white-wash detailed times of services.

'Freddy will be here, I'm sure of it. It's rather his domain.' Dr Moon took a huge set of keys from the pocket of his greatcoat but appeared to reconsider. He returned them and twisted the cast iron handle on the door to the church. 'Should be open. It's Candlemas Day tomorrow, and the ladies shall be sweeping and garnishing, no doubt.'

'You keep it locked?' asked Phyll.

'It's necessary, I'm afraid. My men need absolute privacy, and we can't have the locals roaming about the grounds as they please. We keep the church open for Sunday services and holy days only.' The heavy door swung open on smooth hinges. 'Red Hollow is a small parish, and our parson also has the living for neighbouring Whittingford. It's one of those villages that's become a suburb of a larger town. The old squire sold the manor and hundreds of new houses were built on the land. These young chaps who work in the Coventry car factories earn high wages and want all the mod cons for their wives. I suppose you know the kind of thing I'm describing?'

William nodded. 'I've been in Red Hollow for seven years, and since my arrival, Whittingford has become unrecognisable. Little remains untouched by the developer's machinery.'

William thought of the neglected graveyard. 'Doesn't it cause ill-feeling? The locking of the church, I mean?'

'No, not that I know of. The regularly devout walk to Whittingford, but even country folk are less superstitious since the war. If you can call the people of Red Hollow country folk. The town is coming for them. There's no doubt about that.'

Inside the church, the air was thick with the scent of oil heaters. In the knave, motes of dust danced in the warm glow of lamplight, but the chancel was muddy with winter shadow. The stone walls were not plain but decorated in an Arts and Crafts medievalism of consumptive angels playing brass trumpets, and a motto in Gothic script, declaring: *Therefore God give thee of the dew of heaven, and the fatness of the earth, and plenty of corn and wine.*

William looked for Phyll's brother but instead saw a woman. She stood beneath the pulpit, snipping the stems of white chrysanthemums, arranging them in a large tin vase with efficient sparsity. They walked towards her, and she stopped her work, pausing, a little wary at the sound of their footsteps, a leggy bloom still in her hand.

'What can you get in February?' It was a rhetorical question and directed at Dr Moon. 'Florists are so expensive and there is nothing in the garden.' A tall woman, she was patrician-slim beneath her sage-green tweeds. Her blonde hair was pulled into a plaited coil at the base of her neck. As he neared her, William caught a whiff of dank vegetation and beeswax.

'You could try silk, or even wax.' It was a typically practical suggestion from Phyll, whom William now knew to be the daughter of a parish priest. He smiled. Despite Phyll's bohemianism, her clerical parentage did not surprise him greatly.

The woman regarded Phyll with feigned confusion. 'I don't believe we've been introduced.' She looked at Dr Moon.

'Oh, yes. How remiss of me.' Dr Moon gestured to William and Phyll. 'Lady Pike, this is Mr William Garrett and Phyll Hall.' There was a momentary pause. 'The manor of Red Hollow belongs to Lady Pike,' he added. 'The men and I are simply the current stewards of the house.' There was a forced, magnanimous tone to Dr Moon's voice which William felt was not unlost on Lady Pike.

'Well, Miss Hall,' began Lady Sabrina Pike, her voice as brittle as ice.

'It's just Phyll,' William and Phyll interjected in unison, so that Phyll's name echoed as a plainsong in the perfect medieval acoustics of the church.

Lady Pike smiled at their interruption. 'Silk has been mooted before by one or two of the more modern parishioners. However, I simply cannot bear the ersatz. And I find wax flowers rather redolent of Brighton guesthouses.'

William was sure Lady Sabrina Pike's slim feet had never crossed the threshold of a Brighton guesthouse, but he appreciated her imagination, nonetheless.

'Foliage, Lady Pike, seasonal foliage. Plenty of greenery, and the like,' said Dr Moon.

'It is not Christmas, Dr Moon. White flowers are traditional for Candlemas, and the village does expect chrysanthemums. It's what one should use the hothouse for, I think.' It seemed to be a pointed remark. The woman's title, her self-confident authority, generations of Pikes in the graveyard, she was county through and through, and Dr Moon was on her patch. Queenie once told William the English gentry were just well-settled French gangsters. They intermarried, played nasty for their money and, above all, kept a closed shop.

Dr Moon smiled. 'Is Mr Hall about?'

Lady Pike pointed towards the shadowy chancel. 'Choir stalls. He's blessing them with his undoubted gifts. Mr Hall,' she called. 'Dr Moon is here.' She glanced at William and Phyll. 'With some people.' And then Lady Pike turned back to her flowers, snipping at them with a meaningful, accurate violence.

A tall man in shirtsleeves appeared from behind the rood screen and cast a spindling shadow on the plain stone floor. 'Hello,' he cried, waving to Phyll, and leaping down the steps towards them in three leggy strides. 'Hello, my darling, it's so good of you to come.' He gave the assembled company a nervous grin of pleasure, but his focus was on Phyll. He bent to kiss her head, pulling her into his chest, and interlacing his long, sensitive fingers about her shoulders. The embrace lasted no more than ten seconds, and yet William averted his eyes, feeling as if he had witnessed a private act of grief or love. Finally, Freddy released Phyll, saying, 'Come over and see the choir stalls. They're fourteenth century, canopied and quite rare.' He spoke as a child showing a treasure, proudly tentative. 'But I found something special behind them.'

'Freddy, are you alright?' asked Phyll, her voice a gentle whisper.

'Dr Moon says I'll be quite myself in no time. I'm not sad or frightened, old thing. I'm simply over-excited.' Freddy waved his fluttering nervous fingers above his head. 'I am, perhaps, a little high. It will pass. All things shall be well, darling girl.'

Phyll came alive at her brother's reassurance. 'Are we about to see the lurid imaginations of some medieval apprentice? I'm hoping for filthy and profane graffiti.'

'You don't know how warm you are, darling.' Freddy turned away from his sister, stepped forward and shook William's hand. 'Freddy Hall. Thank you for being so good to Phyll.'

'There's nothing to thank me for.' William recognised a fellow nerve case in the slim, fragile man before him. Freddy's near-normality was a mask he'd put on for Phyll's benefit. 'Phyll is good to me. I wouldn't be without her.'

'Oh, Phyll is a remarkable person.' Freddy beckoned towards Dr Moon and Lady Pike, raising his voice slightly. 'Please, all of you, I want to show you the choir stalls.'

They followed Freddy through the latticework of the rood screen and into the chancel. On the eastern wall, stood an altar backed with an elaborate Victorian reredos. A Gothic and gilded crucifixion, William hovered before it and shivered, resisting the urge to genuflect. To his left, and in deep shadow, an alabaster knight slept cosy in a niche. A pious Pike praying, a sword by his side, and a spaniel at his feet. Didn't these blokes usually have their missus with them? Not this chap. He was single in death if not in life.

'Down here, Mr Garrett. You've walked too far.'

William turned at the sound of Freddy's voice, tripped over a small black cat sleeping on a discarded overcoat, saw an adze and chisel, smelt fresh sawdust, and then noticed a choir stall that had been pulled away from the whitewashed wall of the church. Freddy lit its base with a large electric torch.

'How could I have missed you?' he asked. The choir stall was tall, and beneath its elaborate canopy were paintings of sinuous bearded men, each one robed and haloed. William thought them to be the Apostles. 'They're remarkable, but didn't the Puritans paint over things like this?'

'My ancestors were not, by nature, iconoclasts but conservationists,' said Lady Pike.

'Well, I'm conserving them as best I can,' said Freddy. 'The painting is still quite good, but years of floor washing has rotted the feet. I'm replacing them with new oak.'

William glanced down and saw thick slices of golden oak dovetailed into the ancient black wood at the foot of each stall.

'If it wasn't for Mr Hall's undoubted skill, much of the church would've gone to rack and ruin. The parson —' Lady Pike paused for what William believed to be dramatic effect — 'is an evangelical from Wolverhampton. He considers church upkeep an unnecessary idolatry. I believe he would prefer to preach in a Nissen hut.'

Phyll grinned and then laughed. William sensed her warm to Lady Pike.

'It's no laughing matter, Phyll.' Freddy's mood darkened suddenly. 'The man is a vandal. He aims to whitewash over the Pre-Raphaelite wall paintings and rip out the reredos. It's taking all of Lady Pike's strength of will to stop his vile sacrilege. And what is worse, I don't believe the man has an ounce of Christian charity in him. All those endless sermons on thrift, blaming the poor for their own poverty. Last week, forty-five minutes of tub-thumping about modern girls and their wantonness, and with not a single word to the horny old goats who chase them. A man of God, but with nothing of God in him.'

'That's enough, Freddy,' said Dr Moon. 'That's quite enough, old chap.'

However, Freddy wasn't finished.

'When he found out old Jane Marsh visited the Spiritualist church in Milby, he quoted Exodus to her in the street. *Thou shalt not suffer a witch to live.* Mr Brooke told me the poor woman was so terrified she's hardly left her cottage since. But that was what he wanted – don't you see? The Reverend Andrews takes pleasure in putting the fear of God in people, but not the love. Never the love.'

'Darling, do tell me what you've found.' Phyll moved forward and touched her brother's arm.

'*Mercy, pity, peace and love,*' Freddy muttered under his breath. William recognised it as a quotation from a poem by Blake. 'I can't bear these cheap fanatics and the harm they do.' Freddy's face twitched into a violent contortion; it lasted for a second, and yet William felt he'd witnessed an accidental flourish of a normally well-buried damage.

'Don't leave us all in suspense, Freddy,' said Phyll. 'Show me your graffiti. After all that speechifying, I'm hoping for nothing less than a Sheela-na-gig.'

Freddy blinked at his sister, swaying – lanky, dreamy – and grinned. Phyll's voice had the effect of bringing Freddy back from the brink. But of what? Religious or artistic mania, genuine moral outrage, or a flaring, bitter hatred for Red Hollow's evangelical parson? 'Phyll, you don't know how right you are.' He lifted his electric torch, shining its white, unnatural beam down towards the rear of the choir stall. 'I want you to look here,' he said. 'On the bottom of the stall, nearest to us.' He passed the torch to William. 'You first, Mr Garrett, kneel down. Then, you'll soon see.'

William hunkered down on his heels and squinted. Beneath the cobwebs, which hung like strands of tattered bridal lace from the blackened wood, was the carving of a figure. About twelve or thirteen inches tall, it was etched deep into the oak. The upper part of her body was that of a curvaceous woman, but her lower half splayed out into a monstrous double tail as feathery and threatening as the tentacles of a jellyfish. She held a mirror and comb, as if challenging the viewer to contradict her beauty, and her hair, flowing like pondweed about the curve of her scales, did nothing to cover the immodesty of her bare, round breasts.

But it was the creature's face which drew William's gaze. Her eyes were wide and staring, and her full, pouting lips formed a strange, alluring grimace around a cavity, an oval-shaped hole carved deep in the dark oak. Around which, displayed in flagrant grotesquery, were the razor-sharp teeth of a predatory fish.

William reached forward, overcome by a temptation to put his finger in her mouth and wiggle it.

'Please don't do that, Mr Garrett. The opening is very fragile.'

At Freddy's voice, William snatched his hand back like a guilty child, stood and shuddered. 'It's a mermaid,' he said. 'A fanged mermaid, of all the bloody God-awful things. I've never seen anything like it before. It's carved into the back of the pew, and it wasn't done recently. Hundreds of years old, I reckon.'

'Yes, yes.' William handed the torch to Freddy, and the man's face became uplit like an actor in a horror film, seeming, in that moment, at once innocent and fanatical. 'Yes, I've found the Mermaid of Red Hollow, and she's wonderful.'

4

Each member of the party took their turn in examining the mermaid in a reverential silence, like medieval pilgrims viewing the relics of some saint. When the observations were over, they huddled together in a conclave and spoke in whispers.

'When did you find her, Freddy?' asked Dr Moon.

'Last night, after tea.' Freddy had lost some of his fanaticism and seemed sheepish.

'I see.'

'It's remarkable,' said Phyll. 'Have you known anything like it?'

'There's one in Zennor,' said Dr Moon.

'And a few other English churches,' said Freddy. 'It's not unusual to have pagan totems as part of church architecture. Old gods die hard.'

'And how old do you think it is?' asked Lady Pike.

'I believe it pre-dates the story,' said Freddy. 'That's why it's so important.'

'What story?' asked William.

'Could it have been faked?' asked Dr Moon.

'It would be difficult, but possible. However, the cobwebs and woodworm are quite genuine. If it is a fake, it's a very old fake.' Freddy paused. 'By that, I mean it hasn't been done within the last hundred years or so. I'd bet my life on that.'

'Please don't say such things.' The electric surge of Phyll's nerves appeared once more. 'It's flippant.'

'Mummy, I have the snowdrops.'

The girl stood a few steps away from them in the chancel. William found it difficult to assess her age, but she was perhaps twelve or even thirteen years old. Dressed in a winter coat too small for her gangling adolescent height, ruddy-cheeked and redheaded, she had none of her mother's cool blondeness. She carried a wicker trug filled with greenery, gardening tools – trowel, fork, a knife – and snowdrops. February rarities of liturgical whiteness, their muddied roots remained intact.

'Well done, my dear.' Lady Pike stepped forward and took the trug from her daughter. 'We shall plant them in pots and place them near the pulpit.' She pointed to the sparse vase of chrysanthemums below the lectern, and said to the adults, as if in apology, 'Everything is rather desultory and pinched. I despair of Puritan parsimony.'

'Where did you get the snowdrops?' Dr Moon smiled at the child. 'They look almost springlike.'

'Near the Red Hollow.' William saw the girl flush. 'It is the very best place for them.'

'Yes, it is.' The doctor nodded in reassurance. 'The Red Hollow is chock-full of life.' He turned towards Phyll and William. 'This is Miss Persephone Pike. Persephone, please meet Mr Garrett and Phyll Hall.'

'I don't know why Daddy lumbered me with such an awful name, and I can't ask him because he's dead.' She glanced at her mother. 'The girls at school call me Percy. I much prefer it.'

'Hello, Percy,' said Phyll. 'When I was at school, all the girls called me Phyll rather than Phyllis. And I stuck with it.'

35

The girl grinned. 'Are you Freddy's sister?'

'I have that honour.'

'He's terribly clever, isn't he?'

'I absolutely agree,' said Phyll, mimicking Percy's beaming adoration. 'Everyone with sense thinks Freddy is the cat's pyjamas.'

Freddy stood to his full height and laughed. 'Steady on, ladies. I shall get a swell head.' He beckoned to the child. 'Percy, do you want to see what I've found?'

'Yes please,' she said, moving towards him. 'What is it?'

'It's a carving of the mermaid,' said Lady Pike. 'Mr Hall believes it to be very old.'

'Oh, is that what you were talking about when I came in?' The girl shook her head, and her smooth brow became furrowed. 'No, I don't think I want to see it. I'm sick of the mermaid. When one is a Pike, one gets her rammed down one's throat, and her story is disgusting. Everything about it is vile and shameful.'

Truthful adolescent passion threw the adults into a moment of uncomfortable silence. Phyll spoke first. 'Are you home for the half-term, Percy?'

It was the kind of question one asked a thirteen-year-old girl of that class, and intended to dispel the tension, yet it only served to intensify the embarrassment.

'Sort of. It's a bit early for half-term.' Persephone blushed, uncertain. 'I might be home for good. I don't know.' She glanced towards her mother, in need of reassurance.

'Take the ivy to the tower, dear,' said Lady Pike. 'If the village know we brought it in here, there'll be bothersome deputations. Country people think it bad luck for it to be inside the church.'

Sabrina Pike bent to organise the snowdrops from the greenery, handing trails of ivy to her daughter. William had no idea that foliage could be sorted into the sacred or profane. The catechism of his Catholic childhood had not prepared him for such mysteries.

'I dare say Mr Garrett and Phyll are ready for their coffee, Freddy,' said Dr Moon, smiling and beneficent. 'Do come too. I imagine cook can rustle up some fruitcake.'

'Yes, alright.' Freddy rolled down his shirtsleeves and glanced at his tools – the chisel, plane and square – left untended at Christ's feet. 'I shall finish this off later.'

'What about your overcoat?' said Phyll, pointing to the crumpled, cat-covered mass of tweed on the floor. 'It's bitterly cold outside.'

'No,' he said, offering the sleeping cat a loving smile. 'Rossetti works the night shift and deserves her rest. I shall be a gentleman and brave the cold on her behalf.'

Persephone, swathed in ivy, smiled and said, 'I'll look after Rossetti, Freddy. I adore her, and I don't think black cats are bad luck at all.'

5

Outside, the clouds, now low and gunmetal grey, skimmed the horizon, throwing the distant pithead into black silhouette.

Dr Moon drew the collar of his greatcoat tight about his chin. 'Definitely snow, Mr Garrett,' he said. 'You're quite wrong about rain.'

'Either way, we're in for some bad weather.' William watched as Freddy and Phyll walked arm-in-arm through the graveyard. Freddy's blond head was bowed — and Phyll's upturned — in a muttered, unsmiling conversation which William strained to hear. Suddenly, Phyll's grip tightened on her brother's hand, blanching her knuckles into an anxious pearl white. 'Exactly how ill is Freddy?'

'Freddy has made a remarkable recovery since his arrival at Red Hollow.' Dr Moon patted the pockets of his army great-coat, and brought out, not a revolver, but a battered meer-schaum pipe which he did not light. 'Phyll will mother-hen him, of course, but Freddy is his own man, and he has great reserves of strength. I can't say the same for my remaining patients.'

'Is there something I should know about Freddy and the Reverend Andrews?' asked William.

'What do you mean?'

'Freddy dislikes him.'

'That's because the Reverend Andrews is dislikeable, poor chap.' Dr Moon turned to William and smiled. 'I doubt the parson is our unwanted visitor, if that's what you're driving at?'

'He doesn't approve of your work here.'

'Correct. Neither does he approve of Freddy's work in the church.' There was a note of sardonic amusement in the doctor's voice. 'But the thought of the man breaking into the building in the dead of night to chisel phalluses into the wood panelling to get back at Freddy for some ecclesiastical slight is almost laughable.'

They walked to the rear of the house. Here, on the lawn, away from the buffer of the church, William felt the fierce nip of an easterly wind. The river ran close by and was bare of bordering trees, and amidst the dead, muddy reeds which edged its narrow course, a few stone steps led to a pontoon. There, a moored rowboat, red paint faded to pink, bobbed softly on the water's swell. And beyond the river, on land as flat as a cricket pitch, the straight cut of the canal was crowned by a low, curved bridge now picturesque with age.

A Victorian conservatory, smaller than the Crystal Palace, but only just, stretched along three-quarters of the rear of the house. William followed Freddy, Phyll and Dr Moon through a glass door too narrow to accommodate his thick frame, and then stepped across a threshold of steam emanating from the elaborate grate which outlined the tiled floor. The focus of the conservatory was a moss-covered fountain of Pan, slim and wicked, playing his pipes. Water trickled through the aperture of the little god's flute and into a deep copper basin full of darting goldfish. An arrangement of elaborate cane furniture stood to the right of the fountain and was partly swathed in the soft greenhouse fog.

And no chrysanthemums grew, for the whole place had been given over to exotics. Plants, like mouldering cottage loaves, pale green and bulbous, ranged on tiered shelves, and huge spiky cacti, typical of cowboy movies, stood so incongruous and un-English in the corners that William wondered if Tom Mix might pop out from behind one at any second brandishing his six-shooter.

'What an interesting collection,' said Phyll.

'Botany is my passion,' said Dr Moon. 'I'm proud of how well the *Carnegiea gigantea* have grown.' He squinted at the larger cacti, and then turned and pointed towards the small spineless specimens. Like grey pebbles or sea urchins, they were the most plentiful in the greenhouse. 'These are my speciality, *Lophophora williamsii*. Yes, my absolute favourite. A fascinating species. And the *Opuntia* are fruiting,' he said, as if both honoured and surprised. 'You may know them as prickly pears. One can eat them.' He caressed the globules of fuchsia pink, which grew like stunted fingers from the flat green palm of the cacti. 'They make a fine marmalade, but I cannot persuade our cook to attempt anything other than orange.'

'Your conservatory is sadly lacking in chrysanthemums, Dr Moon,' said Phyll, smiling.

'Oh, yes,' laughed Dr Moon. 'But why grow what you hate? By her own admission, Lady Pike despises chrysanthemums. She is a woman of extraordinary sensibility but is burdened by a conventional sense of duty. But perhaps I have little respect for the usual hierarchies,' he mused. 'I spent time in the Southwestern United States after the war. There's an honesty to life there. No artifice of class with its confining expectations of rank. A man is simply a man in New Mexico.'

His little disquisition had become plaintive, and for a startling moment, William thought Dr Moon might burst into cowboy song. 'New Mexico?' he asked. 'Like D. H. Lawrence?'

'I had the pleasure of meeting him once. I'm acquainted with a friend of Mrs Dodge Luhan and was invited to Taos. New Mexico is a remarkable place for the student of botany. I aim to return there, eventually.'

William had no idea who Mrs Dodge Luhan was, and he had no interest in botany. 'But what was he like, Lawrence?'

'A fascinating mind, but in frail health.' He pronounced his diagnosis with the gravitas of someone divulging a secret.

'The opposite of me,' said Freddy, breaking his silence. 'I am in rude health, but the old brainbox –' he patted his head with a bony forefinger – 'leaves something to be desired.'

William offered Freddy a reassuring grin; what else could he do? But Phyll resumed her tight grip on Freddy's arm, her face falling into a hard, impassive blank of well-controlled grief. A daughter of the Empire, with a stiffened upper lip, she would never show the world the extent of her pain – and perhaps, her shame.

'Shall we go through to the library?' Dr Moon smiled. 'It's quite comfortable there, and we have a lovely view of the grounds and beyond, if one ignores the spoil heap.'

They passed through a sitting room. It was darkly panelled, and a worn Persian carpet softened the stone floor, but the room's former splendour had faded so that a whiff of the institution hung about the place like a miasma. A modern suite of sofa and chairs, chosen for practicality rather than beauty, stood forlorn in the centre of the room, and cheap glass ashtrays, all emptied but not clean, littered the Victorian side tables.

Above him, a wedding cake of a ceiling sagged with the weight of its elaborate, snow-white plaster, and was bisected by a crack as wide as a grown man's thumb. William stopped for a moment and stared up at the startling black zigzag.

'It won't fall down,' said Dr Moon, noticing William's interest. 'It has been made safe, although not restored. A shame because it's Jacobean, and quite the survival. The damage was caused by nineteenth-century mining subsidence, according to Lady Pike. The family attempted to sue the local mine owners, but got nowhere, of course.'

Dr Moon ushered them into a shadowy corridor. Narrower than usual for a house of such size, the passageway's thick wall panelling, blackened with age, enclosed William like a coffin. Nothing seemed square. Even the floorboards shifted and undulated beneath his tread. He had an uneasy feeling of confinement and disorder, as though something alive and ancient had been shaken into chaos. Then, with almost comic timing, a madhouse groan emanated from behind a distant door. 'What the hell was that?'

'One of the residents is having nightmares,' said Dr Moon. 'Please don't worry, Mr Garrett. Mr Brooke, our orderly, is with him. The man doesn't suffer alone.'

'He sounds like he's in pain,' said William.

'Mr Irwell is doing alright. He's the surviving kind. Don't you worry about him none.' The speaker, a man, emerged from the gloom with a movement so silent and smooth that William, for one lunatic moment, believed he had levitated. William jumped, and Phyll gave out a small yelp.

Dr Moon flipped on a light switch. The electric behaved oddly, and the man's face jumped and flickered into view, queerly uncertain. 'I believe you startled our guests, Mr

Brooke,' he said. 'I doubt they're comfortable with the gloom of these corridors.'

'Work here long enough and you get used to the darkness.' Brooke addressed the doctor, but his words were directed at William. In his early thirties, smallish but handsome, he wore the white coat of a hospital orderly unbuttoned over a decent wool suit. 'Cook wants to be out before three o'clock today. She won't want latecomers for lunch, or she'll never get done in time.' He assessed William and Phyll, sighing. 'Argy-bargying with her will get my timetable all upset.'

'Our guests shan't be staying for lunch.' Dr Moon's clarity of tone was of a man who had once made the grave mistake of upsetting Mr Brooke's timetable. 'However, we would very much like coffee, and perhaps some cake.'

'Cake?'

'I saw a fruitcake in the kitchen.'

'We have one or two fruitcakes at Red Hollow. There's no doubt about that.' Brooke raised his eyebrows towards Freddy. 'But the one in the kitchen is for Miss Persephone's birthday. She's thirteen tomorrow, and I made it myself on behalf of Lady Pike.' Adoration oozed from each word. 'I daresay cook can rustle up some digestives. The woman's good at opening tins and packets.'

'Well, yes, then digestives will have to do.' Dr Moon mustered a crumb of authority. 'Tell cook I want good coffee, Mr Brooke. None of that bottled muck.'

'If you want good coffee, I'll have to make it myself. She's incapable of anything other than stewed tea,' said the orderly. 'I suppose it's alright to leave Mr Irwell on his own for five minutes. He's been playing up again, silly boy.'

The doctor nodded, and Mr Brooke disappeared as he had entered, silently. And although his capacity to present obedience as an insult was lost on no one, Dr Moon, stalwart and unafraid, still called after him, 'We shall take our coffee in the library as soon as possible, Mr Brooke.'

No bigger than a large office, the library walls were lined from floor to ceiling with bookshelves, and, unlike the sitting room, a fire had been laid. Logs, not coal, burned in the elaborate grate, and the resulting warm glow gave the room an air of timeless comfort. Dr Moon, at home once more, moved to switch on the green-shaded standard lamps which stood in each corner, and then the modern brass reading light on the large central desk. Four early Georgian windows, each as big as a door, offered a grand view of the same lawn, riverbank and canal as before, but from a different angle and seen through a mist of dried silt from a previous heavy rainfall. But again, industry, in the form of the pithead, loomed. William wondered why Lady Pike was not coal-rich like the rest of the gentry in this part of the county. It must have been a humiliating reminder of her own relative poverty to have another man's colliery hovering on the margins of her estate.

'Despite later additions, this is the oldest room in the house,' said Dr Moon. 'I believe it's been a library since the sixteenth century. Please, do sit down.' The doctor motioned to the chairs at the desk, and then walked to the bookcase nearest the door. Pulling out a cloth-bound book, he flipped through the pages, and handed it, open, to William. 'You were asking about the story of the mermaid, Mr Garrett. As I have said, I am not a believer in the supernatural, but I do think it has relevance to your enquiry. This account of the mermaid was written by Sir Leofric Pike, Lady Sabrina Pike's father. It's fair to say it's from the horse's mouth, so to speak.'

William glanced at the cover. The book was perhaps thirty or so years old and was titled, with the comic grandiosity of the Edwardian era, *Annals of Arcane Warwickshire*. He began to read, but nonetheless the doctor, now seated opposite William, delivered a precis.

'Sir Divinity Pike, seventeenth-century squire of Red Hollow, returned from the Civil War a broken man,' began Dr Moon. 'Drunken, dissolute and exhausted from battle, Sir Divinity developed a dangerous obsession with a young village girl.'

Annals of Arcane Warwickshire was written in fruity, but enjoyable, prose, and so the doctor's voice was a vague commentary on the margins of William's consciousness.

'The maiden, however, did not reciprocate Sir Divinity's passion, refusing his attempts at lovemaking. And so, one Candlemas night, somewhat emboldened with brandy, Sir Divinity took matters into his own hands,' said Dr Moon. 'He spotted the girl while she was out tending the sheep in lamb and rode her down. Then, at the banks of Red Hollow pool, he raped her. During the violation, it began to rain, and eventually the pool burst its banks. After he'd finished, Sir Divinity left the girl for dead at the water's edge.'

There came a soft, sudden thud – as if a child had thrown a snowball – against the picture window. Dr Moon stopped his story and frowned. William turned. The view of the lawn, river and pithead was clear, nothing had changed. He rose, handing the book to Phyll, and glanced outside and down at the stone pathway. There, a magpie, stunned into a self-protecting ball, twitched in pain and shock. Bad luck birds, William's mother would count them on her way to Mass. 'It's just a magpie. It flew into the window and brained itself,' he said.

'One for sorrow.' Freddy had joined William at the window and was now bending his lanky frame to unfasten the latch.

'We should try to save it, or at least move it out of Rossetti's way. I should hate for her to find it and have her fun. Cats can be merciless.' However, at Freddy's words, the magpie rallied, stuttering into flight. Both men watched the bird's low, tentative glide towards the ancient copse, and its quivering red pool. 'Red Hollow looks bleak now, Mr Garrett, but in May, it's the greenest place I've ever been. The water makes everything quick with life. Nettles, bindweed, cleavers, they're thigh high. I sometimes think a man could stand by the banks of the pool and dream for an hour, and the greenery would engulf him.' Freddy pinched his nose with forefinger and thumb, as a swimmer does after coming up from a dive. 'I can't bear the idea of a burial, but such a death would be the appropriate culmination of life. A man would be of use to that vast expanse of brilliant green.'

'Do continue, Dr Moon.' *Annals of Arcane Warwickshire* lay open on Phyll's knees. Her head down, she was making shorthand notes. But her voice was cool and clear; her message was pointed. 'Billy, if the bird is alright, you should sit down now.'

William and Freddy glanced at each other and smiled at Phyll's instruction, then both men returned to their seats.

'Well, the girl drowned in the flood, of course,' continued the doctor. 'But in her death throes, she cursed Sir Divinity and all the drunken, lascivious men of the parish. Sir Divinity died a year to the day later of dropsy, an old-fashioned term for congestive heart failure. However, it is said the mermaid returns to Red Hollow during heavy rainfall to wreak vengeance on the parish reprobates. She comes in the form of a freshwater mermaid, of course.' Dr Moon paused as if gathering his thoughts. 'You're both intelligent people. There's a peculiar cruelty to our intruder. They use the power of the story to interfere with the very valuable treatment we do here at Red Hollow. Why terrify innocent men? It's perverse.'

Sir Divinity died from heart failure, and the young girl drowned. William recalled the patient who died in his bath, Mr Trent. The manner of his death held an eerie resemblance to the folk tale, but Dr Moon's patients must have been wound tight to see this as anything other than a sad coincidence, let alone reason to leave his care. William shifted in his seat. The doctor was leaving an important fact left unsaid. Again, it was something Sir Leofric hinted at in the written account. 'What did the writer mean by "revenge of the most personal and humiliating kind"?' he asked.

Before Dr Moon had time to answer, Mr Brooke entered the library. Encumbered with a huge, silver coffee service, he placed the tray on the doctor's desk and began to fiddle with the coffee cups. 'I made the coffee myself and managed to find a half-pack of digestives.' Brooke glanced at the copy of *Annals of Arcane Warwickshire* on Phyll's knees and removed the plate of biscuits from the tray.

'Thank you, Mr Brooke.' Dr Moon gave the man a peremptory nod. 'I shall pour. Please return to Mr Irwell.'

Brooke straightened up and eyed the doctor with servile contempt. After a few long seconds, he left the room silently.

'Brooke makes good coffee.' Dr Moon poured once the orderly had gone. 'He's a better cook than our current incumbent, and it's a matter of pride to him. He was brought up in service, you see. His own father was valet-butler to Sir Leofric, and I believe his mother was an upstairs maid before her marriage. Now, I know how Phyll and Freddy like their coffee, but what about you, Mr Garrett?'

'The mermaid has vagina dentata, that's what Sir Leofric means.' For a moment, Freddy's fingers fluttered near his temples; then he tamed them, interlacing his hands about the knee of his crossed legs. 'She lures men to their own emasculation. Rapists, wife-beaters, and woman-haters, you know the type. The poor, debased creature has resorted to a sad, bloody kind of vengeance. But then vengeance so often is both degrading and brutal. *Wound for wound*. It says so in the Old Testament.'

6

It took William three seconds to guess the meaning of the Latin. He winced and crossed his legs. 'Bloody hell,' he said. 'No wonder you're all so nervy if that's the local fairy tale.'

'Well, yes, a wandering mermaid equipped with a vicious set of vaginal teeth is disturbing, of course.' Dr Moon smiled, perhaps a little uncomfortably, and glanced at Phyll, whose face was impassive and pale, drawn. 'The Red Hollow mermaid isn't alone, by the way. Women with the power to emasculate men during coitus is an ancient, but not uncommon, myth.'

'And the story of the girl, is it true?' William asked.

Dr Moon reached for a pipe, filled it with tobacco, lit it and began to suck on its stubby stem, meditatively. 'The rape and murder, you mean?'

William nodded.

'There is probably a good deal of truth in the story, yes. Soldiers coming back from war, it happens. And it seems our culture is riddled with narratives of *droit du seigneur*. But it doesn't really matter if an actual girl was raped and drowned or not.'

'It mattered to the girl,' said Phyll, placing the book down on the desk. 'The whole story is about woman-hatred. It drips with it. Why am I not surprised?'

'You misunderstand me, Phyll. I only meant that what is important now is not the truth of the thing, but that the story terrifies my men.'

'What about you, Freddy?' asked William. 'Are you terrified of her?'

William heard the crows caw out in the pasture beyond the canal. Phyll's coffee cup rattled in her saucer, as, palely silent, she reached for her brother's hand. Finally, Freddy spoke, flashing William an honest, boyish smile.

'I have nothing to fear. The mermaid and I have already met, and although I don't think she'd be on friendly terms with any man, she wouldn't harm me. I've never laid a hand on a woman in anger. I believed she sensed this when we met.'

'Do you think the mermaid killed Mr Trent, Freddy?' asked William.

'Who knows what passed between them.' Freddy's shrug was unusually casual. 'I've no idea what sort of man Trent was. I imagine the mermaid had an inkling, though. And Dr Moon would know all about Trent's past, I should think.' Freddy nodded towards the doctor but didn't meet his eye.

Here lay the madness. To Freddy, the mermaid was real in tooth and claw, but not a threat because the man did not beat or rape women. William felt a vague sense of shameful triumph: his own shuddering, neurasthenic nightmares were small fry compared to conjuring up an imaginary fishy friend. He turned to Phyll. 'Did you know about this?' William's tone was accusatory, he knew, but the hedging secrecy about Red Hollow, Freddy, the mermaid, irritated him. No one, including his partner, was willing to give him the full picture.

'Good God, no.' There was an honest outrage in her voice. 'Dr Moon told me Freddy had a disturbing encounter with an intruder. That is all.'

'The intruder is responsible for Freddy's encounter with the mermaid. I told the truth.' Dr Moon's tone was defensive. Phyll remained tight-lipped, but avoided meeting the doctor's eye, her pale face flushing pink. 'Although Freddy and I disagree on, shall we say, the corporeality of the mermaid, he has worked hard on correcting his own over-responsive fear instinct.' William came to the conclusion the doctor's professional tone was tactical, and perhaps used to avoid too much scrutiny. 'However, not all my men are so advanced in their psychotherapy. My men fear emasculation, and they fear the wrath of a vengeful woman. The mermaid's violence is directed towards men only, and the intruder, I believe, is deliberately destroying the peace of our small community. She is, to put it frankly, terrifying to them.'

Terrifying, William thought. Dr Moon often used that word when describing the mermaid. Yes, terrified enough to empty an entire round of ammunition into a frozen pond. It wasn't just Dr Moon's patients who were stiff. William's instinct told him the man was keeping more secrets than the peculiarly sexual nature of a folk tale. 'Have any of your patients been violent towards women, Dr Moon?'

'I'm not at liberty to say, but I understand the importance of the question.' Dr Moon offered them cigarettes from a box on the desk, but William refused. 'Many men, not just my residents, have guilt complexes, and somewhat, shall we say, unhealthy experiences with, and opinions about, members of the opposite sex. When men suffer, Mr Garrett, women and children often bear the brunt.' William knew the truth of this from his own childhood experiences. 'I can also tell you that no one man has been the focus of events. Our intruder is indiscriminate.'

'Good grief,' said Phyll. 'This is all so tiresome; I don't know quite what to say.' Her exhaustion with the discussion was palpable, and the cause of the blushing was not embarrass-ment but rising fury. 'I've known women who were raped. The men who did it are living the life of Riley. Female ven-geance is about as mythological as your mermaid.'

'I am a man of science.' The doctor addressed Phyll. 'Therefore, I do not believe in the existence of gynaecologic-ally afflicted freshwater mermaids with the uncanny ability to slither, I suppose, around a Midlands village enacting revenge on the local lecherous drunkards.' His tone was authoritative and sardonic, and he seemed mildly amused by Phyll's outrage. 'However, fear is real. We all fear something.' Dr Moon glanced at William. 'And there are those amongst us whose fears will always seem odd or illogical. Misogyny, I would suggest, is just as illogical a fear as arachnophobia or –' he paused – 'aquaphobia.'

'Sir Leofric believed in the mermaid.' William nodded towards the book. 'He enjoys the violence of the story. He's salacious.' There was something of the fanatical true believer in the narrator's tone which had made William uneasy.

'Sir Leofric was a dedicated occultist and a follower of Mr Crowley.'

'Aleister Crowley? The sex magick bloke?' William guffawed. 'Jesus, this just gets better and better.' Then he dropped his favourite fact like a bomb. 'He's from Leamington Spa.'

'Is he really?' asked Dr Moon, smiling. 'Why am I not surprised the wickedest man in England is from Leamington Spa?'

'I always thought there was something funny in the water in Leamington Spa.' Freddy, gently comic, raised his eyebrows.

'And in Red Hollow, if you and Sir Leofric are to be believed.' Phyll squeezed her brother's hand.

Freddy laughed, and William had a sudden insight into the strength of their relationship. 'Ain't that the truth, old girl,' he said.

'Phyll has rather elegantly brought us back to our point,' said Dr Moon, gesturing towards the river with the stem of his pipe. 'Sir Leofric spent much of his time attempting to magically summon water nymphs, and there were rumours of Bacchanalian frolics near Red Hollow pool with a coterie of local women. In fact, the man had a terrible reputation for debauchery.' The doctor paused, as if in reflection. 'Perhaps Phyll is right. It's all rather priapic and self-regarding, the mermaid story, I mean. Either way, the Pikes have such rotten luck. Scandal dogs them.'

'When did Sir Leofric die?' asked Phyll.

'Before the Great War when Lady Pike was Persephone's age. He is *persona non grata* in the hamlet, so if you were to ask Lady Pike about him, she would stay tight-lipped.' Dr Moon resumed his meditative smoking. 'Sir Leofric was a queer one, that's for sure. His sort of personality is all id. It thrives on chaos. The Pike family tree is somewhat incestuous, I'm afraid. Their eccentricity may be due to inbreeding. Even Lady Pike's late husband was a cousin. He was a solicitor from Melton Mowbray, I believe, before he inherited the title. You've probably gleaned that she's quite impoverished. Of course, all county families have their black sheep, but their relative poverty makes the Pikes vulnerable to gossip. Sir Leofric's mischiefs had that peculiarly sexual quality which meant the family were snubbed at hunt balls, that kind of thing. After the war, Captain Pike became sensitive to the family's fall from grace, and Percy's recent outburst suggests she has inherited her father's delicate nerves.'

William wondered if neurosis were hereditary, like eye colour, haemophilia or weak ankles. The thought worried him.

There was a lull in the conversation which Dr Moon used to refill his pipe. He lit the bowl once more, took two great puffs and looked at William, Freddy and then Phyll with challenging consideration. Pipe smoke once more filled the air, and it cloyed like incense.

Phyll was first to break the silence. She turned to her brother, placed a gentle hand upon his knee and said, 'It's about time you told us what happened last night, Freddy darling. What on earth did this mermaid do to you?'

Freddy smiled. 'Don't get too cut up about it all, old thing. My masculinity is still intact. Just.'

7

'It happened after tea,' said Freddy.

'Tea is an informal but compulsory meal,' interjected Dr Moon. 'It is our final analysis session of the day, and it starts at six o'clock sharp. We eat communally and discuss our progress on the road to wellness. It is an opportunity to talk through our problems in a spirit of fellowship.'

William winced. The shared meal, the compulsory talking, Dr Moon's over-hearty euphemism; it turned William's stomach.

'It's not as bad as it sounds,' said Freddy. 'There are not many of us now.' He glanced at Dr Moon. 'Anyway, with so few men in attendance, the talk was easy going.'

'No arguments or any difficult discussions?' asked William.

Freddy shook his head. 'The cook prepared a decent spread before she left for the day, and Tom Sherbourne and I are old hands at talking through our looniest moments. The new fellow, although in a frightful state, seemed alright.' He stretched his elegant fingers towards the communal box on Dr Moon's desk and flipped open the lid. William watched as Freddy lit a cigarette. If he once had the shakes, Dr Moon had cured them. William's own hands were tremulous, forever betraying him. 'Irwell and Tom couldn't pull a stunt like the one last night, honestly.'

'And after tea?' Phyll took notes, her practicality a stark contrast to Freddy's strange, visionary madness. If, as Dr Moon believed, a flesh-and-blood evil was behind the haunting of Red Hollow, then Phyll, in all her smartness, would uncover it.

'We all went our separate ways.' Freddy's mouth puckered as he pulled hard on his cigarette, and with this one swift action something of the man's blond boyishness disappeared. 'I went to my room for a bit. Tried to read, but the book was a duffer, and I couldn't settle. Then I wandered about and ended up in the sitting room. Dr Moon and Tom were listening to a Brahms concert on the wireless, but it's not my thing. Irwell had retired for the evening, and I was rattling around with nothing to do.' Freddy paused, his hand, still holding the cigarette, resting across the knee of his crossed leg. 'In all fairness, I was itching to do something creative, even practical. I remember thinking it would be ridiculous not to work on the choir stalls while the muse was upon me. I wanted to get them finished before Candlemas, and I had spoken earlier to Lady Pike, and we had hatched something of a plan to get St Chad's looking tiptop before Easter. So, I decided to go AWOL.'

'AWOL?' asked William.

'The men are confined to barracks after tea.' Dr Moon flashed a smile which William did not return. 'It's for their own safety. We do not allow them on the wider grounds after eight o'clock in the evening unless accompanied by a member of staff. This includes the church. Our rules are not draconian, but most of our residents –' he glanced at Freddy – 'if not all, are in the grip of addiction. We must do our best to give them appropriate care.'

'And this is when you lock both the main gate and the house?' asked William.

'Yes, I lock up. Or, on rare occasions, Mr Brooke does.'

However, Freddy's mild insubordination revealed the laxity of Dr Moon's security arrangements. William wondered how many addicts sloped off to the stable block with their favoured contraband of an evening or walked the few miles to the nearest pub as soon as Dr Moon settled down with his pipe and his Brahms. Surely it was nothing to shin over a fence or wade the river to find yourself a drink and some company? And if the patients were free to wander the grounds at night, what about the outside world?

'And it was you who locked up last night?' asked William.

Dr Moon nodded.

'What time did you go AWOL, Freddy?' asked Phyll.

'Half-past eight or so,' he said. 'I keep my electric torch in my room and my carpentry tools in the church crypt. They're out of the parson's way down there. He doesn't like me to keep them in the vestry. In fact, he doesn't much like me hanging about the church at all.' Freddy stubbed his cigarette out and ran his hands through his blond hair, one of Phyll's mannerisms. 'I have a key to the church. That's quite legitim-ate. Everyone knows it.'

'How did you feel when you entered the church?' asked Phyll. William was struck by the intelligence behind the ques-tion, as it was designed to gauge how much of Freddy's story would be coloured by his imagination.

'As I keep saying, I was quite alright.' Freddy reached over and squeezed Phyll's hand but, tellingly, he did not release it. 'Outsiders think Red Hollow an eerie sort of place, but it's been my home for over five years, and I see nothing frighten-ing or sinister here. The church is my domain, and I'm rarely uneasy. However, I'm not a particularly observant sort of person. Unless something was very much out of place, I simply wouldn't notice a change.' Freddy's voice became suddenly distant and reedy, like the sound of a gramophone record heard from a far-off room. 'What I do remember about last night is being terribly engrossed in my work. I was at a place of perfect peace, and absolutely focused on the wood, my tools, my hands, the process of cutting and carving. It was beautiful and revelatory, and this sensation of wonder, and yes, oneness, only intensified when I saw the carving of the mermaid.'

Dr Moon banged the bowl of his pipe once more against the ashtray, dislodging a dirty lump of spent tobacco. William jumped, as did Freddy. Dr Moon looked up as if wondering why the storytelling had stopped. 'Do go on, Freddy,' he said.

'She was like a bride behind all those cobwebs. I remember moving them to one side to reveal her, lifting her veil, as it were. Reaching beneath them to touch her seemed something of an invasion, but she was beautiful, and there was an uncanny quality to the polished smoothness of the wood. I experienced – I know this sounds ridiculous – a connection to the man who carved her. As though he and I thought the same, spoke the same language, looked alike. I had lost my sense of self because I was at one with this craftsman. I knew this not on a verbal level, but precisely and deeply, as one does a religious calling. It was all wonderful and of profound significance. Last night, my understanding of the world, and my craft, had become more expansive.' Freddy's smile was nervous but in no way as intense as his words. 'I'm unsure how long I stayed by the choir stalls. Time seemed irrelevant, but eventually I packed up my tools.'

'And when did this sensation of contentment end?' asked Dr Moon.

'When I returned my toolbox to the crypt. I'm not usually afraid of such places.' Freddy closed his eyes, and the lids, near purple with fatigue, fluttered like a trapped moth. 'The dead do not scare me. However, as soon as I entered the place, I had a terrible feeling of paranoia, as if I were being watched by a sinister force. It was as if all those Pikes were scrutinising me from their graves, and it undercut the elation I felt at finding the mermaid. I got the wind up, immediately. Felt it in my stomach, you know, physically.' Outside, the sky darkened further to an ominous gunmetal grey. And in the subtle change in light, the faint lines about Freddy's mouth and eyes became dark ravines of suffering. 'My skin pricked, and each nerve was on alert, as if I was in for a bad show.' Freddy opened his eyes and looked at William. 'You know?'

'Yes, I do know.' The moment before the danger. Fear, tight-wound in your body, until the whistle blew, and you were over the top.

'That's when I smelt it. A waft of air, as though someone had opened a door to a stale room. It was a terrible stench of dank, and it became suddenly worse, as if there was something wrong with the drains.'

'Is there another door to the crypt?' asked William. 'Did you hear footsteps or a creak or any indication of an intruder?'

'There is a door you can use from the outside on the north wall, but I didn't hear it open. And the smell came as if from nowhere and was overwhelming.' Freddy let go of Phyll's hand and reached for another cigarette. Dr Moon leant over the desk, lit it for him, and nodded in reassurance. Freddy took a soldier's drag – a deep, and much-needed, hit of tobacco – and continued with his story. 'When Phyll and I were children, we came across a dead sheep in a drainage ditch. It was bloated, and fly-ridden. The ditch was putrid with rotting

59

greenery. Oh God, the stench of it. That was the first time I ever saw death, Mr Garrett. I mean saw what happened after death, in tooth and claw. Of course, I've seen plenty since.' Freddy flicked ash into his empty coffee cup. 'Perhaps more than a man can take.'

For just a moment, all became hushed in the artificial twilight of the library.

William broke the silence. 'Do you have a problem with the drains?'

Beside him, Phyll guffawed. 'Good grief, that's a good 'un. So well timed.'

'It sounds insensitive, I know,' William continued. 'But it's best to be clear about things from the start.'

'Not that I'm aware of,' said Dr Moon. 'As a matter of fact, I was checking the drains this morning when we first met. The crypt has been known to flood, but flooding is the norm here. It might be politic to call a plumber. Our plumbing is somewhat complicated.'

'It always is in old piles like this,' said Freddy. 'I bet those smart little semi-detached houses in Whittingford have magnificent drains. Our mother was obsessed with the vicar-age drains, but cholera killed off most of her siblings in infancy. She was of that generation. The old girl had that sanitary, Victorian attitude to things.'

'Poor old Mummy,' said Phyll.

Freddy reached for his sister's hand once more. 'One can put a strange smell down to nearly anything,' he continued. 'I'd have been quite alright if it was just the smell, but of course, I saw her. I saw her and I felt her, and by God, I even heard her. And she was quite real. Rather more than real.' Freddy let out a hollow laugh. 'She had a terrible mask-like face, and fallen into a palsy, like the victim of a gas attack. Her skin was deathly pale, but her lips were red, like a rosebud. But I'm sure that was because her face was heavily made-up, like the prostitutes one saw on the streets of Paris during the war. Beneath her pallor, her artificial pallor, her skin was a strange green colour. And she saw me. That is what was so terrifying about the whole experience. She was no unthinking spectre, but a sapient being.' Freddy turned towards Phyll, speaking directly to her. 'There was intelligence behind those monstrous green eyes. Unblinking eyes, like that of a horrid bird. And she spoke to me, as if prophesying – no, not prophesying but foretelling, for me personally.'

'And what did she say?' asked Phyll, her voice quiet and soft as if speaking to a child terrified of some nebulous bedtime monster.

'She quoted from a poem by William Blake. *Prudence is a rich, ugly old maid courted by incapacity. The cut worm forgives the plough. Dip him in the river who loves water.*' Freddy recited the lines like a schoolboy, and then paused for a moment before continuing. 'That was the worst bit,' he said. '*Dip him in the river who loves water.* She spat those words out. I was transfixed, not by her words, but by her grin. It was a terrible grin, fixed and wicked.'

Freddy knew, and could quote, Blake. Hadn't he muttered a few lines from *Songs of Innocence* in the church? Of course his mermaid was a Romantic grotesque of a vision, thought William.

'Her grin?' asked Phyll.

'She had the rotting mouth of a hag. Her teeth, what few she had left, were sharpened, and by that, I mean artificially filed to points. I got the feeling that she wanted me to stare. That she demanded my gaze. Then she snarled and bared those grotesque teeth.' Freddy gave out a long, deep sigh. 'It was a low, humming purr at first. God, that terrible, fetid breath. Then she inched closer, still emanating her protective snarl.' Freddy paused to examine the tip of his cigarette, shifting slightly away from Phyll. 'We were nose to nose for quite a while. She sniffed me, and then put her hand between my legs. Felt me, my manhood, I mean. She had no shame. Squeezing hard. Hard. Sniffing at my face. Twisted. It was shocking and painful. I was powerless, you see. Mute with shock.' Freddy writhed at the memory, a face-contorting squirm. 'She cackled as if I were hilarious to her. It was a screeching, animal-like laughter, and she wouldn't stop. She pushed me away. Rejected me, I suppose, and I ran. I got out of the crypt as fast as I could and fled the building. By the time I got back to the hall, I was in a bit of a state. I won't go back to the crypt again. I'm leaving my tools in the church. I'm alright there. I cannot go down to the crypt again.'

'Christ,' said William. 'Christ almighty, that's quite the story.'

And it was. But it was a story of a gentle man's sad, grief-stricken life. Of a childhood spent in a country vicarage with a germophobe mother; of horrifying gas attacks after which exhausted furloughs were spent with elderly French whores; of a man with a Blakean, mystical sense of God, living in an age of poison gas, machine guns and strategic bombing. William didn't need Dr Moon's qualifications to see the truth in Freddy's story. However, had Freddy's strange vision been sparked by a flesh-and-blood encounter with the intruder? And if so, what were they up to in the church?

'She touched you intimately, Freddy?' asked Dr Moon, placing fresh tobacco in the bowl of his pipe, and, in William's opinion, feigning indifference. 'You didn't tell me this.'

'Yes, I'm afraid she did.' Freddy shuddered. 'She didn't like me, but she didn't want to harm me. She thought me quite comic, and not worth the trouble. I think the story is right. The mermaid only hurts men who have hurt women.'

Phyll said nothing, but stood, bent down, and wiped the blond hair away from Freddy's forehead. Then she clasped his face in both her hands and kissed him. Phyll returned to her seat. And Freddy, William and Dr Moon made as if this private show of affection had not happened.

'Who else has keys to the church?' asked William.

'Myself, the parson and Lady Pike,' said Dr Moon.

'And who has access to the hall and grounds at night?'

'Lady Pike lives in the tower.' Dr Moon pointed to his left with the stem of his pipe. William remembered one crenellated corner of the manor house, thick and tall and ancient. 'The tower is converted to a quite separate apartment. She and Percy have their own entrance and there is no access from the tower to the hall. The former connecting doors are all locked and boarded. However, she and Persephone have free access to the grounds, including the church and other outbuildings.'

'How many outbuildings are there on the property?'

'Numerous. Stables, an icehouse, two dilapidated follies and a boathouse. Not to mention the various tool sheds and shepherds' huts.'

'And the Pike family are the only people who have access to the grounds?' William asked the question, but it was Phyll who took notes.

'No,' said Dr Moon. 'Mr Brooke has keys to both the front gate and the manor. My secretary, Miss Moore, works afternoons and cycles in from nearby Milby. She has no key. Our locum, Dr Lynch, who works in the nearby asylum has keys to the hall and gate, but not the church. He covers my days off. The parson has a key to the front gate and the church, but not the house. None of the residents have keys. At the moment, because of our uninvited guest, only Freddy is resident, as is Mr Sherbourne, and our newish man, Mr Irwell.'

It was a free-for-all, thought William. Everyone or anyone could have given Freddy a fright.

'But anyone could wander about the grounds at night,' said Phyll, voicing William's concerns. 'There's no gamekeeper with a shotgun, I suppose?' she asked.

'We rely on the villagers' goodwill and sense of propriety. It would be very easy to break into the grounds.' Dr Moon tamped his pipe once more. It was like a nervous tic. 'Not the church. And most definitely not the external door to the crypt. We keep that door locked and it's never used.'

Never used by you, William thought.

'Did it rain here last night?' asked Phyll. It was an important detail. In the mermaid story, she sought revenge when the Red Hollow burst its banks, and Mr Trent died during a storm.

Dr Moon and Freddy shook their heads.

Phyll made a final note, returned her book and pencil to her overcoat pocket, and then glanced at William, her face pale.

'No,' said William. 'But it will rain tonight.'

8

William didn't believe in the existence of vengeful mermaids, but he knew neurosis behaved like a contagion. He remembered one endless, panic-ridden day during the war. Rumours of a future offensive spread through the trenches, mutating, with speed, into terrifying fact. Men felt themselves doomed. Most shook, or wept for their mothers; one young subaltern bolted into barbed wire. There was a touch of this at Red Hollow. Hysteria brought about by human action. But to what ends – old-fashioned mischief or something more purposeful? William wondered if Mr Trent's heart attack, and eventual death by drowning, were as natural as the coroner, and perhaps Dr Moon, believed. He turned to Freddy and the doctor, saying, 'I'd like to talk to Phyll alone for a moment, if that's possible.'

'Yes, of course you must.' Dr Moon smiled and placed his empty pipe in the desk drawer. 'Freddy and I will leave you to discuss your work.' Then he reconsidered, and reaching once more towards the drawer, he pulled out his pipe and tobacco and placed both in his pocket. 'If you need me, I shall be with my cacti.' He turned to Freddy. 'I suppose you want to finish the choir stalls, old chap.'

'Yes, I do,' said Freddy, eager to please, for facing your fears was part of the therapy, William supposed. 'What doesn't kill me, and all that.'

Phyll flinched but said nothing.

William rose and walked over to the window. On the flat marshy land beyond the river, crows pecked, hunched and murderous, at some smaller creature. It was a world of death and black water, this countryside. The city, of course, had its own chaos, but it was nothing compared to the anarchy of the country.

'Does it look like rain?' Once more, he felt Phyll's quiet presence by his side. 'If you're right about the weather, old sailor that you are, then she'll make an appearance tonight?'

'Yes, it'll rain alright.' William moved to the cigarette box, lit one and drew hard. 'And tomorrow is Candlemas. The anniversary of the mermaid's death. Dr Moon and his patients know this. They're all wound so tight the intruder could wreak havoc without hardly lifting a finger. She'll have something special planned.'

'We should stay the night.'

'I don't like this job. It's all psychology.' William tapped his head. 'We're not taking the case.'

'What on earth are you talking about?' Her pale face reddened. 'You promised me this morning that we would take on the case, and now you're welching.'

'We'll take Freddy back to Birmingham with us now and find him somewhere better to live. Bloody hell, Phyll, Red Hollow is one great big fucking mess. It's understaffed, the grounds aren't properly secure, and it has a history which could give the sanest man nightmares. We'll take Freddy with us today and leave Dr Moon to deal with the yampy bastard playing at mermaids. Let's stay well out of it.'

'Yampy? That's a new one.'

'It means mad.'

'I gathered that.' Phyll's face flushed further; her voice hardened. 'I can't take Freddy away with me, Billy. I simply can't.'

'Dr Moon can cause all the fuss he likes over fees and three days' notice. We'll get Shifty on the case. He can prove Freddy's health is in danger if he stays. Let's face it, Red Hollow is on its last legs anyway.' But his words hadn't worked. Phyll had fallen into a tension so tightly drawn William felt he could twang her like the string of a violin. 'This mermaid business is too complex for us to deal with, Phyll. We're not properly equipped or experienced.' William attempted a reassuring smile and a tone of clear authority. 'We're not that kind of detectives.'

'Then what the hell kind of detectives are we, Billy?'

The authoritative tone hadn't worked.

'The finding-a-beloved-lost-dog kind. The finding-a-less-beloved-errant-husband kind. Small fry and minor tragedies, that's our game.' William held out his cigarette, clamped between his treacherous fingers, and watched it tremble. 'I'm the nervous kind of detective, Phyll love. I just can't take any more shit.'

Phyll's angry pink face softened. 'Oh God, Billy, you don't understand, do you?'

'Then it's about time you bloody well told me.'

Smiling, she took William's cigarette from his shuddering hand, and said, 'Freddy lives here for free. The family money I used to pay for his care ran out two years ago. It's why I took up with Quince. He paid so well for his vulgar little pictures.' Phyll took a few puffs of the cigarette and stared out onto the flat black bleakness of the lawns. She hadn't mentioned the pornographer since last summer, and neither had William. He glanced at his knuckles, thinking of Quince's broken nose. Trouble was brewing. The magpie was a sign.

'I'm six months in arrears with Dr Moon. I know he's rack-ety, and more than a little eccentric, but Dr Moon is a dear, kind man, and he saved Freddy's life. He hasn't said a word about the money I owe and will pay us properly if we take on this job.'

Phyll's voice was heavy with guilt and gratitude. William paused, but then said what he wanted to say nonetheless. 'But he took everything you had, all of your inheritance, in fees.'

'It wasn't much, but yes. Everything Freddy and I had, but it was worth it.' Phyll took another draw on her cigarette, and he noticed the thin skin beneath her closed eyes had purpled. Then there came a momentary tell-tale twitch of exhaustion. 'Freddy was at Passchendaele.' William raised his eyebrows. Bloody, muddy Flanders where young men fell with the ubi-quity of autumn leaves. 'He led rescue and recovery missions into no man's land, despite the heavy shellfire. The other men called him Four Leaf Freddy because he had such good luck. But his luck ran out, eventually, and he got buried under a lot of Belgian mud. He doesn't know how long for. He thinks days; the army says hours. I believe Freddy. His men dug him out, but by then he was a wreck. He was at Seale-Hayne Army Hospital for a year, and they diagnosed him with complete retrograde amnesia, mutism and hysterical paralysis. Eventually, he came round, and they sent him home, quite alright other than having a peculiar form of agoraphobia. If anxious, he would hide away in confined spaces like a fright-ened cat, only feeling safe if something quite solid was about him. When Father died, Freddy retreated to his wardrobe. Mother and I would try to coax him out, but he wouldn't shift. He did eventually, when our mother died, and that was to try and take his own life. After that, he was put in an asylum. He could hardly bear it.' She moved to stub her cigarette out in the ashtray on the library desk. 'Dr Moon was with Freddy at Seale-Hayne, and when he returned from America, he asked Freddy if he'd like to join him at Red Hollow, rescued him. Dr Moon worked a kind of miracle on Freddy. The only thing is, he can't leave the grounds. He can't allow himself to go beyond the gate. It's as though the bounds of the manor are a barrier he can't cross. That's why I can't take him away from Red Hollow. That's why I have to make this place safe for him again. He's happy here, thank God, if not completely normal.'

'Oh, fuck me, Phyll. No one is completely normal.' Phyll gave him a wide, and thankful, boyish grin, and reached over to squeeze his hand. 'Alright, we'll take the case. We'll do our best to give Freddy a bit of peace, but we can't stay overnight.' William looked at his feet, schoolboyish. He was about to give what seemed a weak excuse considering Freddy's story, but it was the truth. 'We have the christening tomorrow.'

'We can easily be back for the christening, Billy. You know that.'

'If we're even a minute late, Queenie will have our guts for garters.'

'We will be there, Billy. I wouldn't miss it for the world, honestly. We can be home in half an hour. It's an easy journey.' Phyll reached towards the box and lit them both another cigarette. Neither one felt any shame at chain-smoking, and William took pleasure in watching her grateful inhalation. 'Besides, Queenie's bark is bigger than her bite.'

'Bollocks,' he said. 'Queenie's a notorious biter. She's worse than that fuckin' mermaid.'

'Then you go back to Birmingham, and I'll stay here and keep an eye on things. I promise I'll be in church first thing. You go home. The two of us don't need to be here. I suppose

I want to stay for my own peace of mind, and I have an inkling that having an actual private detective poke about a bit here might prevent another attack.'

'Or provoke one, Phyll,' he said. 'So for fuck's sake, watch your back.'

'Don't worry about me. Freddy is my big brother, and despite his troubles, he's actually very brave. Did I tell you he has the VC?'

Day Two

9

Friday, 2 February 1934

Queenie, the proud new owner of a driving licence and a spanking Rover 10, drove assertively. She motored down Bennett's Hill, which was still thick with black ice, passed the Sun Life building at speed, and sounded her horn at the Inland Revenue, giving William a grin and a quick wink as she did it, too. 'That'll show 'em,' she said. 'Poking their noses into my bloody books. They can stick their slide rules up their arse.'

William kept his mouth shut and his arms about his son. Wrapped in an elaborate white shawl, the baby slept, an innocent. The other three kiddies, all trussed up in church clothes, were on the back seat, giggling and yelping at every bump in the road, and every sudden turn.

'Weren't a bad service, were it?' She took a sharp right onto Curzon Street, and so wide that they hurtled straight into the path of oncoming traffic.

'Christ almighty, be more careful,' he said. 'You'll bloody kill us.' William pressed the baby to his chest with his left arm, flinging his right back to stop two of the other children tumbling hard onto the handbrake.

'What's up with you?' Queenie weaved her Rover between

the trams and buses with an unrestrained glee. 'Spill it. I cannot bear a mardy bloke.'

William did as he was told, and out it poured.

'Your choice of godparents wasn't much to my liking.' William thought back to the service. The priest whizzing through the Latin, poor bastard scared shitless of half the congregation; the northerner with the gold tooth and his brassy missus declaring they would renounce Satan, and all his works, and all his pomps, on behalf of William's only son. 'I don't reckon those new friends of yours were quite respectable, Queenie bab. I doubt they'll instruct young William here on how to walk the straight path of right-eousness.' William chuckled, but it was mirthless. 'You promised me the clean-living Bob Stokes. Where was Bob, by the way?'

'Bob weren't available no more.' Queenie waved a dismis-sive hand. 'He had to go away for a bit, short notice. And we still got Arthur and Edie. I was struggling for Catholics, and my new Mancunian friends were a good choice. Bestowing the honour was a sound business move. Northerners are senti-mental bastards. They cry more than we do.'

'I just didn't want him christened in the first place,' he said.

'All my babbies are Catholic.' She frowned at the road; her first scowl of the day. 'I couldn't have Billy die unbaptised.'

'Are we nearly there, Mom?' Queenie's eldest called from the back seat.

'Any minute now, bab.'

'Die? Jesus, Queenie.' A violent surge of panic swelled like a great wave and lodged itself in William's throat. He glanced at his child's closed eyes, his pursed pink lips, the rise and fall of his tiny chest beneath the shawl. Queenie was medieval. This was what he was up against, this backward, tribal bullshit.

His baby wasn't going to die. 'Why the hell would you say a thing like that?'

'They do, Billy.' Her voice was gentle, motherly. 'Lots do. You know that.'

'Shut your trap, Queenie. I don't wanna hear it.'

The giggling children became silent at hearing William's cheek. 'I'm gonna let that lie,' she said. 'But only because I'm in a bloody wonderful mood today, and your funny nerves ain't gonna stop me from celebrating.'

Curzon Street became New Canal Street, the terraced houses stretching up to the railway bridge and beyond. The Woodman, a corner pub, came in view. Queenie used her right foot, at last, and they drew to a halt with a jolt that made William's stomach turn. She looked about her, jumped out of the Rover and then opened the rear door. The three children tumbled out, scooting to the pavement at Queenie's instruction.

'Come on, love.' She smiled at him, nodding towards the Woodman. 'The day's over, all bar the shouting, and there's going to be a lovely spread. Hand over the little one.' William passed the baby to Queenie, who loosened the swaddling and sniffed at the child like a mother wolf. A small pink hand appeared from beneath the shawl. Queenie kissed it and placed it back beneath the wrappings. 'Keep your donnies in, me babby. It's bitter out.' William shut the car door and stood, tall and awkward, three steps away from Queenie and her children, a superfluous patriarch. 'He ain't done a poo yet,' she whispered. 'I told you it was a good day. Where's Phyll, by the way? Was she sitting at the back of the church? I couldn't see her.'

Yes, where was Phyll? William had woken early that morning in a cold sweat and with Phyll's name on his lips. He had telephoned through to Red Hollow Hall to speak to her but had got no answer. William shook off the rising feeling of unease and blamed the trains. Phyll was stuck outside of Water Orton and would arrive in time for Queenie's party, no doubt. 'She didn't turn up, Queenie,' he said.

Queenie, busy straightening her eldest son's cap with her left hand, said, 'Of course she did. You were just too wrapped up in your nerves to notice her. She was at the back because she's posh, and she ain't Catholic. She was being polite.' Job done, and child duly uncomfortable, she turned to William and smiled. 'It's just like her, ain't it? She's nice, ain't she? She ain't the type to take centre stage?'

William glanced at the sky. Clouds, as leaden as foundry smoke but pregnant with moisture, darkened Birmingham, and along New Canal Street the gaslight flickered from the windows of the terraces with an eerie will-o'-the-wisp light. He had been wrong. It had not rained. William shivered and pulled the collar of his overcoat tight about his neck, and said, 'No, love. I was on the lookout for her, but she weren't there.' However, Queenie had not heard him, for she was already ten steps ahead, high heels click-click-clicking on the frozen pavement, as sure-footed as a Sherpa on the ice, his baby safe on her hip, and her children trotting obediently at her side. He cried out once more, 'Queenie, love. I'm getting worried about her.'

Despite the cold, the door to the main bar of the Woodman was wedged open. Still not quite opening time, the pub was empty of customers. A mahogany bar, chestnut rich with decades of polish, ran along the far wall. Pumps, rails and drip trays, all brass and gleaming with hard graft, glimmered with the prospect of a good time. Backed by a trio of etched and gilded mirrors, the bar spoke of the gin palaces of a bygone era: of railway stopovers, navvies drinking away their pay, floozies in feathered hats. The only concession to modernity was a brand-new Bakelite telephone perched, in sombre black, next to an enormous and gaudy Victorian till.

In the corner, a sparrow of a woman scrubbed at the tile floor, but she didn't look up from her work. The landlord, however, was all attention at their arrival and moved towards them with an unlikely grace. He was a tall, broad man in his early fifties. Clinging to the last vestiges of his good looks, he patted his slick, artificially black hair, and flashed his eerily white false teeth before greeting Queenie. 'Congratulations on your new arrival, Miss Maggs,' he said. 'You know you're always welcome at the Woodman.' Queenie nodded. The landlord took her hand and stroked it reverently, as if it could cure scrofula. 'There's a lovely spread in the function room, all laid on special. Our Iris is there to serve; she's a good girl, quick and clean. Just ask her for anything you need.'

He nodded to William and shook his hand, then ushered Queenie through the bar to the rear of the pub. William watched as he placed his big, ex-boxer's palm on the base of her spine, and, standing too close and breathing too heavily, waved his free arm as if to indicate the festive opulence of the function room. 'Ain't it just the ticket,' he said.

Butted up against the far wall, beneath a mirror advertising *Gordon's Gin*, stood a large table, weighed down with a vast quantity of food: celery in pressed glass vases, plates of triangular sandwiches, sausage rolls, slivers of livery pressed tongue, fat pink radishes and a cellar of salt. Two urns, generous with chrysanthemums and spikes of fern, flanked a huge cake, hard with white icing. And above the unmistakeable note of tinned salmon in malt vinegar, the scent of stale beer and Jeyes Fluid lingered. Function room or not, they were in a Digbeth pub.

'You've done me proud, Mr Baker.' Queenie surveyed the room but did not smile. Instead, she pointed to the empty leather bench opposite the buffet table, and said, 'You kiddies sit nicely, and this man'll get you all a pop.' The children obeyed; three pairs of wide eyes were now fixed on Mr Baker.

'Pop.' Mr Baker offered the children a weak, avuncular smile. 'Lemonade, kiddies, is that what you want?' The land-lord stood for a second, simpering, and William wondered if the man might tug his forelock. Finally, he said, 'You just ask for anything you need, Miss Maggs. You know you have friends at the Woodman.'

'Just the pop, Mr Baker,' she said.

The landlord returned to the bar with due deference.

Queenie loosened the baby's shawl, and placed him, now fully awake, on her hip. William watched as she faffed about at the table, straightening plates, peeking under serviettes, inspecting the sandwich fillings. William, superfluous, stood with his hands in his pockets, fingering his loose change. She turned to him and said, 'It's what they call a running buffet, you know. It means there's more food to come.' She was proud of herself, for this was Queenie's idea of grand. 'There'll be hot baps and then cake for sweet.'

'I'm going to phone Phyll,' he said.

'What? Why?' Queenie, distracted, sniffed at the flower water. 'If she ain't here already, she'll probably be coming along with Arthur.'

'Why the fuck would she want to travel with Arthur Stokes? Not everyone trusts your muscle as much as you do. Besides, Phyll doesn't even know him. Use your brains, Queenie.' He had change enough to put a call through to Red Hollow. He would do it now, if only to put his mind at rest. 'I'm going to the bar.'

'Well, tell Mick Baker to hurry up with the pop while you're there,' Queenie called after him, undisturbed by either his language or his panic.

Queenie's guests had arrived. They stood in groups at the bar, clutching pints and chatting in low murmurs, or waited to be served with a silent stoicism. Two or three broke from the pack, taking a dignified slow walk to the back room and Queenie's running buffet, and then the telephone was revealed. William edged through a small crowd of suited men and called out to the landlord, 'I need to use your phone. Local call.'

'Tuppence in the jar and knock yourself out,' said Mr Baker. The landlord had a moneymaking sweat on, a heady combination of over-exertion and glee. 'But no more than five minutes or I'll come along and cut the call for you.'

William made a show of placing his coin in the jar and rang through to the exchange. The operator was prompt, and the call to Red Hollow rang out. William felt a draught on the back of his neck, a chill strong enough to make him shiver. From the corner of his eye, he saw Arthur Stokes enter, holding the door open, not for Phyll, but the northerner and his missus. William stood full square to the bar and watched the new arrivals reflected in the tawdry glamour of the Victorian mirror. Still the call rang out. 'Answer the fuckin' phone,' he said. 'Answer the telephone, someone.'

The giant till clanged and clattered. Mick Baker gave William the side-eye, and then pointedly examined the gold fob watch dangling over his incipient paunch. From his left, there came a squeal of rasping laughter, like the bark of a fox. He glanced at the woman; her eyes sparkled as men circled. The Mancunian and Arthur Stokes's chatter became a babble of hearty dialect, the two accents strangely melding into one.

William became once again conscious of his own shallow breathing, a constriction in his chest. 'Answer the phone, for Christ's sake.'

'I'm sorry, caller, but I am unable to connect you.' The operator's voice was high and reedy. 'Do you want me to try once more?'

'No, no thank you. I'll call later.'

William put the receiver down and steadied himself against the weight of the bar. Something terrible clawed at the edge of his subconscious. He took a few steadying breaths, inhaled deeply through his nose, and glanced at his reflection in the bar mirror – death warmed up. Mick Baker was watching him; he saw it from the corner of his eye. The big landlord sidled over. 'What can I get you, pal?'

'Double brandy.'

'No spirits on the tab. Arthur Stokes's orders.'

'I pay my own way.' He handed over a few shillings, and the landlord soon returned with his brandy. William took a gulp and turned away from his own reflection. He was nothing but an over-anxious fool, he told himself. Hadn't Dr Moon complained of being short-staffed? There wasn't a problem at the hall. They simply had no one available to man the telephone. Phyll would arrive any minute, red-faced and apologetic, muttering something about the trains, and all would be well.

He returned to the function room, hard booze sloshing about in his empty stomach, and realised, for the first time, that the place was full of men. And men William did not know. Queenie's old guard had dropped by the wayside, and only the Stokes siblings remained.

Few women were at the Woodman, and those in attendance made themselves invisible in plain coat and hat, and chatted in corners with low, respectable voices. *Just a drop of port and lemon, for now.* Their men were solicitous, handing out plates of food, but obviously wishing the wife would get off home. And each man had something to say to Queenie, who, baby still on her hip, responded with discreet nods and one-word whispers. Queenie's older children sipped pop from half-pint glasses and picked at their sandwiches, looking restless and eager to leave. It was no place for them. This wasn't a family event. Queenie turned as he entered and handed over the baby. 'Give me a break with him,' she said. 'He's getting heavy.'

Surely the baby would need a feed and a nap soon? William looked about hopelessly, as if a bottle and a cot would become manifest at his thoughts. All he knew was his son was too young for a Scotch egg and a kip under a copper-topped pub table. He hovered next to Queenie, unsure and anxious. Then in came Arthur Stokes with a large whisky in hand and acting as if William did not exist. He placed his thick body between William and Queenie. William didn't move.

'I spoke to Mick Baker,' said Arthur Stokes. 'He'll keep a tab open for two hours. No spirits, just beer.' He downed his drink. 'You're generous, but you're not stupid.'

'But you're taking good care of our new friends?'

'Double whisky at the bar. His missus drinks neat gin. Never known it. Didn't even want a dash of lime cordial.'

'Not everyone's as ladylike as me.' She looked over Arthur's shoulder. William followed her gaze and saw Edie Stokes, head held high as she sailed into the room with a huge black pram. A luxury liner on wheels, she docked it near the open window. 'Good girl, Edie,' said Queenie. 'Give him his bottle and put him down for his nap now. We'll let the kiddies have another hour at the party, and then you take 'em home. I got a bit of business to do.' She nodded to William, who handed over his child without a word. This is impotence, he thought.

Then, boom, into the room came the Mancunian. Red curls like a Tudor prince, big and handsome, gold tooth glittering like Christmas, all heads turned. William's hackles rose. He'd never seen a less sentimental-looking man, but he was the affectionate kind. Taking Queenie by both shoulders with his great paws, he did not lean in, but moved her body towards his, planting a long, wet kiss on each of her powdered cheeks. It was an obvious assertion of power, and not lost on Queenie.

The man's little fur-clad missus slipped in between them like the fox she was. Grinning with gin, she took Queenie's hand, sisterly, and said, 'Me and Sammy are having a lovely time. Birmingham ain't as horrible as people say it is, is it?'

'Some say it's like Venice,' said Queenie.

'Now, love, that's not quite true,' said Sammy the Manc. 'What they say is you've got more canals than Venice.'

'You're right.' Queenie lifted the netted veil of her cloche and fixed her big green eyes on the man. 'It's what we have in common, ain't it, canals and commerce.' Queenie paused, her voice becoming breathy. 'And we both have a reputation for making brass.'

Sammy considered her as a butcher does a side of beef, and then said, 'You're a clever one. I like clever women, don't I, Violet?'

Violet, the gin-swilling fox, smiled. 'He likes brains, like other men like tits.'

Queenie had met her match.

Then the big man took a step to his left, peered into the baby's pram, and pulled back the covers. Breathing whisky breath into the child's face, he pinched the baby's cheek between his thumb and forefinger, and said, 'Ain't my godson a little angel. Ain't he just precious.' The baby rumbled into an indignant cry. Sammy the Manc stepped back, in faux shock. 'Sensitive little fella. I don't think he likes me.'

The room was full of sweat and lies and egg sandwiches. William's brandy-filled stomach soured, and his nausea rose with a pulsating anger. He glanced at Queenie. He was angry with her, not only for allowing this recent violation, but for the whole, wasted day. This, he realised, was why he had been so desperate for Phyll's company. With Queenie, his moral compass spun in a constant, anxious rotation. Phyll was his north. He moved forward, plate of beige stodge still in his hand, and said, 'I'll take him out into the fresh air. It's a bit crowded in here.'

'You're a funny-looking nursemaid,' said Sammy, flashing the gold tooth. William wanted to prise it out of the man's gob with pliers, pawn it, use the money to buy the baby something nice. A deposit on a house, maybe. He placed his plate on the top of the pram, grabbed the handles, and reversed through the crowd, saying:

'I'm his father, pal.'

'I didn't know the poor little bastard had one.'

Foxy Violet hooted.

William halted, felt the fury swell and roil. A brawl would do him nicely right now, clear his head, free him up from the chaos of the day, and teach that arrogant Manc fucker a valuable lesson.

Queenie slid over, stony-faced. 'Have a bit of cake, Billy.' She pressed a hunk of fruitcake into his free hand. He knew what she was doing. Women had been placating angry men with food and sex and comforting words for millennia. He shook his head but watched as the northerner sank his glittering teeth into a large slice, and ate open-mouthed, defiant.

'When you're ready, Queenie,' said William. 'I'd like a word.'

The baby was asleep before William left the public bar. Outside, William sat on his haunches, head resting against the cold, red brick of the pub wall, and ate a sausage roll. In the distance, plumes of smoke and steam floated from beyond the neoclassical façade of Curzon Street station. He heard the clamour of the goods trains loading. Near a mile long, they took Brummagem off to London in a matter of hours. The canal, and its way of life, he knew, was enduring a long and lingering death. Extinction loomed.

Suddenly, he felt the fur of Queenie's best winter coat brush against his cheek, smelt her heady French perfume, too. 'It's the oldest railway building still standing in the country,' he said, nodding down the road.

'You've always been a clever one.' He offered her a cigarette, but she refused. 'I want you to know, I didn't like it either. Him mucking about with our Billy. Pinching his cheek, and all that. But love, never show what you really feel. It ain't a healthy thing to do if you move in my circles.'

William shrugged and said, 'You can't control that sort of bloke, Queenie. It's like trying to make a pet out of a fighting dog.'

'With dogs, when they've finished scrapping, you put 'em down.'

'So, that's how it's going.' He sighed, stood and pulled the pram towards him, peered in at his sleeping son. It was a soft, puffing sleep, open-mouthed and innocent. William thought his heart might rend in two. Love was a dangerous thing. 'I hope you know what you're doing.'

'Don't I always?'

'Keep your business away from the baby, Queenie. I mean it.'

There came a great rumble, a low thick growl. It was a disconcerting sound, and it came as if from the surrounding air.

Queenie frowned. 'Trains or machinery?' she asked.

'Goods yard, I reckon.'

'Strange, weren't it?'

'I left my bit of christening cake in the pub,' he said. 'I missed out because I was in high dudgeon.'

'It's alright,' she said. 'I've got you another piece.' Queenie reached into the pocket of her coat and passed him a wrapped hunk of cake. 'Where's Phyll? I've not seen her all day.'

'Christ, love, I keep telling you. She didn't bloody turn up.' And who could blame her? She was sensible to distance herself from it all. At least, he hoped Phyll had ditched him and this whole sorry shit-show. He hoped it with all his heart. William bit into his cake and was immediately comforted. 'This is moist.'

The air rumbled again. There came a weird, electric crack, an unseasonal fizzle of summer.

They paused, listening to the sound.

Queenie broke the silence. 'Bullshit,' she said. 'You just haven't seen her, that's all.' She pulled her fur coat tight about her chest and began her walk to the Woodman. 'Christ almighty, Billy. You never looked properly. I'll find her.'

'She's not here, Queenie. I'm telling you.'

She halted in her tracks. 'Where is she then?'

'On a job, I think.'

'For you?'

'Who the fuck else for?'

Queenie returned, and considered him for a moment with her shrewd, secretive face.

'Phyll stayed overnight on the job,' William added. 'She said she'd catch the train to Birmingham first thing. She promised me she wouldn't miss the christening.'

'What kind of job?'

'A funny one.' He proceeded to tell her the details. Dr Moon's rest home, the folk tale, the church, Freddy's visitation, everything. 'My hackles are up, Queenie. There's something about this case that's playing havoc with my gut. I reckon that intruder means business. I never should've left Phyll alone.'

'Then we go to this Red Hollow place and find her, and if we have to fillet the odd mermaid in the process, we will.'

A stream of men trickled out of the pub, nodding to Queenie as they passed.

'We?'

'Yes, we.' It wasn't a challenge, or a matter of discussion, but a confident affirmation that William would do as ordered. 'I've got Edie to look after the kids. We'll check out Phyll's flat, and then go to Red Hollow. We'll take the Rover.'

'Why the interest?'

'Phyll's a good girl,' she said. 'You know I look after my own.'

'Alright,' he said. A few drops of water fell on William's cheek. He held out his hand; yes, it was beginning to rain. 'But I'll drive. There's no way I'm putting my life in your hands again.'

There came what William thought to be the sound of great iron doors clanging in the goods yard, or perhaps the boom of a foundry press. The noise echoed down New Canal Street, hollow and eerie. And then, from between the sagging clouds, as purple and vivid as a fresh bruise, came the unmistakeable flash of lightning.

'That was thunder.' Queenie looked up at the clouds, frowning. 'Have you ever heard of thunderstorms in February?'

Then the scattered raindrops became a deluge, and they ran with the pram for cover, back to the open doors of the Woodman. Much of the crowd had dispersed. Arthur stood at the bar, slightly apart from Sammy the Manc, who held court with a few of Queenie's men. He told blue jokes and slapped backs, swilled back brandy and enjoyed the younger men's awe. Arthur stubbed out his cigarette and moved forward at their entrance. Sammy clocked Queenie, but feigned ignorance of her arrival – and her status.

'Fetch me Edie and the kiddies,' she said to Arthur Stokes. 'And then get that big bastard and his smart-arse whore back to Manchester as quick as good manners allow. I got summat to do.'

Arthur, good dog that he was, nodded and left.

William gazed at his sleeping child. He was precious to him, and the burgeoning love, new but fierce, lodged deep beneath his ribcage. The child had a place there, alongside his love for Clara. Criminality was not his boy's inheritance. Criminality and violence as a family tradition – what kind of life was that to lumber on a child?

Edie Stokes entered the bar with the kiddies in tow. William watched as Queenie whispered to the woman, who moved forward impassively, and wheeled his son away from him without a word.

For the last time, though, William swore. No more would Edie Stokes act as de facto mother to his son. He glanced about the bar, took in Queenie's lads, brash in smart suits, their pockets bagged out with knuckledusters; Violet, hair all awry, slowly swaying with gin; Arthur sweating adoration and obedience; Sammy, a man who wouldn't piss on you if you were on fire. No more of this, he thought, no more.

IO

Queenie was saying something, but he couldn't hear a word. The downpour was deafening. Blinding, too, for little was visible beyond the immediate wall of rain, and the Rover's wipers were ineffectual against the strength of both the water and the whipping wind. The fields and farmhouses familiar from the previous day's journey were now blurred and distorted, each house and barn a warped, disconnected vision, as if seen through the bottom of a beer glass. They crawled along Watling Street, not stopping, but wading onwards through mucky rain, which at any moment threatened to cut the engine, and isolate them in the midst of the storm.

'Hope for the best, expect the worst.' Queenie's voice came once more, but this time as a deep yell. William merely nodded. They had spoken little since leaving Phyll's, as it turned out, deserted flat, but there was nothing to be said, even if they could make themselves heard. As the journey progressed, he had sensed Queenie's usually soft body stiffen, and become poised, muscles taut, nerves on high alert, as if readying herself for battle. Boadicea in a Rover 10. And there was something about Queenie's concern for Phyll, and her interest in Red Hollow, which worried at the edge of William's consciousness. Queenie rarely paid attention to his business unless it turned out to be her business too. 'Are we nearly there?' she asked.

'Five minutes to the turning, perhaps ten in this weather,' William said. 'Look out for the sign on your side.'

Queenie merely nodded and turned her head to the left.

'Now,' she called. 'The turning is coming up.'

He flipped the indicator and drove down the lane which now seemed a shallow, fast-flowing brook. As they passed the village houses, William noticed a bulwark of sandbags protecting each front door from the rising water. Light shone as a dull distortion from the cottage windows. These were the only signs of life. He glanced at the patchwork of fields to his right and wondered if the drainage ditches continued to do their job, but saw, to his horror, that the river had burst its banks, and the spindling willow and beech were bent near horizontal by the brute force of the wind.

'Not far to the hall. It's to the left, but we need to cross the ford,' he said. 'And it might not be so low now.' William was unsure if this commentary was for Queenie's benefit or his own. She simply nodded.

He made the left-hand turn along the trackway, now thick with mud, and moved the Rover down to a crawl. Traction was already poor, the rear wheels sliding, unable to keep a grip on the slick red clay. Soon they would be upon the ford, and William knew he would be unable to gauge the depth of the water. He was unsure how fast he should take it. Yesterday Phyll had slowed down, and so William shifted the car into first gear.

They plunged into what seemed a river. He felt the power of its force against the pathetic efforts of the engine. Water, black and sliding, seeped in through the bottom of the car doors. William saw, in the rear-view mirror, a tree fall slowly, as if managing its own landing with grace, and he realised there was no returning to the village by car. They were cut off.

'Put your foot down,' Queenie yelled.

'What difference will that make?' William was unable to mask his panic. Water tickled his ankles. What if they became stuck in the ford, unable to get out of the motor? Trapped in this deluge, the water rising ... And yet he did as Queenie said – that was his nature – and moved the car into second, accelerated but heard the agonising grind of gears above the heavy drumbeat of the storm. He felt Queenie's grip on his left arm. The Rover spluttered forward and came to a halt.

William caught his breath. They had made it through the ford, but only just. He sat for a minute, watching the downpour, which came in sheets of silver against the gunmetal storm-grey sky, and then he turned the ignition, and to his horror heard nothing but a splutter and scrape of the waterlogged engine.

William pulled up the collar of his overcoat and turned down the brim of his hat. 'Wait here,' he said. 'I need to see how far we are from the ford.' He stepped from the car and out into a furious winter darkness. Icy rain, driven near horizontal by the wind, whipped at his cheeks, punctured the weft of his overcoat, entered his shirt, his underclothes. And then he lost his hat, and the rain became blinding.

The lane was ankle deep with fast-flowing water, and the Rover teetered mere inches from the edge of the ford. If they were to save the car, they would need to push it to the side of the road and as far as possible onto the high verge, and then make their way to the hall on foot. Neither he nor Queenie would contemplate turning back, even if they could. This he was sure of.

He tapped on the window on Queenie's side. There was no use sitting in the car. Queenie opened the window a few inches, pulled her body away from the blast of rain that entered the motor. 'We're gonna have to walk it,' he said, glancing at Queenie's patent leather heels. 'Have you got any rubber boots?'

She shook her head. 'How many miles?'

'No more than two.' If they made it. The sky, the bare hedges, the trees, the whole country seemed in the grip of some ancient frenzy. Only the marshy fields, now shallow glassy lakes, were eerie in their stillness. He glanced to his left. Beyond the creaking oaks that bordered the lane hunkered the patch of woodland and the Red Hollow. Had the pool burst its banks? Was it the prospect of flood or superstition about the mermaid which made the villagers barricade themselves in their homes? He shook off the thought. 'You got an electric torch in the glove box?' he asked.

She shrugged. 'Why should I?'

'I dunno. It's helpful when breaking and entering. You can wallop nightwatchmen with 'em.'

'Don't be like that,' she said. 'Can we manage without one? Is the road ahead alright?'

'We'll manage, but we need to try and save the car. Slip over to the driver's seat and take off the handbrake. We're going to steer the car into the passing place to the left. It's about a hundred yards or so away and on higher ground. Do you understand what I mean?' She nodded. 'I'll push and you steer, yes?'

He moved to the back end of the Rover, and saw her small, gloved hand give him the thumbs up from the window on the driver's side. William put his shoulder to the rear of the car and began to push. At first, he couldn't get traction, his feet slipping in the clay and the slaty gravel of the lane. Then it shifted, and off they went. For a moment, he was tempted to push the car for the two miles, simply to keep Queenie dry. There was a time when he would have broken his back for her, but William's days of chivalry were now long gone. Suddenly, the car halted with a bump on the grass verge, and out came Queenie, slamming the door behind her, needing no white knight. She looked down the lane and fastened the top button of her coat. 'Fuck it,' she said. 'We've got no choice.' And she tottered forward, leading the way.

They trudged along for half an hour in bleak silence, soon becoming inured to the relentlessness of the weather. No more than a hundred yards or so down the lane, the gates to Red Hollow Hall were open a crack, the threatening cast iron spikes slick with water. William pointed towards them. 'We're nearly there,' he said. 'A quarter-mile at the most.'

Queenie nodded.

And all seemed devoid of life. No crows circled, and the sheep, grazing on the pasture only a day before, had disappeared; moved, William thought, to higher ground at the first hint of heavy rain. He did not see the house in the distance, but only the jaundiced light which glowed from each window. William gestured to Queenie. 'Lights from the hall,' he said. 'Not long now.'

Queenie picked up pace, as a marathon runner gets a second wind when the finish line is in sight, and they soon neared the house, which proffered a blank, unblinking face against the rain. There was no movement behind the half-closed curtains. No sound other than the enveloping storm. No sign of life.

Queenie turned to him and frowned. 'You didn't tell me it was this house, Billy,' she said. 'Can you remember when we passed through here as kids? I loved this house. I thought it looked like a castle, like the ones painted on the cabin doors of the *Little Marvel*. I used to dream of owning it. Perhaps I still do. Can you remember when you and Ronnie stole those crates of jam from—'

'I don't want to talk about him, Queenie. I can't take it.'

He had spent the walk worrying that she would remember Red Hollow, and the worst had happened. Ronnie's name had been mentioned, and so the ghost materialised.

'Why?'

'Why? Are you mad? Because of what happened last summer.' His childhood faith suddenly surfaced like flotsam; it was the christening and the biblical weather. 'All that sin. All that mortal sin.'

'But don't you know? Divorce, perjury and fiddling with yourself, they're all mortal sins.' Queenie laughed. 'I reckon that means you're fucked, bab.' She gestured towards the church tower. Red stone, liver-like in the strange light; it seemed a sunken island in the flood-land. 'We're all grave sinners, Billy. Sometimes I reckon Jesus is on his tod up there. He rattles about in heaven like a marble in a pop bottle.'

'I told you, Queenie. I can't take it.' William marched ahead. Queenie saw the world differently, he knew. She wasn't immoral, or amoral, she was simply a dangerous pragmatist.

'Well, you're gonna have to.' She caught up with him, trotting at his side like a pretty, panting Shetland pony. 'What we did was mete out justice. Think about what would've happened if we hadn't cleaned up that whole bloody mess. We did a hard thing. But we did it because someone had to.' To the right of Queenie, the mermaid weathervane spun, her golden tail flapping, frantic at the mercy of the wind and rain. 'Make peace with God, Billy, if you still believe in Him. And if you don't, make peace with yourself. We've made our bed. We just have to fuckin' lie in it.'

William glanced heavenwards. A peculiar lavender shimmered between the crevices of the black storm clouds, as if the sky had dressed itself in Victorian mourning. Then he looked behind him, assessing the water's incursion. On either side of the drive, the sleek surface of the flooded parkland reflected the overhanging branches of the oaks as monstrous curves. Soon, he knew, the pathway would be gone, and if a stretch of river upstream burst its banks, then there would be no escaping Red Hollow unless by boat. William blinked away the rain from his eyes, squinting at a patch of strange shadow beneath the trees. A bobbing hump of black, it bumped heavily against the thick, low branches. It wasn't a shadow; it had heft. It was a dead sheep. No, it was the wrong shape. Longer, narrower and with what looked like trouser legs swaying in the shallow water.

A vision of Phyll, smart in a dark suit, surfaced. And then William ran.

The rain fell, vivid and lustrous against the darkening horizon as William skidded along the gravel drive. When he came to the lower ground of the park, the water became deep, pushing against his shins, and slowing him down in what seemed an act of deliberate frustration. Queenie was a few squelching steps behind him. He turned and called out to her, 'It's Phyll. It's her. She's under the trees.'

'We've just come from there. How could we have missed her?' Queenie's panting, panicked voice came in fragments over the sound of pouring rain.

Because we were arguing, William thought. Wrapped up in each other, always, like a pair of cats scrapping in a bag.

William slowed, wading now as he neared the body. It floated face down, overcoat billowing on the water like the fins of a great, black stingray. William bent, and grabbed the waist, turning the torso upwards and away from the water. He worked in the dark, Queenie hovering gravely silent at his side, seeing none of the body's features in his panic, but sensing the heft of the corpse and the hard muscle under the heavy tweed and the thickness of the abdomen. 'It's a man,' he said. 'It's not her.' And he let out something akin to a small yelp in relief.

William lifted the dead man's head above the water and moved the snaking trails of mud from his wide forehead and bulging eyes and clogged nostrils. There was no saving the poor bastard. Confusion mixed with relief, as William had half-expected the face to be Freddy's. He reached into the inside pocket of the unbuttoned coat, fingers clumsy with cold, searching for a wallet and some form of identification, found nothing, but saw the unmistakeable white strip of a clerical collar glimmering amidst the dark of the man's sodden black suit.

'It's a priest. A dead priest.' Queenie sprang upright and crossed herself. 'All that talk of God, and mortal sin, and we've found a dead priest. Holy Jesus, I don't like it. It's bad luck.'

'I doubt this poor bugger likes it much either.' William wiped the mulch of dead leaves, grass and gravel from the pale, rabbity face. 'And don't get your superstitious knickers in a twist. He's not a priest. He's a Protestant. The parson no-one around here much likes. The Reverend Andrews, I reckon.' He nodded to the church in the distance. 'That's his church. God only knows what he was doing all the way out here on a Friday afternoon in this weather. He must've had some very good reason for his visit.'

'It's Candlemas. He'd be here to bless the candles.' Queenie's voice held a note of relief. She squinted through the rain towards the manor and winced. 'It'll take us ages to lug him back to the house. You grab the shoulders, and I'll get the ankles. Did I tell you I lost a bloody shoe in this mud?'

I I

William shook the raindrops from his eyes and rang the electric doorbell. No one answered. He glanced at Queenie. Bent double in exhaustion, the hem of her fur coat caressed her mud-caked feet. William pressed his forefinger hard against the buzzer, then counted to ten, and listened for any sound of life coming from behind the door.

'Try the handle,' panted Queenie. 'The lights are on, so someone must be home.'

William stepped forward and examined the door. Pockmarked with the scars of musket balls, it had no handle, only four wrought-iron hinges. He pushed against it, but the door held fast. 'There's no handle. It must be locked and bolted from the inside.' He used his fist and hammered against the oak in five sharp raps. 'Open up. It's William Garrett.' He knocked again, his gut now churning in alarm. 'Open up!'

Suddenly, as if moved by the power of his own panic, the door swung open. William blinked dumbly against the sallow light emanating from the hall. Mr Brooke, a slight figure framed in the centre of the arched doorway, stood silent and assessing, as an actor does before a hostile audience. 'This is a private residential home,' he said. 'And we are not open to casual visitors.'

If the greeting was designed to throw William off-kilter, it was successful, at least until he noticed the wicked glimmer of a smile in Mr Brooke's dark eyes. But William was too exhausted to muster the outrage needed to play Brooke's game. 'We've found a dead body in the flood. We think it's the Reverend Andrews,' he said, gesturing beyond Queenie to the crumpled mass of black clerical wool lying bent on the porch steps. 'Get Dr Moon, immediately.' William stepped forward, toe-to-toe with the orderly. The rain, undeterred by his bulk, sleeted through the open door, spattered Mr Brooke's brogues, pooled on the stone threshold. The orderly glanced at his shoes, and then blinked dumbly at William, but did not move. William resisted the urge to slap the man into action. 'Now, Mr Brooke.'

Brooke's face wrinkled into a disbelieving grin. He tiptoed, stretching his small, dark head to see over William's shoulder, and then fell flat back on his feet, and frowned. Moving aside, he opened the door wide, and said, 'Leave the corpse outside. He's not going anywhere, is he? I'll get Dr Moon. You pair can wait in here.'

The entrance hall was large, square, partly panelled, and crammed with country-house detritus. Umbrellas and shooting sticks had been shoved into a Victorian elephant's foot, and a series of brass hooks held cracked oilskins, shapeless tweed jackets, and a decent, navy-blue overcoat. Huge taxidermy fish, mounted on oak plaques, were hung on the crumbling paintwork; the tail of a fox, its arse-end manacled in silver, dangled above a badger and her cubs in tableau; a glass case containing an adult swan, posed in such a stance to suggest it could break a human arm with a flap of its massive wing, stood on a refectory table. 'I don't much like this room,' he said. 'What is it about the landed gentry and killing stuff?'

'Mastery.' Queenie's answer came quickly, naturally. 'But who am I to talk? I've committed my sins.' She glanced down at her muddied feet and shivered so powerfully William saw her body tremble beneath her sodden fur coat. 'In all honesty, I'd give my eyeteeth to have been born one of them, and have a smidgeon of their class, breeding. I'd be kind to my servants, though. I'm a benevolent mistress. Ask Arthur.'

'I'd rather shit in my hands and clap than ask Arthur Stokes anything.' William nodded to the coat hooks. 'Take off that fur before you catch your death of cold. I'll get you another coat.'

Queenie removed her fox furs and ratted cloche. William placed the bits of ragged city glamour on the hooks amongst the country tweeds and ancient oilskins, and reached for the navy-blue overcoat. He twitched, and held his breath. Then, he ran his thumb and forefinger over the good wool, and, as he did so, that cold fullness, weighing heavy in his chest since the christening, lifted. William exhaled. Phyll. She was here, at Red Hollow. 'This is Phyll's coat, Queenie,' he called out. 'She must still be here. Unable to leave because of the flood.'

'We live in hope, bab.' Queenie nodded to the oak door, and the corpse beyond.

There came a polite cough from the doorway to the corridor. Dr Moon entered the hall and smiled frowningly at William. 'Mr Garrett, I'm afraid we're in disarray. Water has entered the kitchen. Disastrous in these old places, don't you know.' The doctor wore no shoes, and his trousers were rolled to the knee, exposing the thick scarring on his injured right leg. He held out his hand in greeting. 'My dear chap, if you needed to speak with me, why not telephone through?' The doctor shot Queenie a quick, clinical glance. 'Is Phyll not with you?'

William's anxiety welled at the note of bewilderment in Dr Moon's voice; he let go of Phyll's overcoat, and said, 'This is Miss Maggs, my associate. Phyll is—'

'Birmingham seems awash with lady detectives.' Lady Pike's smile, thin-lipped and achingly polite, was directed at Queenie. 'What progress we women have made since the war.' Rubber-booted, the hem of her tweed skirt sodden, she entered the room with Mr Brooke hovering at her side.

'Lady Pike, I'm afraid we found a dead man, and Phyll Hall is—'

'The telephone lines are down, Dr Moon,' interrupted Mr Brooke. 'I've been trying to get through to the Coventry agency since midday, and the night nurse hasn't arrived for her shift. I doubt she'll be with us tonight. You're going to be horribly short-staffed. What with Miss Moore calling in sick, and, you do remember, it is my evening off.'

'Dead? Who's dead?' Dr Moon held up a silencing hand and looked at Brooke. 'Why on earth didn't you tell me about this in the kitchen?'

'I couldn't mention stray corpses in front of Mr Irwell.' Brooke shrugged. 'The silly boy's nerves are already quite ragged because of the flood.'

'It's the body of a clergyman. I believe it's the Reverend Andrews. Miss Maggs and I found him in the floodwater on our way to see you.' William gestured to the shoeless, trembling Queenie. 'He's outside. We carried him here.'

Queenie shuddered, violently. Pale and exhausted, she remained silent.

'My dear lady, please sit down.' The chivalry of Dr Moon's class – passed, William supposed, from father to son, like power – kicked in, and he took Queenie's arm. 'Mr Brooke will fetch some hot water, clean towels and blankets.'

'Oh, shall he now?'

'And the lady shall have my bedroom slippers, Brooke,' said Dr Moon.

'She's got you all hot under the collar, hasn't she?' Mr Brooke grinned, and indicated to Queenie, bobbing his head towards her like a young crow. 'In all your ardour, you seem to have forgotten about the poor dead vicar.'

Before Dr Moon could reply, Mr Brooke, practised at theatrical exits, left through a door so discreet it could hardly be distinguished from the wainscoted wall.

The doctor rose from Queenie's side. 'Mr Garrett, you say it's the Reverend Andrews?'

'It's probable, but I've never met the man. We left him on the front steps. You need to identify him, and then take a proper look at him.' William spoke the last words with emphasis, not wanting to say out loud what he feared.

Dr Moon broke out into a nervous smile. 'On the steps?'

The doctor, William realised, was momentarily useless.

'No, we must bring him inside. You'll need light to examine the body.'

Freddy and two other men appeared in the doorway, peering into the entrance hall like children spying on a grown-up party. One man was young, barely out of his teens, with a mop of fair, curly hair. The other was a man William's own age. All moustache and sideburns, he looked like the hero in a novel by Thomas Hardy, but his rural handsomeness was undercut by a complexion the wrong side of ruddy; the man was a drinker's pink.

William crooked his finger, and the men inched into the room.

'Freddy, you and Curly clear the refectory table of the dead swan.' William barked his orders like the sergeant he once was.

'Then, move the table so it's directly underneath the light.' He waved towards the wrought-iron chandelier, modest but electric, dangling from the ceiling. 'We'll put the body there for Dr Moon to take a look at. The light, at least, seems decent.'

'Body?' Freddy blinked, twice.

William nodded. 'A clergyman. Drowned in the floodwater.'

'The mermaid. She's struck again.' The youth crossed himself, and his skin blanched to a delicate parchment against his bony skull. 'We must close up the house. Stop the water's ingress.'

'We must do as we're told, Mr Irwell.' Freddy grabbed the boy by the jacket sleeve and nodded towards the cased swan.

'You.' William pointed to the drinker. 'I need help getting him inside.'

'Alright.' The man stepped forward, wiping his hands on the sides of his trousers. 'But my name's Tom Sherbourne, and the bloke you call Curly is Vincent Irwell.'

Outside, the sparse light from the entrance hall cast a sallow sheen on the stone steps. There, face down, lay the Reverend Andrews. His fingers, waxy, pale and poignant, stretched out of the cuffs of his grey shirt; his bent left leg dangled in the flooded drive, so the clergyman appeared, for one appalling moment, as if he were crawling out of the water with his last breath.

'Whereabouts did you find the poor bastard?' asked Tom Sherbourne.

'Over by the oaks on the other side of the driveway.'

Tom squinted through the sheeting rain. 'Christ almighty. What on earth was he doing out there?' He turned to William. 'You and the woman carried him?' William nodded. Tom bent and readied himself to lift the Reverend Andrews by the shoulders. 'I'll take the weight. You look knackered out.'

William stepped down into the water, wincing at the cold, and grabbed the parson's bony shins. They heaved on 'three' and hauled the corpse into the entrance hall. A few slick steps in, and William skidded, his city shoes no match for flagstones treacherous with water. He bumped, floundering, into Lady Pike and dropped the dead man's leg, so that his heavy brogue thudded against the glass case of the mute swan. The sound wobbled, echoing through the room like a dinner gong. William and Tom stood for a moment, catching their breaths before they hoisted the Reverend Andrews, finally, and face upwards, onto the refectory table.

At the arrival of the corpse, Freddy took three efficient steps back but remained alert, standing guard, his shoulders erect and ready to assist; the army training was never forgotten. Mr Irwell hovered near the doorway to the corridor. He chewed his nails and shot hungry glances at Queenie's now stocking-free legs.

'God have mercy.' Lady Pike bent tentatively over the corpse, and then glanced upwards to the returning Brooke. 'It really is him. It really is the Reverend Andrews.'

Brooke raised his eyebrows but didn't reply to Lady Pike. Blankets and towel slung over his shoulder, a pair of bedroom slippers snug in his armpit, he carried a basin full of steaming water, which he laid at Queenie's feet. Then, he turned to Dr Moon, and said, without his usual air of disdain, 'I'll fetch your bag.'

William was grateful for the decorous hush that descended on the group. Up until now, the Reverend Andrews had been an inconvenient dead weight, a distraction from the search for Phyll. But now, inside and laid out before a doctor, he had been transformed into some mother's son. Dr Moon also understood the age-old etiquette surrounding the treatment of the dead. Tenderly, he shifted the body on its side, and squinted at the gore-matted dent at the base of the parson's skull.

'He's terribly caked in mud, isn't he?' Freddy wiped his nose with his forefinger and thumb – a tic, William thought; a war wound. 'Wretched stuff gets everywhere.'

'Steady on, old chap. This is the Reverend's tragedy and not yours.' Dr Moon spoke with the tone of a kindly, yet essentially unworried schoolmaster soothing a pupil's examination nerves. 'All will be well.'

'How can you tell us that?' Mr Irwell's voice was a skittish northern whine. 'When he's obviously been got by the mermaid. Oh Christ, she'll have us all before the night is out.'

'Don't talk rubbish, Irwell,' said Tom. 'The bloke never had a sniff of a barmaid's apron. And besides, I carried him in, and he's intact.' He screwed his face, glancing first at Lady Pike and then Queenie. 'Not that I've been fiddling about with his flies.'

'He was a terrible, tub-thumping woman-hater, though.' Freddy's fingers fluttered against his temples. 'I've never known a man use the word *whore* so often. This could be the mermaid's work. Yes, quite easily.'

'The poor bastard obviously tripped and drowned, Freddy,' said Tom. 'Don't fill Irwell's head with any more of this mermaid tripe. It's just a story meant to keep little boys away from floozies and booze. Christ, it never worked on me.' He peered at the dead body and frowned. 'I just can't understand what the fellow was doing here. He was hardly a friend of Red Hollow.'

'He was here for Candlemas,' said Lady Pike. 'He never liked the rite and told me it was popish. We often have – had – these tussles. I assumed he had used the flood as an excuse not to conduct the service. Now I feel terribly guilty that he should've braved the storm and met such an end.'

William considered, and then discounted, the likelihood of an evangelical parson traipsing two miles in a raging storm to conduct a service he thought too Catholic. And surely, with Red Hollow's villagers secure in their houses, sandbagged against the storm, there would be little to no congregation to preach to.

'The Reverend Andrews wouldn't be the first to drown himself in a flood, would he now?' Mr Brooke had returned; he handed a battered medical bag to Dr Moon. 'There's plenty of precedent.'

'Mostly drunkards, though, Mr Brooke, and the Reverend Andrews could hardly be called that.' Lady Pike turned and addressed Queenie. 'My husband drowned in similar circumstances during the great flood of 1921. Poor Redvers; his name meant *place where the rivers meet*. I haven't quite got over the irony of his death.'

'You mean *tragedy*, Lady Pike,' said Freddy.

'No, she don't.' Queenie, wrapped in blankets, her feet in a bath of warm water, had rallied. Besides, she was no respecter of death, or anything other than God and money, and had perhaps recognised a like mind in Lady Sabrina Pike. William suddenly longed for Phyll and all her decency. His panic swelled at the thought of losing her.

'We must telephone for the police immediately.' Dr Moon looked up from the corpse and spoke directly to William. 'This is all rather serious, I'm afraid. The head wound is large, deep. Blunt force trauma. A police surgeon will be needed to determine the cause.'

At Dr Moon's words, the electric light above the muddied, bloodied body of the Reverend Andrews flickered and blew with a static fizz. The chaotic chatter of the small group ceased, so that in the dense, sloshing blackness, William heard nothing but the rattling storm, and the squelch of rubber-booted feet fidgeting on wet flagstones.

The silence lasted for a scant second.

'Oh God. I can't take much more of this.' Mr Irwell's nasal voice rang out in the echoing dark. 'The mermaid is coming to get us. Just like she did Mr Trent and the Reverend Andrews. She'll swim through this bloody floodwater and pick us off one by one.'

12

'The generator has packed up, Irwell.' Tom Sherbourne's strong, practical voice came as a relief. 'Water in the engine room, probably. I should be able to get it started again, but I reckon you fellows will need to sandbag the doors and low windows of the house. That's where we're most vulnerable. Not much point in concentrating on the flooded pantry now.'

'I think we should telephone for the police.' Dr Moon repeated.

'The lines are down,' said Mr Brooke. 'Are you hard of hearing?'

'I'll walk over to Whittingford and fetch the constable,' said Tom.

'But you're the only one here who can fix the generator.' Mr Irwell's adolescent petulance had grown into full-blown hysteria. 'I'm not staying here without electric light. It's bloody medieval to be in the dark. Trapped in this godforsaken place and surrounded by water. The mermaid is out to get us. We're sitting ducks. Christ, I wish I had a gun. I'd sit on the roof and take potshots at her. I honestly would.'

'Mr Irwell, I think you'll be more comfortable in your room.' Dr Moon's words held a note of authoritative exasperation.

'Alone in the dark and pumped full of muck. No bloody fear.'

With Irwell's words, the electricity quivered nervously into action.

'Why on earth should this be a matter for the police?' Lady Pike's voice was stiff with outrage. 'We should telephone the man's family, and his own doctor, of course. The Reverend Andrews must be returned to the parsonage at Whittingford as soon as possible.'

'I disagree, Lady Pike. The Reverend Andrews has sustained a suspicious head wound. I believe the police must be informed.'

Dr Moon's words only confirmed what William suspected already. The Reverend Andrews had been murdered. And the connections between the parson's death, Phyll's disappearance, and Red Hollow's strange, watery vandal were plain to see. William raised his voice. 'Phyll Hall is missing. She didn't appear in Birmingham as planned this morning. I'm here to find her.'

'What are you saying about Phyll?' Freddy's voice was tremulous. 'Where is she?'

'We're worried about her, Freddy.' William lit a cigarette. 'When did you last see her?'

'Not since last night.' Freddy's blanched blondness flickered beneath the wavering light so he appeared, in all his panic, ethereal, ghostly. 'Phyll told me not to see her off in the morning as she was going to get up early. She didn't want a taxi into town, you know. Said she'd walk the three miles to the train station. Oh Christ, where is she?'

William's stomach lurched at Freddy's heartfelt plea; the man knew nothing of his sister's whereabouts. 'I think she's here.' He nodded towards Phyll's overcoat, which, in the draught blowing in from beneath the weather-warped door, billowed on its hook as if alive. 'She wouldn't leave for Birmingham on a February morning without her coat. She wouldn't set foot outside without it. Phyll could still be in this house.' William glanced at the dead Reverend Andrews. 'I hope to God I'm right.'

Freddy removed the coat from its hook, sniffed at the wool, and cradled it as one would a child. 'It smells of her.'

'Freddy's sister looks like a boy, doesn't she?' Irwell, twitchy with fear, spat out the words. 'She looks just like a delicious young boy. A nice little snack for that filthy bitch of a mermaid.'

'Shut your disgusting mouth, Irwell. I mean it. You're showing your true colours, man.' Freddy twisted the dark wool of Phyll's coat. 'And for God's sake watch your language in front of the ladies.'

'I'm not offended by his language, but I could do without his bullshit.' Queenie had the knack of making herself invisible when it suited her, and would wait, watchful and always listening, until the time came to command the attention of the room. This, she now did. 'Phyll could be in bed with a fever. Has anyone checked her room today?'

No one answered Queenie's question, but the whole group, a sea of blank, expectant faces, turned to Mr Brooke.

'I'm not the daily help. It's not my place to see to the young lady's room.'

Outside, the church clock began to strike. Mr Brooke waited until the chimes stopped before turning to the doctor. 'It's four o'clock and my evening off, Dr Moon. I should like to get home to Mother.'

'We have no night nurse, Brooke.' Dr Moon tried, but failed, to keep outraged frustration from his voice. 'You can't leave me completely without staff. Phyll is missing, and the poor Reverend Andrews has been —' the doctor hesitated, searching for the correct word — 'killed. I am sure your neighbours will be good enough to look in on your mother.'

'Mr Brooke, really,' said Lady Pike. 'You simply cannot leave the doctor now.'

'Miss Sabrina, I can't stay tonight. Mother is terrified of the flood. I must go before it gets any worse.' Mr Brooke paused, as if gathering some inner strength, and then spoke quickly. 'You know she is quite childish. I don't even know if she'll allow Mrs Morris in the house. Mother forgets such a lot, and she can be very naughty at times.'

William ached in frustration. The clinging drag of damp clothes pulled on his skin; numbing cold nipped his feet; a shiver of exhaustion rattled his teeth. The conversation scattered like buckshot, and each disparate volley of talk wasted precious moments in the hunt for Phyll. He turned to the orderly. 'You're the only one here who can go for the police, Mr Brooke. You know the country and are used to the water. Dr Moon can't leave Red Hollow because of his patients, and Lady Pike has Percy to consider.' William glanced at the fizzing filament of the electric light. 'Tom will be needed to fix the generator. Meanwhile, I aim to find Phyll, so I'm going to search the house. This you must understand.' The note of brisk authority in William's voice was designed to secure the attention of a mob. 'And Dr Moon, it should be your priority, too.'

'Priority? What a joke.' Irwell was frantic, near tears. 'Dr Moon's priority should be his patients. The woman is lost and it's her own bloody fault. If the mermaid has gobbled up Burlington Bertie, then better her than me.'

William's skin itched in a strange, cumulative outrage. The day, this hysterical boy, the awful circumstances of Phyll's disappearance appalled him. 'Toddle off to bed now, Mr Irwell.'

He paused, and took a long draw on his cigarette, considering his words. 'Let the doctor give you a sedative. You need one. Go now, before your big mouth gets you into trouble.'

'I won't have a stupid fat Brummie talk to me like that.' Irwell straightened his young, broad shoulders, and squared up to William. The action was surprising, and it jolted William into a muscle-tightening alarm. 'Who the hell are you to butt in here, anyway? I'm a fee-paying guest.'

'Gentlemen, we must show a little respect for the dead,' said Lady Pike.

William paused at her words, ashamed, and glanced at the damp, twisted figure of Reverend Andrews laid out on the refectory table.

'No, just belt the little idiot, Billy.' Queenie ran her fingers through her curls and stood. Her bare feet in Dr Moon's slippers, she made a strangely casual figure next to Lady Pike's haughty composure. 'We need to get on with the job, and the lad is wasting our time. He likes the attention, that one. Sucks the air out of the room with all his nonsense. Knock the kid out, and save the doctor his dope.'

Irwell stared at Queenie, thin-lipped, hands twitching with a feral, ready-to-pounce hatred. William stepped forward and ruffled Irwell's hair – hard. 'Don't even think about it.' The younger man squirmed beneath his paw, but William held fast, bent in close, and felt the heat of his own breath as he whispered in Irwell's ear. 'If you ever lay a finger on her, or any of the women here, I will bite your fuckin' ear off.' William turned to the rest of the group, with Irwell, animal alert, still in his grasp. 'Miss Maggs and I will start our search in Phyll's room,' he said. 'I suggest the rest of you look to the generator and then secure the house against the flood. The villagers have sandbagged already.' William let Irwell go; the boy slunk into the nearest corner like an injured fox. Then, stubbing his cigarette out on the glistening flagstones, William beckoned to Freddy. 'Freddy, you come with us.'

'I'm happy to go for the police if I can call in on Mother first, Mr Garrett,' Brooke said, and William nodded at the compromise. 'I'll only be a few moments with the old dear, and then I'll be straight off to Whittingford. I would never want to hinder your investigation.' The orderly gawped cheerfully at the juddering Irwell and pulled an oilskin and a set of waders from the coat stand. 'I'm not scared of the water, and I've got quite the clean sheet with the ladies.' Once more, he shot a pointed glance at Mr Irwell. 'So what do I have to fear from the mermaid?'

13

No one bothered to knock. They simply walked straight into a square room of good size illuminated by the light of the corridor. A small double bed, its pristine counterpane like virgin snow, stood a few feet away from a marble fireplace laid with kindling and logs, but not lit. The curtains, chintz, were drawn back, and the window, open just a crack, let in the gusting storm. And, for the first time since his arrival at Red Hollow, William smelt a lurking note of the rest home beneath the beeswax-scented, country-house domesticity.

'Phyll's room,' said Freddy.

William switched on the wall light and blinked against the hard white glare. Phyll was not there. Not in bed sweating with influenza. Not doubled up with appendicitis. 'If she was ever in here, it wasn't for long.' He spoke his thoughts aloud and couldn't take them back. They were out in the open now. 'Do you think her bed has been slept in?'

'I doubt it,' said Queenie. 'A trained woman has made up that bed, and Phyll's never been in service.'

And yet, the room was full of Phyll. In her absence, her presence was felt with the cloying intensity of a haunting.

'We should look in the bathroom and the lavatory. She may have collapsed or something.' Freddy had been carrying Phyll's overcoat, like a child does a favourite blanket. He placed it on the dresser, and then opened the door once more; framed by the doorway, he was poised to go. 'Shall I do it?'

'Yes,' said William. 'That's a good idea.'

The note of hope in Freddy's voice was painful. He watched him disappear into the corridor, and as he did so, something of Phyll's boyish kindness left too.

Queenie nodded towards the door. 'What's he in here for? He seems alright.'

'He got knocked senseless by a ton of Belgian mud.'

'Ain't that what happened to all of you blokes?'

'Only the really unlucky ones.' William closed the door after Freddy. 'He's sane enough, except he sees mermaids after tea. Tom Sherbourne seems alright though.'

'He'll fall into the lap of the nearest barmaid as soon as he leaves here,' said Queenie.

William nodded. There was no better judge of drunken men than Queenie Maggs. 'It's that mad little bastard Irwell we need to watch out for,' he said.

'You should've belted him out cold when I told you.' She blinked, impassive, but her steady, focused quiet, he felt, was disapproving. 'I wish you hadn't sent that Mr Brooke out for the coppers.'

William was half-expecting this. Men in blue uniforms brought Queenie out in hives. 'There's a murdered vicar in the entrance hall, didn't you notice?'

'Country plod ain't gonna do no one no good.' Queenie began the business of examining the dresser drawers. She banged them shut after each thorough inspection, and they rattled in an irritating emptiness. 'You could've persuaded the doctor that the Reverend just fell in the flood and hit his head, like Lady Pike's husband. She didn't want the constabulary here either.'

'You and Lady Pike are alike. Apart from she has better grammar, and you have better tits.'

'I can't help my station in life. Or my figure.' Queenie wriggled her toes in Dr Moon's slippers. 'Who haven't I met?'

'Only Persephone. She's Lady Pike's daughter, a child,' he said. 'They live in the tower. It's been converted to a separate flat.' It will have to be searched, William thought, eventually.

'No other servants or members of Dr Moon's staff?'

'Red Hollow is a big, bloody mess, as far as I can tell. The place is run on part-time and agency staff. The doctor employs three daily women for the housework.' William reeled off the facts as if delivering a report to a superior officer. 'Miners' wives, they like to be home by four o'clock. The cook cycles in from Milby each day, but she leaves early too. And it looks as if the night nurse won't arrive tonight because of the flood.'

For the first time since he had entered Phyll's room, William looked from the window. He adjusted his eyes to the dark and saw, between the river and the hall, that the land shone with creeping water. 'The rain ain't stopping. The house will be an island by the end of the night. Phyll's disappearance, dead vicars, bollock-chomping mermaids, it's all variations on a theme of mad bastardy. We could be too late.' William winced at the constant scratch of the storm, and the pricking humiliation of his own war-weakened nerves. 'Did I tell you Dr Moon thinks the intruder is either a patient or a member of staff?'

'It's a likelihood, ain't it? We need to brace ourselves for a shitty night, because there ain't no easy escape from here in this weather.' Queenie then spoke with a sham detachment. 'You like that Dr Moon too much, Billy. He's got something to hide, that one.'

'Jesus, Queenie. Ain't we all got something to hide? That's the crux of the whole bloody problem.'

The bedroom door opened a gap. Through it came a mop of blond hair, tousled and boyish. William felt the pulse of Queenie's joyous gasp, but this shared relief was momentary; it was Freddy's loping frame, and not Phyll's compact elegance, that emerged into the room. William shot Freddy a pleading glance, but Freddy merely shook his head and mouthed, 'No.'

'Then, we do a proper search of this room before we do anything else. Wardrobe, under the bed, everything.' William, becoming Sergeant Garrett once more, issued his orders. 'You never know what people leave behind. If she was in here, or taken from here, anything could help us. A slip of paper, a cigarette end, anything at all.'

It was as if someone had fired a starting pistol. They all sprang into action.

Freddy opened the doors to the wardrobe, clattering the wooden hangers. 'Empty as a drum.'

Queenie stepped forward and pulled back the bedcovers, removing the pillows with one healthy fling of her arm.

William rolled the rug, a thirty-second job, and found nothing more than a speck of dust. 'Did anyone check the pockets of her overcoat?' He moved to the dresser and patted the coat down. 'Nothing.'

William turned at the sound of the china ewer rattling in its basin. Queenie was performing a hefty shimmy beneath the bed, the motion of her movements designed to free herself from low springs and tangled sheets. She emerged, red-faced, hair awry, and cross-legged at first, a bottle in her hand. Then she stood, teeteringly, to face William.

William knew from the label it was a bottle of Glenfiddich. Half-empty or half-full, it had been Ronnie's brand. He took two steps forward and steadied himself at the foot of the bed.

'God, I'm cold,' said Queenie. 'Why is it so cold in here?'

'You're shivering, Miss Maggs. Do put this on.' Freddy placed Phyll's coat tenderly about Queenie's shoulders. 'And please sit down, you're obviously exhausted.' Queenie obeyed, wrapping herself in Phyll's overcoat, and perched on the end of the bed. 'Whisky is strictly *verboten* at Red Hollow,' he said. 'I'm not here because of alcoholism, but even I'm not allowed a drop. Dr Moon is fanatical about keeping any intoxicant in a locked cupboard.'

William brought himself to examine the bottle. He squinted, holding it up against the light. 'There's something more than whisky in here.' He moved closer to the lamp. 'Yes,' he said. 'There's something heavy in the bottom of the bottle. Whatever it is, it's turned the whisky an odd colour.' It was not the usual rich amber of Ronnie's favourite drink, but a golden yellow. Motes of red-black danced in the liquid. William shook the bottle. There came a muffled clatter amidst the more expected glugging slurp of the whisky. Nails, rusted nails, at the bottom of the bottle. He uncorked it, and it opened with a comical *pop*.

'Good God in heaven.' Freddy gagged.

Queenie covered her mouth with the back of her arm, burying her face into Phyll's tweed coat.

William turned away, momentarily, then recorked the bottle and placed it on the bedside table. He took two steps back, distancing himself from the madness of the thing.

A great weight of silence hung heavy in the room.

Freddy was the first to speak. 'Could she have been caught short?'

'And piss in a bottle full of nails?' Queenie's fury at the question came as a spitting sibilance. 'There ain't a chamber pot in the room, but I've never met a woman who could, or would, do that. And, by Christ, I've known some bloody types.'

William, too, was dumbfounded, unable to fathom the motives of such an action. 'Who in the hell would fill a whisky bottle with piss and nails? What kind of lunatic would do such a thing?'

'The mermaid,' said Freddy. 'It's just the kind of foul, degraded thing she would do.' He glanced towards the window, the hammering rain, and the great watery transformation of the land. 'The Red Hollow has burst its banks on the anniversary of the mermaid's death. The veil between her world and ours is thin tonight. So thin, so fragile, the mermaid can lift it, slither through. She'll come again tonight, and God knows what she has planned. The only hope I have is that she doesn't hurt women.'

William knew human bastardy was less morally constant than Freddy's supernatural mermaid. 'The mermaid isn't real, Freddy, but she is mad. She's doing mad things, like cracking parsons on the back of the head, chiselling obscenities in the walls, pissing in bottles full of nails. That kind of person would take pleasure in hurting Phyll. And, let's face it. They're on the loose. I have a horrible feeling they're still in the house. Like you said, the anniversary of the murdered girl's death is important to them.' He patted his pockets for his cigarettes. Damp. 'We need to search the house, and now. Start with the attic rooms and then work our way down. Turn this place upside down if we must. And when we find Phyll, we teach the fucker who took her a valuable lesson. We'll be the stuff of their nightmares.' William let out a long, expulsive sigh. 'It ain't much of a plan, but it's the only one I've got. Oh God, I can feel the hatred at work. It bothers me.'

'You think you can sense evil, Mr Garrett?'

At Freddy's words, they were thrown into a black so rich William felt he could drink it like stout. The generator had failed without a warning flicker from the electric light.

'I wonder if there are candles in this room?' Queenie's voice came as a hoarse whisper. 'There should be, surely. Or an oil lamp?' He heard the static rustle of Queenie's slip, the creak of the bedsprings. 'Did I see an old-fashioned oil lamp out in the corridor?'

Her words worked like magic, and a white glare, queer and shuddering, flooded the room. William blinked, eyelids sore with misery. He rubbed them with his clenched fists like a child. 'Tom Sherbourne must be at work.'

'Nightmares,' said Queenie. 'This whole rotten day has been like some kid's nightmare.' She stood and shuddered. Her face impassive as she bent to lift her skirts, Queenie exposed a small, silver pistol wedged between her white thigh and the candy-pink elastic of her garter clips. 'Well, at least we can be thankful for the electric light.'

'Thank heaven for small mercies, you mean?' Freddy blushed at the glimpse of thigh. 'You have a pistol, Miss Maggs?'

'Call me Queenie.' The Derringer glimmered in the soft lamplight until it disappeared into the pocket of Phyll's overcoat. 'And I never go nowhere unprepared.'

14

'I've never been to the attics before,' said Freddy. 'I don't even know if they're kept locked. I assume we just climb upwards.' They came to a door hidden in the panelling at the end of the corridor. Freddy opened it onto a hallway already illuminated by electric light. 'The whole place is a warren of staircases and passageways, though. Easy to get lost here, don't you think?'

William nodded at the pitiful note of hope in Freddy's voice, knowing that it would be equally easy to hide the body of a murdered woman.

They followed him up a flight of stairs flanked by a pair of stout newel posts, each one topped with a huge, perfectly carved oak ball, and capped with an elongated pyramid. William touched the forbidding spike gently with the palm of his hand as he passed. Here, a falling man would land, and be impaled. Along the staircase, wooden walls were adorned with portraits of bosomy, heavy-eyed women, imperious, and pale with powder. The husbands and sons of Red Hollow were a contrast to the strong Pike women, for the men peeped weak-chinned from their pictures, their dark eyes rheumy with port.

Freddy came to an abrupt stop at a door, baize-lined, through which was yet another staircase. Stone now, with a steep tread, its pine handrail had smoothed with wear. As the door closed, the light faded and all became a gunmetal grey; the stairs were dimly illuminated by the high window of the landing above them, and through that window, black clouds scudded across a purple sky.

'The garret, Mr Garrett,' said Freddy, turning to the left at the top of the steps and towards a narrow corridor of Victorian doors and sloping ceilings. 'It looks like the servants' quarters were here in the Pikes' time. Just the women, I should think. I doubt they've had indoor male servants at Red Hollow for over a hundred years.' Freddy paused, his long fingers searching the wall. 'There should be a light switch. The whole house was electrified in the 1890s when the generator was purchased.'

William thought it unfathomably cheap to leave the maids without electric light when the rest of the house glowed with it, but unfathomably cheap the Pikes were, because Freddy found no switch.

'Is this the very top of the house?' asked Queenie.

'I should think so by the camber of the ceiling. But you never know in this place. One's bearings are invariably mistaken.' Freddy turned the handle of a Victorian door the colour of England in winter, a cold, mucky green tinged with grey. 'Locked,' he said, twisting the handle once more, rattling it in frustration. And then, without a word, he brought his shoulder hard against the door, pounding at it, once, twice, a third time until there came a great splintering crack. Freddy took two faltering steps into the room, powered by his own momentum. 'I can't see a thing,' he said. 'Should I run down and get my electric torch?'

Queenie brushed past William and moved further into the room. 'Hand me your matches,' she said.

William fumbled in his jacket pocket, but Freddy got to her first, passing over his lighter. A click, a rasp, a flash of blue flame, and then illumination. Queenie stood before them, holding a brass chamberstick, complete with candle. Her pale skin glowed golden, and a halo of light shone on her forehead, skimming her dark curls. She held the chamberstick before her and surveyed the room which brightened with each swoop of her arm in a warm glow.

A pair of matching iron bedsteads, their stained ticking mattresses bared of linen, stood either side of a tile-topped wash-stand. In front of this, a worn rag rug offered scant comfort to the naked toes of former maids. The walls, papered in an in-offensive floral print – posies of violets – had only two adorn-ments: an embroidered Victorian motto and a small mirror, blemished with damp. The fireplace had been set off-centre on the far wall. A pigeon, and its fallen nest, mouldered in the grate.

'It's like the bloody *Marie Celeste*.' William worried that some black-clad servant, some Annie or Kate, might pop up before him and bob a curtsy. 'I doubt anyone has been up here for years.'

'Not since the war.' Queenie held the candle before a post-card propped up on the mantelpiece. '*Christmas Greetings from the Fifty-Sixth London Division, 1917.*' She flipped over the card. '*Cheerio! All is well, Bert.*'

'I imagine that's when it all went west for the Pikes,' said Freddy. 'Dr Moon opened up shop in 'twenty-seven.'

'She's not here, is she?' asked Queenie. 'This room ain't designed for secrets. It's all bare. Privacy breeds sin, don't it?' She pointed towards the ubiquitous chamber pots. 'You couldn't even piss in peace. Christ, I'm glad those days are long gone. Well, for me, at least.'

'There isn't even a wardrobe to hide in,' said Freddy.

But a large pine chest stood at the foot of each bed. They were the kind where the maids of his mother's generation kept their Sunday best. William bent to open one, and as he lifted the lid, he heard a familiar glassy clatter. 'Empties,' he said. In the bottom of the trunk lay some half a dozen whisky bottles. 'One man's stash of booze. All the same brand, I think, judging by the shape of the bottles.' Queenie came in close and held the chamberstick over the wooden trunk. 'Glenfiddich.' William shuddered. 'Christ, I hate the stuff.' For a scant second, William believed his subconscious had seeped into the very substance of the house, so that in each room a reminder of his secret anxieties would float up like flotsam. This was what it meant to be haunted. 'It's recent, too. There's one half-full. If our secret drinker left in January, he forgot his poison.' William paused, screwing his face in thought. 'It's likely the late Mr Trent used this place.'

'And, where the mermaid found her bottle, do you think?' asked Freddy.

'If the mad bastard has a key to the room,' said Queenie.

'Well, if you're correct, Mr Trent probably did,' said Freddy.

'I bet you ten bob there's an opium pipe and a couple of bottles of Bass in the second box, but I'm hoping for a good Napoleon brandy and a copy of *Lady Chatterley*.' However, once opened, William found, the trunk contained only the old newspaper which lined it. 'This girl must've arrived in 1912.' He picked up the crumbling shards of newsprint. 'Look, the *Titanic*. There's a metaphor about sinking ships I could try and formulate.'

'Don't. There's a good chap. Phyll is missing. It's no joking matter.'

Queenie shot this second chest a quick look and dragged it to beneath the only window, a high, mean navy-blue eye on the apex of the room. She stood on the box and peered out. 'I can't make out where we are,' she said.

'Does the window open?' asked Freddy.

Queenie tried, and with her second great shove, the window clattered open. She stood on tiptoe, head outside, twisting her body and looking upward, wetting her now near-dry curls with the sleeting rain. 'This isn't the top floor. There are more rooms upstairs. There's gotta be another staircase.'

'There might be one along the corridor. We should go now,' said Freddy.

'I feel like I need to try the floorboards or something.' Still teetering on her trunk, Queenie had turned to face them.

William reached for the chamberstick and circled it over the floor, kicking the rag rug out of his way. 'Thick with varnish. They've not been lifted for years.' There was a short, disappointed silence. 'We should move on,' he said. 'Work as fast as we can.'

'You do know you've already told the probable murderer your plan of action, don't you? If he's got any sense, he'll be a few steps ahead of us. This is a wild bloody goose chase.' Queenie paused her diatribe and frowned. 'Look.' She pointed towards a floor-to-ceiling corner cupboard. Covered in the same violet sprig wallpaper as the rest of the room, its narrow door was only identifiable by the brass knob which glimmered in the candlelight.

Freddy moved over and twisted the handle, pulling hard, rattling it. 'Locked,' he said. 'And difficult to break down. It's designed to swing outwards.' They hesitated for a moment, as a group, staring at the door as if it were one more puzzle to be solved. 'But if Phyll was in there, surely she'd call out.'

'Not if calling out was impossible,' said William.

Queenie moved over to the cupboard. She stood on tiptoe, stretching her right arm to feel for a key hidden on top of the door casing. William was unsure of her reasoning but searching for a key was worth a shot. He glanced at the fireplace. Above the decomposing corpse, and on the mantelpiece, was a Staffordshire figure of Britannia, her helmet badly chipped. William lifted it and peeked under her robes. 'The key,' he said. 'I think I've found it.' He felt foolish at his own excitement. Soon they would unlock the cupboard, and what were they likely to find? Discarded maid's uniforms, no doubt.

'Well done, Mr Garrett.' Freddy took the key from William and tried it in the door – successfully.

What appeared was not the neatly starched aprons of William's imagination, but a narrow staircase. Blackened oak, and older than the door which concealed it, its steep tread was too thin to accommodate a man's feet. William moved in closer, took one step, and looked upwards. He was immediately encased in wood. His shoulders grazed the panelling on both walls. Halfway up, and a man could not turn and run. There would be no easy escape. William stepped back, returning to the room.

'Christ, she could be up there.' Queenie's voice came as an excited whisper.

'It's just the staircase to more attic rooms,' said William. However, he too lowered his voice.

Freddy assessed the width of the stairs in the scant candlelight. 'I should go first. It's a precipitous climb, like the steps to a belfry. I'm used to clambering about these old places in the dark.'

'No,' said Queenie. 'It should be me.'

'I don't think this is the proper time for ladies first, Miss Maggs,' said Freddy. 'In fact, it might be best if you wait down here.'

William understood Freddy's desire to protect Queenie, but from what? Mermaids or flesh-and-blood murderers on the loose? Perhaps there was some part of Freddy which held on to his sanity. Or was it simply instinct? Chivalry was as much of a marker of Freddy's class as a mania for cricket.

'Don't you worry about me. I'm the one with the pistol, remember.' Queenie climbed onto the first step; it creaked under her weight. She stopped. Nothing more could be heard but the rattle of rain on roof tiles. Queenie moved forward. Freddy, holding his candlestick with solemnity, processed behind her like an altar boy. Slowly, they travelled up a flight of thirteen steps.

Queenie reached the top of the flight. William, three steps down, craned his neck to be confronted by another institutional, Victorian door.

'Oh, fuck it. I'm beginning to get sick of locked doors,' he said.

'I ain't gonna shoot the lock, if that's what you're suggesting. It ain't safe.'

'I could break it down.' Freddy passed the candlestick to William and squeezed himself next to Queenie.

'Hold your horses, Douglas Fairbanks. Let me try the knob first.'

And Queenie did. The door swung open, without a sound.

15

Queenie did not enter but paused on the threshold. William knew she was assessing the unknown. He moved to her shoulder and held his chamberstick aloft, illuminating the room in shadowy fragments. The first thing he noticed, on top of a high mahogany wardrobe, was a small stuffed monkey. A wizened brown creature, its wide, startled eyes stared out at the visitors. Fur slightly moth-eaten, it bared its protruding teeth – in a smile or a grimace, William couldn't tell. The monkey clutched a black silk parasol with its small, strangely human paws, the fringe tickling its nose. On top of the animal's head was a red smoking hat, the kind favoured by the louche Victorian aesthetes of *Punch* cartoons.

The monkey was flagrantly male.

'Bloody hell.' Queenie stepped across the threshold. 'What on God's green earth have we stumbled on?'

'Dr Moon's secret taxidermy collection, by the looks of it,' said Freddy, gazing down at the tiger-skin rug on the floor. The big cat's open jaws faced the door, and its huge striped pelt covered most of the polished boards.

William shone his candle upwards, along the walls, in the corners, drifting further into the room towards a small mahogany desk which stood beneath a dormer window. On it, he found a modern Corona typewriter, a blank ream of foolscap, and what he thought to be a Georgian candelabra complete with beeswax candles, the worn silvering the colour of a hunter's moon. As William bent to light it, he glanced outside onto a narrow strip of flat, lead-lined walkway slick with rain and bordered by the hall's crenellations. They were at the rear of the house. Dr Moon's conservatory must have been directly beneath them. William craned his neck but could only see the church tower. Its gilded mermaid weathervane swung belligerently against the storm.

He lit two cigarettes with the flame of his chamberstick and offered one to Freddy. Freddy accepted, but both he and Queenie were transfixed by a glass-fronted display case, too big for the room, on the wall opposite the window.

Gathering the candelabra, he edged towards them, avoiding the raised scalp of the tiger, and gazed into the cabinet. At first, the contents seemed like any other country-house collection – the kind one paid a shilling to see on a bank holiday – but on closer inspection were far more disconcerting. On the middle shelf, a large glass ball, the colour of Queenie's eyes, reflected the shifting distortion of their faces as the light guttered in an unknown draught. Above it, and laid out on the top shelf, its mouth forming a rictus, its body twisted in desiccation, was a dead cat. Below the cat, in a coffin-shaped box, was a root, a sort of hairy parsnip, simply classified *Mandrake*. Next to this were four vials of clear liquid. Unlabelled, but William thought, almost immediately, of morphine. There was enough in the cabinet to kill several men.

'What the bloody hell is this place?' asked William.

'A black museum, I should think,' said Freddy. 'A Victorian collection of esoterica. Such things exist. Knowledge and power.' His voice had become a whisper. 'There's a certain kind of man for whom this stuff is a lifeblood. Once it grips them, they've had it. Do you think it belonged to old Sir Leofric?'

'Well, I doubt it belonged to the Reverend Andrews,' said William.

Queenie, now hunched forward and squinting, muttered an oath. She stood upright and crossed herself, taking a step back. 'Holy Mary, Mother of God, have you read that, Billy?' She pointed to what looked to William like a used kid glove. A man's glove, ancient, twisted and dirty grey. And so well-fitted to its former owner that William saw the echo of knuckles and veins on the toughened leather. Next to it lay an index card on which was written in ink faded to brown:

Hand of Glory

It must be cut from the body of a criminal on the
gibbet; pickled in salt, and the urine of man, woman,
dog, horse and mare; smoked with herbs and hay for a
month; hung on an oak tree for three nights running,
then laid at a crossroads, then hung on a church door
for one night while the maker keeps watch in the
porch – 'and if it be that no fear hath driven you forth
from the porch ... then the hand be true won, and it
be yours'.

'My God. A human hand. Why would a person do such a thing?' asked Freddy. 'It doesn't bear thinking about.'

'Urine, again,' said Queenie. 'Any maid has an endless supply of the stuff.'

Yes, all those brimming chamber pots of yore. Secreted under beds until a girl-child came, in white cap and apron, and made the shameful muck and mess disappear like magic.

Meanwhile, on a table covered in crisp linen, the master and mistress breakfasted on devilled kidneys. Decades of hatred had bled into the bones of Red Hollow Hall. Surely this was what unnerved him. It was England, with all its genteel, repressed inequality, manifested in bricks and mortar.

'Are you thinking the bottle in Phyll's room was put there as part of some ritual?' he asked.

Queenie shrugged. Freddy drew hard on his cigarette and nodded.

William stubbed out his fag on the polished floorboards. Hand now free, he moved forward and twisted a small brass key, its silk tassel wavering, in the lock of the cabinet. As the heavy Victorian glass clinked open, the curiosities trembled, as if in anticipation, at the movement.

'Bloody hell. Don't touch the God-awful thing,' said Queenie.

William reached for it, but Queenie slipped in front of him, and pulled out, what looked to William like a child's rag doll. She stood, for just a second, examining it and then released it from her grip, dropping it as if it were alight.

William bent to pick it up. The doll wore Edwardian garb and was an almost perfect replica of a maid. Delicately sewn, the tiny stitches of her embroidered face – pink lips, blue eyes – were nearly impossible to see in the candlelight. Each strand of her silk hair was pulled back into a mop cap; her full-skirted black dress reached to the tip of her little felt shoes. And hammered above her groin, sullying her apron, was a blacksmith-made nail. The kind used for shoeing horses. Rust spread onto the white cambric like blood.

'Christ almighty.'

'I hate witchcraft. Curses, and the like. It ain't fair play.' Queenie glanced at William. 'Cards and tea leaves, palmistry,

I'm all for. It's good to know what's coming at you. But this lot, I ain't keen on the mind behind it. It gives me the creeps.'

'It tells a story, though, doesn't it? And not a supernatural story,' said William. 'It's dark and human and sad. How old is Mr Brooke?'

'He was thirty-three in November,' said Freddy. 'He made a cake for all us chaps.'

'So his mother is, what, fifty-five or sixty.' William did a quick calculation: the woman would have conceived her child in February.

'Too young to have gone childish,' said Queenie, always astute.

'She's not yet fifty, but she's always been fragile,' said Freddy. 'She lives in a grace-and-favour cottage. Lady Pike looks after Brooke and his mother. Tom Sherbourne told me all about it.'

William placed the doll back in the glass case as carefully as if it were a child, and, as he did so, glanced at an ancienct carving, about the size and shape of a tea plate, but domed. Flakes of vibrant paint still clung to its surface. The ink on the label had run, splodged with rain and mottled with damp, so that the copperplate was near illegible. 'Freddy,' he said, squinting. 'Does this say *mermaid*?'

Freddy reached in and took the carving. 'My God, it's a boss from the church. It's meant to decorate the ceiling.' He handed it to William for examination. The boss was fully and elaborately carved with one sinuous curve of female torso flaring into a fish tail. Framed with an intricate border of oak leaves, it was gilded in parts and had once been richly painted. William guessed it was medieval. 'It's a terrible sacrilege for it to be here,' said Freddy. 'Amongst this disgusting gimcrack profanity.'

Freddy hesitated before putting the boss back in the cabinet.

William's eye was drawn to the bottom shelf, on which stood some kind of gilded mask, or headpiece. He reached for it. About the size of a man's head, its edges nibbled with age and wear, it was made, William supposed, from papier-mâché.

In this object, William believed the mystery of the intruder was solved, as the mask was in the form of the head of a predatory fish.

Each silver and bronze scale painted by hand with skill and devotion, the round, glassy eyes, were reminiscent of the taxidermy creatures in the entrance hall. William touched the fish's crowning glory: blonde hair, the real tresses of an expensive wig, had been fixed to the top of the fish's head. The whole monstrosity was designed so that the wearer might see through the mouth. And terrifyingly, embedded in the creature's pouting lips, were rows upon rows of rusted pins: its makeshift teeth.

William returned the mask to the bottom shelf, and at his movements, the cabinet shifted slightly, letting out a soft, tinny clatter. He fastened the glass door and locked in the weird, vibrating objects. Now, he knew who the mermaid was, and what a terrible mistake he had already made. A mistake which had put Phyll in grave danger. 'I've fucked up,' he said.

'Do shut up,' said Freddy. 'Be quiet. Listen.'

Immediately, there came a noise; a muffled, panicked patter. Again, a strange, muted scurry, too big for mice. He turned and saw Queenie staring wide-eyed at the wardrobe. She touched William's shoulder and placed her hand to her lips, gesturing for the men to ready themselves, pointing to the desk, and nodding to William's candelabra. Freddy and William, understanding her mime, deposited their candlesticks where Queenie indicated. Queenie held out her

Derringer and pointed it towards the wardrobe. Freddy looked at the pistol and shook his head. 'Phyll,' he mouthed.

'I know,' she whispered. But still Queenie held the Derringer straight at the wardrobe. If a man was in there, she was aiming at his head.

The rattle came once more. Queenie gave a sharp nod. William took one swift movement forward and flung open the wardrobe; the door clattered heavily. The stuffed monkey toppled, and floated down to the floor, its silk parasol an eerie parachute. It settled momentarily, teetered and then fell, smoking hat comically askew. And then something swift and dark, hiding among the skirts of several white dresses, leapt out with a screech and landed with grace on the tiger-skin rug.

'A cat,' William exclaimed in relief. 'A bloody great black cat.'

'My God, woman, you were about to shoot Rossetti,' said Freddy, laughing. 'How on earth did you get up here, old girl?'

'Cats can get everywhere,' said Queenie. 'And I wouldn't hurt that little lady for all the world.' Queenie placed the Derringer back in her pocket. 'She's not that big, Billy. She's a dainty little thing.' She smiled up at Freddy. 'I've a fondness for cats.'

Rossetti, in turn, had a fondness for her. The cat weaved in between her ankles, rubbing her cheeks against Queenie's bare legs. Queenie returned the favour, bending to fuss the cat's ears. For a moment, the two creatures were in sympathy, but Rossetti, bored with Queenie's attentions, leapt up onto the desk beneath the window as if she wanted to be let out. Queenie followed, and leant forward to unclasp the latch, but stopped, saying, frowning, 'What on earth is that?'

'What?' asked Freddy.

'The light.' She fussed absent-mindedly at the cat's ears. 'From over there.'

William squinted. The rain came down like silver needles. A single gleaming eye of a light, yellow and sickly, flamed out onto the wet. 'It's the church. There's a light on in the church.'

Then, as if prompted, a bell tolled, a lonely, singular sound echoing out into the night; to William, it seemed like a voice, solemn and mournful over the flat, cold land. Bells, like cats and mirrors, were things to be spooked by. Queer things, they buggered up the senses, skewing human perceptions of movement, sight and sound. 'Who would be ringing the bell on a night like this?' he asked.

'Someone in trouble,' said Freddy.

'Phyll.' Queenie let out the name as a cry of relief.

16

Outside, the flood was ankle deep, and the rain had become a near-horizontal, cheek-burning sleet, needling through the weft of William's jacket. The church clock rang out the hour above the resonant tolling of the bell. Ahead of William, Freddy halted, rubbing at his temples. William touched his shoulder. Freddy turned, shuddered and, wiping the rain away from his eyes, gazed at William as if he were a face from the past whom he couldn't quite place. Suddenly, the clock stopped striking. 'My God, Freddy,' said William. 'Can you believe it's only five o'clock?'

The clouds shifted, allowing them a scant glimpse of moonlight, and Freddy smiled. 'It's been a damned awful day. I thought these sorts of days were over for me,' he said. 'I was thinking of William Blake. *Some are born to sweet delight; some are born to endless night.* Do you know it?'

'Yes, I do,' said William.

They trudged on; Queenie, now in a pair of Freddy's rubber boots, led the way. Moonlight reflected on the white marble of Sir Redvers Pike's grave, and beneath the yew tree's looming shadow, fallen berries shone like rubies. A yellow glow seeped through the glass of the church windows. The bell continued to toll, but with each successive pull the sound became less insistent, as though a dying creature were giving out one last mournful whimper. And there, in the porch, back towards them, twisting at the door handle, stood a man wrapped in a knitted muffler and an army greatcoat.

'Dr Moon,' Freddy called out, his voice thin against the constant wash of the storm.

The doctor turned, and seemed ethereal in the weak moonlight, so that William thought him faded, like a Victorian photograph. 'I can't get the damned thing open.' He rattled the handle of the church door once more, as if to demonstrate, or prove, his words. 'I heard the bell and thought you chaps were in trouble. Do you think it's Phyll? It shouldn't be locked but the bloody thing won't budge.'

'Let me do it.' Freddy stepped forward, edging the man away from the door. 'Damp weather makes it stiff, and you must have the knack.'

The door reacted to Freddy's touch and swung open with ease. 'Hello there,' he called out, stepping forward. 'Phyll, are you here?' William, Queenie and Dr Moon all followed at Freddy's heels, crowding the man, hovering at the threshold, blinking and hesitant. 'Phyll darling. It's me, Freddy,' he called once more, a plaintive eagerness in his voice. But there was no response other than the residual sound of the bell which came as a throbbing of the air.

William moved away from the group and towards a plain font, ancient, by the wear on the stone, and covered in a creeping damp of a bright, almost artificial-looking green. Behind it, the candy-striped plush of the bell rope wavered. And there, by its noose-like pull, and on her knees, filthy and exhausted, was Persephone Pike. Before her lay a circle of candles near burnt to stub, and an array of cards, face down and disorderly, like a kicked-about game of patience. The child looked up towards William, her blue eyes reddened with tears. Her bottom lip trembled as she spoke. 'Oh, Mr Garrett, I've tried, and I've tried, but Phyll won't wake up. I can't get her out of there, and the floodwater is rising. Do come. Come quickly'

William bent and clasped Persephone's small, cold hand, feeling the pinching weight of a heavy silver cross in his palm as he heaved the child to her feet. 'Where is she, Percy?'

'She's on the floor of the crypt. I could only pull her up to the bottom step.' Her voice was high with panic. 'I tried, and I tried for ages, and then I rang the bell for the grown-ups.' She turned to Freddy, voice a breathless trill, and pulled at the man's jacket. 'Come with me, Freddy. I'll take you to her.'

'In the crypt?' Freddy flinched from Persephone's touch and bent his slim frame over the font as if ready to vomit. 'Oh good God, no.' Then his knees buckled, and he collapsed to the floor, crossing his arms over his bowed head. Curled like a woodlouse, Freddy began to rock.

'Freddy, stay calm.' Dr Moon sat down beside his patient. 'Breathe deeply and control your fear.'

'What's wrong with you, Freddy?' Persephone once more tugged at Freddy's jacket. 'Please do stop crying. Stop crying, do. Stop crying, now.'

Queenie moved the sobbing child away from Freddy, and held her to her chest, patting the back of her head in a universal gesture of motherly comfort.

William heard the high wail of Persephone's pleas as he ran down the far aisle of the church. His journey ended at a red, sandstone wall and an elaborate cast iron gate. Unlocked, it swung open onto a set of steep steps. The spare candlelight of the main church illuminated the top of the flight to the colour of a blood clot, but the rest stretched down towards a cavernous black. William stood at the top and called out to Phyll, in hope, but was met only with the pitiful echo of his own rattled voice. And so he took the steps two at a time, soon slipping on the worn, wet stone, and sliding painfully on his hip for the rest of the flight, in the dark, and towards the stinking damp, until his feet touched the crumpled body of Phyll Hall.

William caught his breath and gripped the sandstone wall, hauling his heft away from the motionless Phyll. He waited, for a moment, for the blind panic to subside before inching closer to her, in control, once more, of his body. William blinked, eyes now adjusting to the gloom. On the far wall, as if hovering above the waterline, William saw a window. Nothing but a low arched slit, its scant light defined the shadowy outline of his friend. Face down on the bottom two steps of the crypt, Phyll lay with arms set at awkward angles to her torso, as if she had been crawling out of the wet. William inched forwards. The floodwater shone black and smooth, like the jet buttons on a widow's weeds. There, and eerily reminiscent of the Reverend Andrews, Phyll's hips and legs bobbed, the dark wool of her trousers ballooning and buoyant.

William held her hand. Cold. Deathly cold. 'Phyll,' he called, softly.

There was no response but the strange, and unseasonal, bass chirruping of frogs.

William knelt closer and, turning her head, removed a swathe of clotted hair from Phyll's face. He took a chest-tightening breath and caressed her pale cheek. At his touch, her half-closed eyes flickered and then opened. 'Billy.' Her voice was a hoarse, rasping miracle. William moved in closer and felt the soft warmth of her breath as she spoke his name once more. 'Billy, this is a terrible place.' She made to grab at his lapels but failed, her eyes unable to focus, her grip too weak.

'You were right. We must leave now. We must take Freddy and go.'

'It's alright. Save your strength. Please don't say anything. It's all over now. I've got you.' And as he hushed her, she closed her eyes once more, and that familiar anxiety-driven nausea rose and surged. William did not believe his own words. He once more took her hand, and rubbed at it, warming it with his. Then he wiped her clammy hair away from her forehead, whispering, 'I'm so sorry. I never should have left you.' For one peaceful moment, he was alone with her.

Then a strong torchlight shone above him. 'Don't move her, Mr Garrett, until I've taken a good look at her.' Dr Moon's voice echoed down the stone stairway.

'I'm taking her into the warm.' William moved his arms beneath her body, readying himself to lift. 'God, she's like ice.'

'No, don't move her just yet.' Dr Moon descended the steps. 'Hold my torch while I take a look at her.' William did as he was told, moving away from Phyll, spotlighting the doctor as he knelt awkwardly. 'Let's see if you have any broken bones.' He touched Phyll's body, arms; ran his sensitive fingers through her hair and asked her a few gentle questions. 'Yes, she'll do, but she's had a nasty bump on the head. She may have injured her legs, ankles. I'll see to that later. And you're right. She's rather cold.' Dr Moon nodded an order to William. 'Mr Garrett, if you'd be so good as to carry Phyll into the house.'

William gathered Phyll in his arms, and cradling her soft light body, he carried her up the steps and along the far aisle, towards the font and a waiting Freddy. Blankly staring and seeing nothing, he had the unfocused gaze of a man who'd seen too much. Queenie's left arm was about his shoulders, and with her free hand she stroked Persephone Pike's hair; the child's head rested on her lap.

Queenie was the first to see them, of course. She bent and kissed Persephone's cheek, whispering gently. The child rose and stared at William and Dr Moon. Queenie disentangled her arm from Freddy's shoulder, and took his hand, hauling the man to his feet.

'Don't worry,' William called. 'She's alright. She's in and out of consciousness. We've just got to get her into the house.'

The small group surrounded Phyll, quiet and solemn.

Freddy, teary with gratitude, muttered a prayer; Persephone placed Dr Moon's muffler over Phyll's body; Queenie kissed Phyll on the forehead as though she were tucking her up for sleep at night. This was love. A congregation of concerned humanity; the careful practice of kindness. Surely it was the only thing that mattered, in the end. William sighed in the brief respite. Phyll was amongst friends and safe in the sanctuary of the church. 'Towards the conservatory?' he asked.

'Yes.' Dr Moon nodded. 'The rooms at the rear of the house are well-heated.' He paused and glanced down at Phyll, swaddled like a child in William's arms. 'We need to get her as warm as possible, and quickly. And I'd very much like to take a proper look at that bump on her head.' He bent awkwardly, picked up two cards from the stone floor, and turned to Persephone, saying, 'Tidy up your card game, there's a good girl. And do extinguish the candles. The last thing we need is a fire after this flood.'

17

With each soaking step towards Red Hollow Hall, William's sense of respite faded. The river had burst its banks, and its once bordering trees appeared an incongruous meander of tangled branches in the middle of a flat black lake. A rowboat had broken its moorings and drifted at the mercy of the wind. And away from the buffer of the church, Phyll was no longer safe from the storm, and convulsed, violently, in his arms. William turned to Dr Moon. The man walked slightly ahead and to William's right, lighting their way with his electric torch. 'She's shivering, hard. It's this bloody sleet. It goes right through you,' he called. 'She won't stop shaking.'

'It's dehydration, I expect, Mr Garrett. We'll look after her. Don't worry. She doesn't have a fever.'

Ahead, the conservatory shone a queer green in the moonlight. Its small door sandbagged, Freddy leapt forward and removed the sacks, allowing William clear passage with his precious cargo. Inside, puffs of steam, visible in the dark, shrouded the statue of Pan. Water trickled into the copper basin, and Dr Moon's precious cacti rose like so many bulbous fingers in the greenhouse fog. Music drifted from the open door to the patients' sitting room. A muted trumpet squealed plaintive above the strong alto of the girl singer. *Don't know why there's no sun up in the sky.* William held Phyll close; felt her head bury into his chest; heard the clatter of steps on tile behind him; blinked hard against the dissonance of the American jazz and the cold glare of electric light.

Mr Irwell stood near the gramophone, swaying to the rhythm of the music, a cheroot in one hand, and the flimsy sleeve to the record in the other. He wore a dressing gown and matching slippers; the kind a mother would buy for a child undergoing a stint in a sanatorium, and stared, slack-jawed, as William entered. Then he took an affected draw of his cheroot, and bringing the needle from the record with a static scratch, said, 'Look what the cat dragged in. Such a lot of bother she's put us all to.'

'Keep your stupid mouth shut. I've warned you before.' William didn't look at Irwell, but placed Phyll, his back aching with the burden of her, on the sofa. He knelt beside her, fussing with cushions, ineffectual.

Dr Moon now stood close. The others, William noticed, hung back, concerned and self-conscious, perhaps readying themselves to help.

Phyll opened her eyes and gazed upwards, squinting at the black fissure which bisected the delicate plasterwork ceiling. 'I'm afraid I'm going to be sick.'

Freddy sprang forward, wastepaper basket in hand. He placed it on the floor near Phyll's head, and then took two steps back. 'Use this, my darling.'

'I shall fetch my bag, and some blankets,' said Dr Moon. He turned to Queenie. 'Try to get some of those wet outer things off her, Miss Maggs. And please don't ask Phyll any questions. I don't want to cause her any agitation until I know what's going on with that head injury. I shan't be long.' He paused in the doorway to the corridor. 'Do you understand me, Mr Garrett?'

William nodded, and the doctor left.

Phyll twisted and retched. William held the basket to her mouth, heard the splatter, smelt the bile. 'There was a man. He had the head of a giant fish.' The words came as a mutter as she slumped back into the sofa, eyes closed, lids twitching and blue, like a butterfly's wing.

A man with the head of a fish. It was all as William thought.

'The woman's gone raving mad.' Irwell lit another filthy cheroot and grimaced. 'It's quite the stink she's making.'

William stood, stiffened and fixed Irwell with a warning stare.

'Put a lid on it, Irwell.' Freddy nodded towards William. 'I won't stop him if he goes for you.'

Queenie came forward and touched William's shoulder. He moved a few steps backwards, allowing her room to undress Phyll. She did so with a tender care, peeling each woollen layer from her body with the practised expertise of a mother. 'She's frozen right through to the bone.' Queenie began to rub vigorously at Phyll's pale, shivering flesh. 'We need to get her into a warm bath. She needs food and something to drink.'

'I'll make up the fire.' Freddy, twitching and quick with nerves, threw a log onto the embers in the fireplace. 'Then I'll make some tea and sandwiches. Yes, Miss Maggs is right. Food and a hot drink, that's what she needs.'

'She needs a nip of whisky,' said Persephone, standing a little apart from the rest of the group, cramming the cards into her pockets. She raised her voice. 'Mummy says it's the best thing for a cold or a shock.'

'In this place?' Irwell spoke with a spitting violence. 'She should be so bloody lucky.'

'Go now, Freddy,' said Queenie. 'Make her some tea, very sweet, and toast.'

Freddy shot from the room, bumping into the returning Dr Moon, who made his entrance like a country physician in a play: his black bag perfectly battered, a tartan blanket over his arm, his face the epitome of steadfast concern. William and Queenie stepped away from the sofa, giving the doctor the stage. Dr Moon covered Phyll with the blanket, used his stethoscope and frowned. He took Phyll's pulse and muttered. Then, suddenly, he lost his air of self-consciousness and became engrossed in examining Phyll's head wound, captivated by the clump of clotted blood which mangled her blonde hair, and enthralled by the small gash on top of a walnut-sized bump on the back of Phyll's skull. Phyll winced twice at his examination, but her body remained horribly still. William held his breath. 'She needs nursing more than doctoring. A bath, bed, something nourishing to eat. Perhaps a sedative later to help her sleep.' Dr Moon rose from his crouching position and rubbed absent-mindedly at his gammy leg. 'You are made of strong stuff, Phyll Hall. And you have led your friends a merry dance.'

'What in God's name were you doing in the crypt, bab?'

'It's best not to press her, Miss Maggs. You and Mr Garrett may ask your questions tomorrow morning.'

'We must catch him. Before he does more harm.' She tried to rise from the sofa, pushing herself up by the elbows, but slumped back into the cushions once more. 'God, I feel sick.'

'Don't tax yourself, love. It's alright.' William glanced about the room. Irwell lurked by the gramophone, now thankfully quiet of 'Stormy Weather'; Persephone hovered respectfully at Queenie's side; Dr Moon packed away his bag; and Freddy would be back soon with tea and toast. This was neither the time nor place for true confessions. William released the breath he had been holding in one long, soothing exhalation.

'It's still vile out there.' Tom Sherbourne had returned. Oilskins dripping, he bent to warm his big red hands against Freddy's fire, and then turned, smiling at the sight of Phyll, and said, 'Oh my God, you've found her.' He straightened to his full height, brushing the damp, dark hair away from his face. 'Oh, I'm glad. That's a good end to a bad day. Are you alright, old thing?' Tom moved towards Phyll, who blinked at him, unsure of the near stranger in all her wariness and exhaustion. 'The poor kid's done in. Needs food and a good kip, I reckon.'

'Tom, where's my mummy?' asked Persephone.

Tom Sherbourne's red face reddened further. 'She's been helping me sort out the generator. We bailed out and sandbagged. It'll last the night out now, I hope.' He shot Persephone a reassuring smile. 'I'm sure she'll be along here in a minute. She'll be worried you're not in the tower. You shouldn't really be here, you know, amongst all us—'

'Loonies.' Freddy entered the room, finishing Tom's sentence. He placed a tea tray on the occasional table and began to pour out.

'Not a word we use at Red Hollow, Freddy,' said Dr Moon.

Tom Sherbourne let out a great guffaw. 'Well, I was going to say *men*, but both words are apt. Even if one is forbidden.'

'Freddy,' Phyll called. 'Is that you, Freddy darling?'

Freddy shuffled forward and steadied a teacup against Phyll's chapped lips. 'I'm here, Phyll. I'm so very sorry. I'm so sick I got you mixed up in all this mess.'

Phyll's hand trembled as she held the cup.

A wave of exhaustion swept over William. He became sensitive to the strange quiet of the room: the soft rustle of Queenie's coat; the tinkling of Phyll's nails on the teacup; Tom Sherbourne's puffing breaths; the crackle of logs on the fire.

And everyone watched Phyll, her tense face relaxing with each sip of tea: the hot drink, the warmth of the room, the compassion of the group, Dr Moon's reassurances, all worked their magic. Then she rested her head back on the sofa, and Freddy removed the teacup from her lips. 'Before I bathe,' she said. 'I must tell you about Mr Brooke. While it's all still so fresh, so real.'

18

'Mr Brooke is a very dear and loyal man.' Lady Sabrina Pike entered the room from the conservatory with all the deportment of a medieval queen, and rested her hand on Persephone's shoulder.

William wondered if the chaotic nature of the night meant the Pike women felt free to trespass.

'We should let the girl speak,' said Mr Irwell, stepping away from the gramophone. 'It's about time someone told the truth about what's going on here.' His voice was high and petulant, and he played with the cord of his dressing gown. 'I'm sick of all this mystery and running around and whispering in corners.'

'She's not a girl. She's a woman of thirty-two.'

William didn't know Phyll's age, but Queenie did. Did she know everything?

'No one has been whispering in corners, Mr Irwell.' Dr Moon's words held a note of restrained irritation, and at them, Irwell slumped into the nearest armchair, like an adolescent after an unhappy day at school.

'I don't know everything, and I can only really remember fragments of last night,' said Phyll. 'It's like flicking through a half-empty photograph album.'

A spattering crescendo of rain burst against the window-panes. Tom Sherbourne chucked another log on the fire.

'You don't have to say anything. Not unless you feel strong enough.'

'It's alright. Believe me, Dr Moon, I think I must do it now.' She blinked and her hand hovered, trembled, above her head. 'Otherwise, it'll all be lost.'

'Very well, Phyll.' Dr Moon lowered himself into a chair. 'Start with last night. What happened after you went to bed?'

'I didn't go to bed. It seemed to me that since your intruder did their work at night, I should stand sentry for a while. It wasn't that I was expecting to catch anyone in the act, you understand, I simply wanted to get a feel for the place, or even, I suppose, act as a deterrent.'

'But the mermaid did come, didn't she?' Persephone's voice rang out, clear and terrified. 'She came because you look so much like a handsome boy.' The child flushed at her words.

'Percy, the mermaid is nothing but a pernicious fairy tale.' Phyll pushed herself up on her elbows, searching around the room to meet Persephone's eyes, and spoke forcefully. 'Men are far more dangerous than ghosts and monsters, darling girl. And it was a man who hit me on the head last night, and it was a man who left me to drown in the crypt.' She slumped back into the sofa. 'Oh God, I'm suddenly rather desperate for a gasper.' William stepped forward, lit his last two cigarettes, and placed one in her lips. She took a long, deep pull. 'Delightful. All one needs is a good cup of sweet tea and a cigarette. They're both terribly curative.'

'Who hit you?' William asked.

'Oh, it was Mr Brooke, of course. Where is he?' There was a note of panic in Phyll's voice. 'The man is a maniac.'

'I sent him off to get the police. The storm brought the telephone lines down. You were missing, and the Reverend Andrews is dead. Head staved in and drowned.' William drew hard on his cigarette. 'Brooke is probably halfway to Southampton now. With his dear old mum, of course.'

'Oh God,' she said, resting her head back on the cushions, and drawing hard on her cigarette. 'I'll press charges tomorrow. I hope the police throw the book at him.'

'Involving the police in this matter is a gross over-reaction.' Lady Pike spoke with an icy authority. 'I'm sure any altercation between you and Mr Brooke was simply a misunderstanding, Miss Hall.'

William didn't know whether to be impressed or outraged by the audacity of the woman. It took a deliberate blindness not to see the similarities between Phyll's and the Reverend Andrews' injuries.

'It's *Phyll*, Mummy.'

Lady Pike ignored her daughter's interruption and continued. 'Once you are properly rested, Miss Hall, I am sure you will reconsider the wisdom of bringing this to the police court. The resulting repercussions, not simply to your own business, but on Dr Moon's work, and all who live at Red Hollow, could be disastrous.'

'Her ladyship is showing us all her cards.' Queenie, her voice low and cool, grinned in an intellectual squaring-up. 'And unless she knows all the facts, she should keep her trap shut. All she's doing right now is telling us what she's most afraid of. And I, for one, am wondering why it's the coppers.'

William twitched at Queenie's acumen. Was Lady Pike protesting too much?

'Bloody hell, Sabrina, you've met your match there.' Tom Sherbourne, laughing, glanced appreciatively at Queenie. 'Take the hint, woman, and keep quiet.'

Lady Pike glanced Tom's way, placed her lithe body in an occasional chair, and crossed her ankles in a ladylike manner.

Persephone edged towards the sofa and sat hunched on the floor between Queenie and Phyll.

'Alright, Phyll, do carry on,' said Dr Moon.

'I'd made sure the house was secure; checked as many doors and windows as I could, and then spent a couple of hours in the corridor outside Freddy's room, making sure he was alright.' She reached for her brother's hand and squeezed. 'I remember the church clock had just strich a quarter to three when I heard a clatter. The noise came from the main staircase. It sounded like something heavy and metallic falling to the floor. I ran down the corridor and bent over the handrail, and saw a figure two flights down. A slight figure, with lots of long, blond hair and dressed in a sort of cassock. For one, very stupid moment, I thought it was a ghost. You know, the girl in the story murdered by Sir Divinity. But my art school training kicked in. Under the cassock was a body with heft, broad-shoul-dered. It was a short man. He turned to his side, and that's when I realised the hair was attached to some kind of mask. A grotesque, Arts and Crafts, fish-head mask, rather like a hobby horse from the morris, but a fish.' Phyll took a long, deep breath, and with a faltering voice said, 'I hope you don't think I'm mad, because even as I recall what I saw, it sounds absurd even to me.'

'Just tell us in your own words.'

'The man was bending down to gather what he had dropped. It seems so bizarre, but it was a large, and rather elaborate sword.' Phyll took in a readying breath. 'Then he gathered up the skirts of his robe and slid down the banister.'

'What the bloody hell?' Tom Sherbourne began to laugh.

'Good Lord.' Lady Pike let out the words as a blushing, involuntary exclamation.

The gleeful theatrics of a ritual magician at play: Mr Brooke was having a special kind of fun that night, thought William.

Phyll continued unabashed. 'It's quite true. He slid all the way down to the hallway. I held back a little but heard the main door to the house open. I waited for a few moments, and then followed him outside. It was such a beautiful moon-lit night, everything so crisp and cool and white with frost. I remember shuddering with cold. I didn't stop to put my coat on, you see. Oh God, I don't believe I've stopped shuddering since.'

Tom Sherbourne came forward. Removing his jacket, he placed it over Phyll with a tender solemnity, and then returned to his position by the fireside.

'I kept my distance, aware he might hear my footsteps,' Phyll continued. 'Noise appears somehow amplified in the cold and dark, doesn't it? He headed for the church, but I decided not to follow him inside until the clock began to strike again, thinking the chimes would cover the sound of my footsteps. When I did go in, I found the place quite empty. I waited for a moment, listening to my own breathing, until I noticed a light, a soft light, rather distant and wavering. It came from the opening to the crypt. The gate to the staircase was open, and I heard a lot of clinking and scraping. I remembered Freddy's story, and I thought, rather stupidly, *I've got you now, old son*. Because it was obvious, wasn't it? This was Freddy's mermaid.'

Phyll's fingertips glanced the floor in search of the teacup. Freddy stepped forward and placed the cup once more to Phyll's lips. She took a few sips and then continued:

'Oh God, and then came the smoke. It drifted up those ancient stone steps like some vile presence, and it gave off such a terrifying stench, like horrid, rotting flesh, mixed with incense. By that time, I was determined to see what he was up to, so I went down there and watched him from the shadows at the foot of the stairs. It was alright for a while. There he was, in his robes, but without the mask.'

'That's when you knew it was Brooke,' said William.

'I suspected, but yes, that was the moment I knew. He was mucking about at the far end of the crypt by the little window, scratching something into the crypt floor with the tip of his sword. He had a battered-looking book resting on one of the old tombs and kept referring to it. I had the impression this was a serious business for him.'

Phyll's cigarette, now a stub, glowed near her right knuckle. Dr Moon bent forward and offered her a smutted glass ashtray. 'Could you see the title of the book?' he asked.

She shook her head. 'The only light came from that awful, smoky oil lamp, so most of the crypt was in deep shadow. I scooted behind one of the tombs, desperate to see what he was up to. Now I was closer to him, the stench of the incense and oil lamp was almost unbearable, and so thick and sickening that I gagged. He'd been drawing some sort of circular pattern with his sword and doing it with remarkable precision. When he'd finished, he put his mask back on, knelt and began to recite. Formal and pompous, it seemed almost liturgical.' Phyll screwed her eyes in an act of concentration and mimicked Brooke's recitation, stumbling over the words. '*O all ye spirits present before the face of God, I, the minister and faithful servant of the most high, conjure ye.*'

'This sounds like Key of Solomon magic. Hermetic philosophy. John Dee stuff.' Freddy's words came as a distracted mutter. His head was bent, and his long sensitive fingers massaged his scalp. When he looked up at his dumbstruck audience, his blond hair stuck out at angles. Every inch the eccentric scholar, he waved his arm about the seventeenth-century splendour of the room and then spoke as if conducting a lecture. 'John Dee was chief astrologer to Elizabeth I and sought, through magic, to commune with angels and divine the future. He wasn't the only Renaissance magician. Faith, the occult, science, it was all one and the same to these men. Alchemists, you know, were treasure seekers.'

'Oh God, yes, it was some sort of magic ritual. Of course it was.' Phyll let out a hollow laugh. 'And that awful atmosphere of hocus-pocus got even worse when those bloody frogs began to croak. Their sound made Brooke jump out of his skin mid-incantation. He'd got the wind up alright, and came poking about where I was hiding. Do you know, he was terribly shocked to see me? It was almost laughable. He stared at me, for what seemed like an age, eyes glowing in that awful fishy mouth, until I made a run for it. I'd got to the bottom of the steps before he caught me. He leapt on my back and dragged me by my hair onto the crypt floor.' She moved her hand to her chest; it hovered over her lungs, her heart. 'It's all so vague from then on. I can recall what my body felt, and all quite vividly, but I have so few detailed memories. Why is that, Dr Moon?'

'The body often remembers what the mind cannot face,' said Dr Moon. William shot him a sharp glance. It was involuntary, but the doctor seemed aware of it and twitched at William's interest. 'And you are doing remarkably well. Please carry on.'

'I put up a fight.' She smiled weakly. 'Squirming, kicking out, doing my best to make whatever Brooke had planned for me hard work. Then he came at me with his sword.' Phyll's fingers fluttered over her clotted hair. 'He hit me, perhaps with the pommel. I'm not sure, but I must've been out cold for ages. Have you ever had that feeling of falling while you're asleep? Well, when I woke it was with a jolt, and I was only half-aware that the crypt had flooded. I vomited and prayed for rescue. Then I must've passed out again because that's all I can remember. Thank God Percy found me. If it wasn't for her, I would've drowned.' Phyll reached out for the child's hand and clasped it in grateful thanks.

There came a collective intake of breath. It was Irwell's nasal whine that broke the silence. 'That's all well and good, but what was Miss Percy Pike doing poking about in the crypt in the first place?' He peered at the child through the smoke of his filthy cheroot. 'That's what I want to know.'

19

'I was looking for frogs, Mr Irwell.'

'Looking for frogs,' Irwell repeated, incredulous, glancing about the room, his pale blue eyes glittering and protuberant with anger. 'What the hell is going on in this madhouse? I can't bear it here any longer. Girls running around, poking their noses where they shouldn't. How can a man have privacy in such a place?' Mr Irwell moved away from his chair and hovered behind Dr Moon, fingering the collar of the doctor's discarded army greatcoat.

'Now, that is interesting, Percy.' Dr Moon rose, rubbed hard at his gammy leg, and ignored the hovering Irwell. 'May I ask what you needed the frogs for?'

'Is this all quite necessary?' Lady Pike rose from her chair. 'Adolescents are apt to have strange interests. Persephone is only just thirteen, and the time between childhood and adulthood is so difficult, particularly for a girl.'

'Lady Pike, I'm sure it is our one chance at getting to the bottom of this business.' The doctor smiled towards William. 'What do you think, Mr Garrett? Phyll?'

William's instinct told him that having the child tell her secrets in front of such an audience was both unwise and cruel. Public confession was for the courtroom, evangelical churches and school – awful places. But before he could voice his opinion, Persephone Pike spoke out:

'You found my cards, didn't you, Dr Moon?' Her face was pale with truculent resignation. 'You know what they are.'

'Cards?' asked William.

Queenie rose, felt in the pockets of her overcoat, and then handed William a crumpled card. It was neither a playing card nor a prayer card, but the Ten of Swords. William's card, his mom had said. He would be pinned down by a multitude of situations, and in danger of receiving deep wounds. *Fear death by water, my babby*, she had warned. William twitched, and he felt it like a convulsion. 'You're reading the tarot, Percy?' he asked. 'Who taught you?'

'Girls learn such silly things at school, Mr Garrett.' Lady Pike moved forward and placed a restraining hand on Percy. 'Of course, I never went myself, but you hear such terrible stories. Ouija boards, table tipping, played for a thrill in the dorm rooms after lights out, no doubt.'

Percy shrugged off her mother's hand, pulled a chair close to the sofa and addressed Phyll. 'It's not a game. It's serious divination. It guides me, and shows me how I must act,' she said. 'Honestly, someone must do something. Mr Trent saw the mermaid twice before he died, did you know that? He told me. She slid out of the cold tap each time he had his bath, just a little minnow at first, but she grew and grew and grew, and tried to smother Mr Trent with her fat, fishy body. She got him in the end, didn't she?' Percy shifted forward towards Phyll, scraping the legs of the chair against the polished floorboards. 'The secret of this house is that the mermaid is real, Phyll. I want to protect Freddy, just like you do. But you can't do that unless you accept that she is manifest. She will come tonight unless we act. We must do something, don't you see?'

The child had been praying the rosary, although not a Catholic. And reading the tarot, although divination was strictly forbidden by the Church. This belt-and-braces approach to preventing the mermaid from visiting Red Hollow spoke of true belief; faith. And William could make a good guess at who was responsible for indoctrinating the child.

'This house is full of magic, and yes, evil.' Freddy nodded, solemnly. 'One can sense it. It's in the bones of the place, the ancient, wild belief of the old religion, and with it something deep and dark. The death wish at the very heart of nature.' He came out of his reverie. 'Is this why you wanted the frogs, Percy? You wanted to do some kind of spell to protect against the mermaid?'

'Nothing else was working. I'd read it in one of Grandfather's books.' The child appeared contrite, wide-eyed with shame. 'I would never hurt an animal, but sometimes Rossetti hunts frogs, and leaves bits of them littered about the crypt. I had no choice but to do the spell. You'd seen her, Freddy. I heard Dr Moon talking about it when I was out gathering snowdrops near the Red Hollow. And you'd discovered that dreadful mermaid carving in the church. I never wanted to upset anyone. All I wanted was to keep Freddy and Tom safe. They're so terribly nice and kind.' The child paused and blushed. 'I was worried that the mermaid would hurt them. I couldn't let that happen. When one is a Pike, one has a responsibility.'

'And that unusual bottle of whisky?' asked Queenie.

'Oh, did you find those?' The child flushed a further pink. 'They weren't meant to scare anyone. They protect the people I like. I was worried the mermaid would hurt Tom – and Phyll too. She looks so much like a boy. I put one on top of Tom's wardrobe, behind his suitcase. And there's one by the mermaid pew, now, especially for Freddy. And there's one behind the gramophone.'

'What do you mean, bottle?' Irwell, now wearing Dr Moon's coat over his dressing gown, peered behind the gramophone. 'I've found it. Whisky, thank God. I could do with a drop.'

William sprang forward and took it from Irwell's hand before he could uncork it. 'No you bloody don't, old son.' Irwell's face screwed in anger, but he remained silent and seething in his resentment.

'What about the obscene graffiti we've been finding? Was that you, Percy?' asked Dr Moon.

'It's not graffiti. It's magic,' said Persephone, the truculence returning. 'They're special protective symbols.'

'Percy darling, really! What possessed you?' Lady Pike crouched beside her seated daughter; her voice was gentle but not without exasperation. 'Such vandalism is rather disturbing for poor Dr Moon's guests.'

Flowers and phalluses carved into the ancient, panelled walls of Red Hollow Hall; secreted bottles of piss protecting grown men from a ghostly, cock-hungry mermaid; witchfraft and Catholicism practised side by side in an English country church. He remembered the chaos of his own adolescence. Was anyone's puberty sane? William coughed out a laugh at the comic madness of it all. The laugh became a shudder, and his temples pulsed painfully.

'I was so terribly worried about the mermaid, Mummy.' Lady Pike rose and placed a hand on her daughter's shoulder. Persephone shrugged it off with a twitch. 'There are books in one of the attic rooms all about how you can use magic to protect people. They're horrid books, but magic so often is.'

'Surely, darling, you don't really believe in the mermaid?'

'I do. And you do too, Mummy.' Persephone's raised voice was a minor display of temper, but one which threw the room into silence. 'Everyone is going on about how horrid Mr Brooke is, but he's not. He told me all about Grandfather and of how he used magic to fend off the mine owners and the filthy land-grabbers. The magic is my inheritance because I am born from this country. Without the Pikes, there is no Red Hollow. I am the land, and the land is me.' A sudden volley of rain, elemental and violent, clattered on the conservatory roof. Persephone continued, her voice lowered. 'Mr Brooke is kind to me. He said he would teach me the proper magic as soon as I was thirteen, and then we could use it, so we would no longer be poor and a laughing-stock. We were meant to do it tonight. It's my birthday today, and everyone is being horrid to me, even though I was only trying to protect people. Say what you like about Mr Brooke, but at least he made me a birthday cake.'

20

William's mouth dried at the shocking vulnerability of childhood. Lady Pike, composure lost, and wordless in her distress, raised her face to look at him. A wave of human sympathy passed between them. The sins of the father were to be laid upon the children. 'Occultism runs in your family, doesn't it?' he said. 'Like weak ankles and haemophilia.'

'The men in my family, Mr Garrett, are either weak or degenerate. It's a matter of heredity. Father was never weak.' Sabrina Pike, in all her exhausted anguish, now appeared tenderly human. 'He was, in fact, a wicked man who lived entirely for his own pleasure. When the rumours of his depravities finally surfaced, we had few friends left in the county. The fact that Mr Brooke has somehow saved the magical collection and is using it for his own means is shocking. Since childhood, Mr Brooke has been my most loyal friend and confederate.' She shot a thin, knowing smile at William, and turned to her daughter. 'However, if he has been filling your head with this magical muck, Persephone, he is no friend, regardless of cake.'

'Brooke is a degenerate.' William gauged Lady Pike's imperceptible nod, and then continued. 'It's probable that he killed the Reverend Andrews. It's been bothering me that an evangelical parson would trudge through a storm to conduct a service he didn't approve of. I think he suspected Brooke of conducting his rituals in the crypt, and knew Candlemas was a special date. The date Red Hollow's mermaid died, yes? I think he wanted to catch Brooke in the act. Instead, he found Phyll up to her ears in floodwater. On his way to find help, probably in the form of Dr Moon, Brooke hit him. He may have dragged the parson out into the storm, but I think it more likely that the Reverend Andrews didn't die immediately. I reckon he rose, dazed, and wandered out into the rain in search of the police, collapsing near the driveway.'

'Oh, listen to Bulldog Drummond!' said Irwell. 'Playing at detective, thinking he knows everything. Weren't you the one who sent Brooke out to fetch the police? Well, the boys in blue won't come anytime soon, will they? Brooke will be miles away by now.'

'True. But isn't that a good thing? At least for the time being, you all can breathe a sigh of relief.' William's need to exorcise the mermaid from Red Hollow became overwhelming. The whole place could do with a disinfecting dose of muscular rationality before the superstition spread any further. 'Mr Brooke is the mermaid – don't you get it? The man wandered about at night wreaking havoc dressed as a bloody fish. He's been the one causing all the upset. And I reckon he's responsible for Mr Trent's death, too. Trent's secret drinking place was at the entrance to where Brooke kept his magical kit. Trent may have seen something he shouldn't and was deliberately drowned because of it. Or, he could've seen Brooke in full regalia while he was sweating out a pint of Scotch in the bath one evening. That would give anyone a sodding heart attack.' He looked at Dr Moon for support. 'Delirium tremens, yes?'

'It makes complete sense, Mr Garrett, yes.' The doctor, seated once more in his comfortable armchair, stretched his legs and brought his filthy pipe from his trouser pocket. 'But what was Mr Brooke's purpose, one wonders. There's a kind of reason behind even the most superstitious thinking, as Persephone has illustrated so perfectly.' The doctor began to fiddle with his pipe, tamping and lighting, tamping and lighting. 'Why was Brooke indulging in these strange rituals?'

'I don't want to speculate.' But that, of course, was all William had been doing. He almost laughed at the irony of his own statement. This detecting lark was actual bollocks.

'The great detective is a prize idiot and doesn't know a thing. He's just showing off.' Irwell stood too close to the women; as he spoke, the cuff of his coat grazed Persephone's cheek. The child twitched, but remained still, in polite, utterly feminine, discomfort. 'Do you believe him, Freddy? You saw the mermaid. Do you think she was Mr Brooke in a mask?'

'It wasn't Mr Brooke.' Freddy spoke to Phyll, stroking the hair from her claggy forehead. 'The mermaid showed me her private teeth.'

Phyll closed her eyes and gulped back spittle; so much of her seemed utterly spent.

'God help you, Freddy,' William sighed, aching in disappointment. Freddy couldn't shake the mermaid germ, and no amount of William's rational medicine would cure him.

'Mr Garrett, don't you see?' Persephone's words came as strange heaving sobs made in time to the rhythmic surge of the storm. 'She'll come tonight and there will be carnage.' William had wished to protect Persephone. Solve the mystery, give her a good dose of rationalism, restore order to the chaos of her small, supernatural world. 'If Brooke isn't here to look after the men, she'll come and hurt Tom, and she'll come and hurt Freddy.'

'She won't hurt me, Percy, and I'm the biggest womanising drunkard in the room.' Tom Sherbourne, eyes closed, leant against the wall nearest the fireplace, smoking. Every inch the knackered, middle-aged addict, he was still twitchingly attentive in all his exhaustion. 'I'm not violent.' Throwing his cigarette into the fire, he gave them a wide, handsome grin, and was transformed, young again. 'I'm a lover, not a fighter. But, by Christ, I've done the women in my life more harm than good. When I'm on the booze, my gob turns nasty. But I'm not scared of the mermaid, Percy. I don't need little girls doing magic spells to keep me safe, because the mermaid doesn't exist.' He turned towards Lady Pike and screwed his face in reluctant disapproval. 'You know me, Sabrina, I'm the epitome of laissez-faire, but keep a better eye on the kid. She can't be coming in here as she pleases, woman.'

Lady Pike rose to leave the room. She paused, smiling, in the doorway of the conservatory and beckoned to her daughter. 'Come now, darling, Mr Sherbourne is quite right. It's time we returned to the tower.' She nodded her polite goodbyes to the company, as if she were leaving the village school after doing her duty on prize-giving day. 'Dr Moon has work to do, I'm sure.'

Persephone moved to follow her mother.

'Oh no you don't.' Mr Irwell stretched out his pale, bony hand and tugged at the child's shoulder, turning her so she faced him. 'You're not going anywhere. I want protecting, Miss Percy,' he spat. 'Why don't you want to protect Mr Irwell from the mermaid? I don't want to end up like the Reverend

Andrews, drowned and God knows what else, and all because he shamed a few tarts in church.' He blinked three times, screwing his face with each spasm. 'You don't know my Christian name. It's Tom this, and Freddy the other, but no thought for Mr Irwell. Mr Irwell isn't handsome enough for you to bother to find it out, is he? Good enough for the mermaid to gobble up, but not good enough to spark your interest. He's always been invisible to girls like you.' Irwell thrust his hands into the pockets of Dr Moon's coat, and smiled as his spittle landed on Persephone's face. 'You're staying with me tonight, and every night, until I can get out of this godforsaken hole.'

Persephone blinked, nonplussed at the man's outburst, but the adults responded with a barrage of remonstration.

'Oh, for God's sake, shut it.' Freddy spoke in a vicious, bone-weary whisper. 'You're so unbelievably stupid, Irwell, I can hardly bear it.'

'Come away from the man,' said Lady Pike. 'Now, Persephone.'

The child turned towards her mother, frozen, it seemed, to the spot.

'Grab her, Billy.' Phyll sat up, alert once more.

Dr Moon rose stiffly from his armchair, waved his pipe towards Irwell and the child. 'Come with me, Mr Irwell,' he said. 'You need rest.'

When William saw the pistol, panic came like a punch to the gut. 'Christ, Dr Moon, the Webley. You left it in your coat pocket.'

Irwell grinned at the chaos he'd created. The boy was in ecstasies of power, his chest rising and falling, and his eyes swam with pleasure. He did not wave the pistol about like some lunatic in the movies; instead, he screwed the metal of the muzzle with rough deliberation into Persephone's soft cheek.

Lady Pike let out a deep, primal groan and lunged at Irwell. Tom took three swift steps forward, holding her back, but the woman sought her child, and her torso became strangely horizontal in Tom's powerful, restraining arms, her fingers outstretched, her feet shuffling on the stone floor.

'My name is Vincent, by the way,' he said. 'After the saint. When he was canonised, the Vatican dug up his body, and it hadn't rotted. I doubt they'll say the same about the Reverend Andrews.' Irwell laughed at his own joke, placed his left arm tight about Persephone's waist, and snuggled in behind her, sniffing at her hair. The child responded like a rabbit trapped by a poacher: eyes bulging wide in fear and shocked into stillness, waiting for the inevitable. 'And you better come up with the goods because you know what it says in the Bible. *Thou shalt not suffer a witch to live.*'

'Vincent.' Dr Moon's voice was professionally calm. 'I can see you're in great distress, but Persephone cannot cure that. Come with me and rest. Then we can talk.'

'I'm pig-sick of your fucking tiresome Freudian bleating.' The electric light quivered, black and light, black and light, so each of Irwell's facial tics appeared delineated, as if frame by frame, like an actor at the beginning of a flickering film reel. 'Don't you know I'm a man of action? Talking gives me a headache.'

There was nothing to be done but land three solid jabs, fast and hard, against Irwell's temple, and so William did. The moment of relief as he belted the little bastard was beautiful, but Irwell rolled with William's third punch. Staggering sideways, he was dizzied enough for his grasp about Persephone's waist to loosen. It took a second for the child to dart to the safety of her mother's outstretched arms.

Irwell steadied himself into a blinking focus, pointing the pistol in William's direction. 'How fucking dare you?' He rubbed at his temple with his left hand, body wavering. 'That's the last time you lay your filthy hands on me. I want Percy. Let me have her. Now.' Irwell screwed his face in pain. Tears formed in his pale blue eyes as he stamped his foot on the floor in a grotesque act of childish anger. William stood slack-jawed, stomach roiling at the abnormality of the man, at the strangeness of the house, and at the violence of the night.

William's stupefaction didn't matter, however, because Queenie was never astonished. Creeping up behind Irwell, and with a practised ease, she cracked him on the back of the skull with the Derringer, finishing what William had started. 'You're not going anywhere, son,' she said. 'You're in here for a bloody good reason.'

For a second, Irwell's face was a picture of outraged confusion. His eyes swivelled back in his head, and his grip on the Webley loosened, so that it spun on the floorboards, scudding beneath the gramophone. Then Irwell's legs buckled, and he dropped to the floor.

And so did William.

The shameful, shivering impulse to vomit returned. Queenie loomed over him. Cold sweat formed on his forehead with the shuddering shame of it all. The weight of his sin. Oh Christ, he'd seen and done too much. Beyond Queenie lurked the black of night, the sleeting rain and the dark scar of the canal. All that damage done, it waited deep in his gut to surge and overwhelm him. The clinging damp of his shirt suffocated William. He moved to take it off. Why couldn't he be a normal man?

Neurotic: it's what they called women and old soldiers.

Red Hollow Hall wasn't a place for women.

He's under the bloody water. Weighed down with pig iron. The bastard pike and tench are nibbling at him.

'Mr Garrett, you must breathe.' William felt Dr Moon's hand press firmly on his shoulder. 'You need some tea and sympathy, my friend.'

Day Three

21

2 a.m., Saturday, 3 February 1934

Dick Powell is singing. Again.

'Shut the fuck up, Dick, I've had enough.'

But Dick doesn't stop. *By a waterfall, he's dreaming too-hoo-hoo-ooo.* Dick is Mr Fancy Pants today, as he wears a white tuxedo delicately touched with Hollywood glitter. Dick's arms are about Queenie and, tenderly, they both sway in time to the music of his sweet, high tenor. *There's a magic melody Mother Nature sings to me. Beside a waterfall with yoooo.* Dick and Queenie perform a dainty tap routine, just a few steps, hand in hand. Neither one is known for their dancing. *Tippity-tip-tap-tap, tippity-tip-tap-tap,* on a slick, black stage. Backdrop all black and wet. Overpowering deep black, but Dick keeps on crooning. He doesn't give a shit about black water.

Queenie and Dick fade out, thank fuck. Girls, thirty or forty girls, all clad in sparkling scanties, dance about a huge red pool. Then in they dive, one by one. Down into the depths, down into the quivering red.

'No, girls. Don't go in there.'

William panics cold sweat. Christ, he has a thirst on.

Up pop the girls, smiling Hollywood smiles. Close your eyes, Billy. Don't look. But William peeps through his fingers because he's nothing but a filthy little Peeping Tom. The girls become a wondrous kaleidoscope of naked limbs. Is he a leg man? William doesn't know. He tells the girls.

'I don't know if it's worth bothering with,' he shouts. 'I can't swim, and I don't even know if I'm a leg man.'

The girls can't hear him, or they just don't care. They form a snake in the red water. A silver, sinuous snake made from smiling women. *Under Germ-Laden Film, Decay Begins.* William rubs his tongue over his teeth; he does the Pepsodent test. Too much sugar. *He who desires but acts not, breeds pestilence. Dip him in the river who loves water.* Persephone drew The Devil from the pack. The goat-god, Dionysus, in bondage to lust, power, violence; a reckoning will be needed.

'There's something funny in the water around here,' he shouted.

William woke, feeling the shout in his sore, dry throat, and knew he was alone in the dark of night, curled like a child before the fireplace in the patients' sitting room. He unfurled himself, knees and ankle bones clicking. He needed to eat more fish. Kippers for breakfast, the doctor had said. Moonlight shone from the picture window, casting streaks of silver, mottled and fishy, on the stone floor. Moonlight; the storm had passed. In the distance, the church clock struck two. William had lost time.

He stood, creaking and giddy, and gathered himself, patting his pockets for cigarettes. No. He had run out. He'd been smoking Tom Sherbourne's Woodbines all evening. William searched for long fag butts in the ashtrays; he'd light one from the embers which glowed like cat's eyes in the fireplace. Christ, he'd done worse. But the room had been tidied, and the ashtrays wiped and emptied.

William shook his head. God, he was thirsty. He would need to find the kitchen, and pour himself a glass of water, a pint or two of water. Sweat trickled cold along the base of his neck. His collar was damp with it, but his feet were dry. He wiggled his toes. He was in his stockinged feet, and he noticed his shoes had been placed before the fire, as you would a child's, to dry out.

There was enough moonlight for William to see the standard lamp in the corner of the room. He bent to turn it on at the flex, his extended hand shaking, shuddering, but the lamp didn't work. William tried the wall light. No joy. The generator had given up the ghost. Tom Sherbourne was the man who could fix it, William knew. But it was hardly worth waking him at this time of night to get the thing going.

God, William had a sweat on. He was ill, he thought, caught a chill from walking in the wet. He would make his way to the kitchen in the dark, drink water, make tea, perhaps. If he got lost on the way, he'd scream for Freddy. Scream for both his company and his electric torch. When was the last time he saw Freddy? William shook his head and glimpsed Freddy waltzing the poignant, solitary dance of a lonely man. *Little boy lost in the lonely fen, led by the wand'ring light.* Shut up, brain.

Everyone, William assumed, was tucked up in bed. He must have volunteered to sleep downstairs. On watch for the return of Mr Brooke? On watch for the rising flood? He had no idea. On watch for the mermaid? Don't be ridiculous. William didn't know why he was downstairs, and William liked knowing things. Knowledge was a comfort to William. Christ, he had no memory. His stomach lurched in panic, and his thirst raged.

William straightened, cricking his back, but the more upright he became, the more his heart pounded in a strange, irregular dancing beat. *Tippety-tip-tap-tap, tippety-tip-tap-tap.*

The room was hot, despite the February night. So hot he could wring the stinking sweat from his shirt.

William heard a trickle. Was it the fountain in the conservatory? A constant musical flow of water; the obscene little tinkle of Pan's dripping flute. He remembered the huge, steaming pipes bordering the glasshouse puffing out their fog. Yes, of course, water was piped in. Of course it was alright to drink.

William walked towards the open door, limbs slow and heavy, and strangely uncoordinated in the moonlight; the patients' sitting room seemed fat with distorted shadows. He missed his footing, as if he'd encountered an unexpected step, or wore spectacles which didn't belong to him. William shook thick sleep from his head and picked his way through the door and into a swimming green light. Outside, the flooded land was flat and calm and cold. Inside, the conservatory was the hot undulating backdrop for Dr Moon's exotica – New Mexico in the Midlands. He walked over to the fountain and allowed Pan's water to trickle into his mouth, drinking it down in thirsty gulps. Then William plunged his head into Pan's basin, relieved his hot, sweaty, summertime headache with the cool of the water. One, two, three seconds. The goldfish caressed his cheeks. Up he came, wiping the wet from his eyes, conscious of the bliss of cool drips against the back of his neck. William went under once more.

Tea and sympathy, that's what they had called it. Tom, Freddy, William and Dr Moon, together in the sitting room. Irwell sedated. Pikes in the tower. Queenie and Phyll in the kitchen. Only the old soldiers were left, drinking tea and talking bollocks. When a precious ceramic breaks in Japan, they don't glue it back together and hide it, ashamed of the damage. They gild the cracks. Gild the cracks, William, don't you see?

And the vase, plate, cup becomes more beautiful than ever. It is broken, but it is precious and valued because the damage is part of the story. Talk, talk, talk, with Dr Moon. Visions of his mother, his son, Clara Morton. He'd told them all his secrets. Shit. He'd told them of his love, and what he'd lost. He'd told them what he'd done. Mortal sin, and that was between William and God.

But God was love and God was beauty and God was truth and we fear God but we must also love Him and His creation and aren't we His creation so we must love ourselves and our fellow man and all the creatures on His Earth? Don't you see?

Mercy, pity, peace and love, they're the only things that matter in the end. Don't you see, Billy? Don't you see? And William saw.

William rose from the water, dripping, refreshed, cool.

'It's alright.' William said it out loud. 'It's alright, because what other choice do we have but to gild the cracks?'

William's thick head seemed full of marvels, but his thick head knew, as if by instinct, all this wonder, all this joy, wasn't normal.

There came a sudden shattering crash of ceramic on tile. William felt panic so fierce he almost vomited. He turned, sharply. One of Dr Moon's cacti, a green cottage loaf of a plant, had fallen. William bent to pick up a pot shard, marvelling at the precision of the hand that decorated it: the miracle of the line, straight but human, so undeniably human, and yet so wonderful. He would glue the pot together and gild the cracks. Thick with God, still, Billy.

Then came a rustle on the plant stand, and a swift, sinuous slither in the darkness. Black-silver, quicksilver.

'Who's there?' No answer came, but something soft, prodding and insistent worked its way against his calves in a come-hither caress. William didn't look down. He was frightened – no, terrified – of the mermaid. 'Who's there? I mean you no harm. I won't hurt you.'

William liked the company of women. William was no debaucher.

Oh, but you were, Billy. You were. And you did it all for money.

The rubbing continued about his shins, and as a lithe glide between his ankles. Sharp claws sank into his stockinged feet – the red, painted talons of a glamour girl. William knew his mermaid had Winnie Woodcock's face: platinum-blonde curls, rosebud lips, a purpling shiner: the last of his divorce cases.

'I'm sorry, Winnie,' he said. 'I thought you'd bounce back.'

William braved it and looked down into the shadows, where a pair of beautiful green eyes glowed. 'I love you, Clara.' She crawled towards him, eyes protuberant, lipstick smudged, a silk stocking wound tight about her pale neck, upturning a bowl of lilies, crushing the petals with her knees, unleashing their rich funereal scent. William held out his arms and called to her, and she leapt, with one, swift, elegant pounce, straight into them. 'I'm sorry I couldn't save you.' He cried as he held her.

Small and soft and black, she purred, a low-humming motor of a purr.

William blinked. A nightmare. A fever dream. William laughed at his own foolishness. Laughed through the tears and stroked the cat's nose and chin, for that's how Rossetti directed him. William kissed the cat. Did he kiss a cat?

William turned, the purring Rossetti in his arms. Five or six easy steps and they were near the door to the patients' sitting room. Perhaps William would put another log on the fire, and watch it burn. It was a pleasure, wasn't it, to stare at a slowly burning fire. Yes, the damp logs would sputter and spark all night, and William would gaze at them, and all with a cat curled comfortably on his lap.

The sound came from heaven as a shatter of splintering rain, and William thought he might die. Rossetti screeched and leapt from his arms. The angel of death had come to take William, but it wasn't Rossetti's time, yet. Sleek, clever cats hid from the angel of death, maintaining their nine lives with swift self-preservation.

The sky had collapsed, and with its descent came a body. A fallen angel of a man, naked torso pale green-grey in the glassy moonlight, he lay arched and broken on Pan's fountain. Glass fluttered down like hard snow and landed on William's upturned face. He brushed it away and watched clouds scud across the moon, and then the glittering tail of a shooting star arc in the night sky, seeming, in that moment, to have gained the time he thought lost.

But the wicked god's water still flowed, trickling, darkened. It mingled with the man's blood, rose like a stream along the legs until it got to the dangling feet and then dripped onto the floor, forming a terrible pool.

William's gaze travelled across the body, stopping at the man's groin. An empty mess of clotted blood and pubic hair, his cock and balls had gone, leaving a gaping red depression, a bloodied hollow. William forced himself to look at the man's face. Dark locks stuck damply to his furrowed forehead, and twirled prettily about his ears, caressing the lifeless eyes, so that, for a moment, Tom Sherbourne, in death, resembled the statue of some Greek hero.

Above William, and from the shattered sky, a wizened brown creature tumbled down like a sycamore seed and landed, teeteringly, on Tom's naked body. The monkey clutched his parasol, but he had lost his red velvet hat in the fall, so that his moth-eaten pate was exposed to the chill night air. He stared at William with wide, affronted eyes and bared his protruding lower teeth. The monkey was angry because he was dead, William thought, but at least he still had both bollocks.

'Count your blessings, monkey.' William touched the back of his head. Deep, deep inside, there had been a disconnection. 'I've cracked,' he said to the monkey. 'I'm cracked.'

Skull full of the thud of his own heartbeat, he turned and vomited. All he had eaten that night, and all he drank, re-emerged in a wave of convulsive, painful retching. Then came shuddering so violent his muscles spasmed in agonising seconds-long contractions.

Men, run for cover. Quick, boys, quick!

William had told Freddy that by the end of the evening they'd both be the stuff of the mermaid's nightmares. But that had been nothing but hubris.

22

William blinked in the hard white glare, eyes watering, painfully.

'You have a shard of glass embedded in your cheek, Mr Garrett. I'm going to remove it.'

'The veil between the worlds has lifted, Dr Moon.' William didn't see the doctor, only the fizzing bulb at the very centre of the torchlight, and a glittering halo of polished steel. 'The world of the imagination has bled into reality like a radio not tuned right so that two separate broadcasts interrupt each other and form a sort of poetry.' William talked and didn't take a breath. 'All the locked doors are wide open, and I know what the mermaid wants. She wants to see England fall. She wants the whole sorry show to sink into the filthy mud. The mermaid is sick of all the beatings she gets in England's name.' He waved his hand as if to indicate beyond Red Hollow. 'I've seen Hell, Dr Moon.'

'I'm quite sure of it, old chap. But do stay still.'

'Have you seen Hell?'

'Many times over.'

'Tonight.'

'Yes.'

'Is Tom dead?'

'Yes, murdered.'

'We must give Tom his dignity.' William attempted to get to his feet, but the doctor placed a restraining hand on his shoulder. 'We must remove the stuffed monkey with his stupid big bollocks. It's a sacrilege.'

'There'll be time enough for Tom. First, we must see to the living.'

'Which living?' William's panic surged. 'Who else has she got?'

'You, my dear fellow, you.'

William's hands grasped his intact groin as if by instinct. 'All present and correct, sir,' he said.

'You have a nasty cut on your face,' said Dr Moon. William heard the clasp of a large bag open, and then a rummage and a sigh. 'I'll take the shard out now, but I think we should go to the kitchen. There are paraffin lamps in a cupboard. I'll light them, and then I can make a decent examination of you.' William felt the cold metal of Dr Moon's tweezers and, for the first time, a sharp kick of pain. He winced and cried out. 'You might need one or two stitches. Pop this against your cheek.' Dr Moon handed William a wad of cotton wool and gauze. 'Do you have glass in your feet?'

'I dunno. How would I know?'

William heard scissors snip at the cuffs of his socks, and then felt the cold blades run down each ankle.

'No glass. You're alright, I think. Let's pop your shoes back on.'

Dr Moon put William's shoes on William's feet; tied up the laces in a nice bow, as his mother once did. 'Warm but damp,' said William.

'Could be worse.'

'Where is everyone?' William hadn't come to his senses; he'd simply found motes of practicality amongst the dancing dust of his awareness. 'Didn't Tom wake the whole house?'

'As far as I know, everyone is asleep, and I hope to keep it that way for as long as possible. Are you alright to walk?' The doctor bent, took William under the arms and hauled him to his feet. 'Coffee, yes? I learnt to make good coffee in the United States.' He looked down at the floor, and then at the specks of egg white on William's shirt. 'I'm glad you vomited.'

'Queenie does a good fry-up. What a waste.'

William followed Dr Moon's bobbing white light through the dark corridors of Red Hollow Hall. The torchlight dipped and shifted with the lilt of Dr Moon's uneven gait. William watched it intently. Beautiful light trailed and danced in radiant variations of white, never true white, but more often a soft yellow, like a baby's hair. William told Dr Moon all about it.

'You're a very observant fellow.'

William thanked him.

Soon, he was sat at the kitchen table. William ran his finger along the smooth pine, salt-scrubbed. He pressed the wad of gauze hard against his cheek, conscious of his dripping blood ruining the kitchen hygiene.

There came the slamming of cupboard doors, and the successive illumination of each corner of the kitchen: the coal-black range; the glossy cream dresser; the refrigerator, pristine enamel, hospital-like; the lead sink containing the snaking tubes of an abandoned stirrup pump. In William's line of sight, the mouthlike opening to the flooded pantry gaped, emanating damp like bad breath. William shuddered. A wave of nausea surged.

Dr Moon placed an oil lamp on the kitchen table, next to his black medical bag. He remained silent, busy with the preparation of coffee.

'Time is strange tonight.' Upon hearing William's words, the church clock chimed the half-hour, and the servant's bells gave out an eerie, vibrating retort. 'When did Tom die?'

'I always think time misbehaves in the early hours.' Dr Moon was at the range, fussing with the coffee pot, filling a pudding basin with water from the copper boiler. 'And I don't know when he died, but I heard the crash about twenty minutes ago.'

'Psychopomps,' William blurted.

'What a very interesting word.'

'My mind is full of interesting words. I saw the mermaid.' William tapped his skull, and the bloodied gauze fell from his cheek, sullying the scrubbed table. 'But I'm not in my right mind, and I don't know why. It's not just the wind up. Did you know I have neurasthenia?'

'Of course I do.' Dr Moon placed the bowl of steaming water before William.

'Look at me shake.' William left his cheek to drip and held out both arms like a monster from the movies, marvelling at his own trembling. 'Look, it's amazing.'

'Gauze on cheek, Mr Garrett.' Dr Moon put the dressing back on William's face. 'Let's get you stitched up.'

'The shakes won't stop,' he said, realising he spoke each thought he had. 'I'm saying everything I think.'

Dr Moon walked to the dresser, and returning with a chequered tablecloth, he placed it over William's shoulders. William sat hunched, hand pressed against his cheek, shawled like a shaman, and attempted a thoughtful, masculine silence.

'I need to see how much glass is in your face, and get you cleaned up properly.' The doctor unclasped the brass fastening on his heavy black bag. 'I can give you something for the pain, but it might not be wise. Can you take it – the pain I mean?'

'I can take it, but I'd like some of that coffee you promised.' William pulled his tablecloth tight about his shoulders, for warmth, protection. 'I bought a good percolator from Lewis's, but I've only used it once or twice. It's a bugger to clean. I like to waste my money on complex machinery.'

'I'm not sure I like the machine age too much.' Dr Moon leant over William, oil lamp in hand, and scrutinised his face. 'A coffee pot is simpler, more elegant. Tilt your head upwards.' William obliged. 'Don't talk now, Mr Garrett. Once I've stitched you up, we'll have our coffee.'

The doctor squinted over him and removed small shards of glass from William's face with the points of his tweezers. After each prick of his skin, William heard a delicate tinkle on a china saucer. Then, warm and wet and chemical, there came a sweeping clean-up with a wad of cotton wool. William saw his blood form dancing poppies in the pudding basin full of water.

Needle threaded and glinting in the golden lamplight, Dr Moon came intimately close, nose to nose, moving in as if for a kiss. William closed his eyes in readiness, and the needle pierced his flesh. 'Two stitches, I think,' said Dr Moon. 'I'm a very dainty seamstress, Mr Garrett. After a few months, you'll hardly see a scar.'

Wadding and tape fattened William's face, and with it came a stinging numbness larger than the injury.

Afterwards, Dr Moon, by way of a treat, placed the promised coffee before William, pushing the sugar bowl his way, too. 'Plenty of sugar, Mr Garrett. It'll do you good.'

William stirred his coffee, watching the sugar – three lumps – float and dissolve until the very last grain disappeared into the glossy liquid. Then he drank to the dregs and rose, moving with the oil lamp towards the pantry, stepping as close to the sloshing black floodwater as he dare. On the wall to his right, the limewash bubbled with damp. William touched it, crumbling the chalky substance between his thumb and forefinger. 'Did we men dance together tonight?'

Dr Moon stood a few steps behind him. 'We did.'

'And eat bacon and eggs and drink sweet tea?'

'Miss Maggs was kind enough to make our supper.'

'Queenie is an all-rounder.' Dried herbs, thyme and bay, dangled between a brace of pheasants. 'She's a good cook and can subdue a madman with the butt of her revolver.' William stared at a bird, his stomach turning at the oily iridescence of the feathers, and the bare, red skin wrinkling about the eye. 'Cock pheasants,' he blurted.

'The archetypal mother figure.'

Beyond the birds, three dead rabbits hung from a hook in the corner. Glassy-eyed, dun fur ruffled at the point of gunshot wound, their small, pointed front paws dangled piteously. William's mother had given him a rabbit's foot for luck on her deathbed. Six years later he had lost it in the mud of the Somme. 'I don't think I'll ever be normal,' he said. 'Normality is an opportunity that passed me by.' A tin bucket bobbed in the floodwater. Tom Sherbourne bent to pick it up. 'Thank you, Tom,' said William.

The dead man played peek-a-boo behind the dangling rabbits, half-concealed in a shadowy corner. Water lapped against Tom's shins, dampening his rolled trouser legs. Tom made as if to bail out, but looked at William confusedly when no water appeared in his bucket. Tom's ghost grinned, and said, 'It's like a game of Murder in the Dark.'

'But it's not a game,' he said. 'You need to be serious.' William closed his eyes, taking a blind step upwards and backwards, straight into the arms of Dr Moon. 'Tom was sleeping with Lady Macbeth.' William looked about for the ghost, but it had gone. 'She'd be all elbows in bed, I reckon.'

'Sabrina Pike?' asked the doctor.

'That's what I said, didn't I?'

'I have a feeling Tom only stayed at Red Hollow because of her. Lovers are rarely as discreet as they imagine. You noticed their little intimacies, I suppose.' Dr Moon turned William away from the pantry, exerting a gentle pressure on his shoulder, like a rider might press his knees against the flanks of a horse to get him going. William trotted on.

'I'm a very observant fellow.'

'Do sit down, there's a good chap.' In the golden lamplight, Dr Moon's red hair shone like the pelt of a fox.

William sat. Dr Moon poured coffee and moved to the refrigerator, returning with a ham and a dish of butter. Then a loaf of bread and a carving knife appeared on the kitchen table as if by magic. Dr Moon brandished the knife, hacking at the meat with a blade so old it had been sharpened to a curve. White bone appeared in the pink flesh.

'Ham off the bone,' said William, salivating. 'Pavlov's dog.'

The doctor turned, waving his cutlass. 'You're hungry?'

'No, I've just been sick.'

Dr Moon topped up William's coffee cup and handed him a sandwich. 'Eat up and drink up, doctor's orders.'

'Tom's ghost is about as real as my mermaid.' William bit into his sandwich, leaving teeth marks in the thick butter. 'I'm feeling quite chipper, considering. Freddy's mermaid and my mermaid are the same, aren't they?' William wagged his finger. 'You're a very suspicious fellow, Dr Moon. Not that I don't like you.'

'I don't know how I shall bear Tom's death.' Dr Moon took a gulp of coffee and bit into his sandwich. 'I've been foolish,

Mr Garrett. I think the Greeks called it *hubris*. And I will have to live with the consequences of my arrogance for the rest of my days. Poor Tom, poor dear Tom.'

'He said you saved his life.' Visions of earnest talking crowded William's mind. Unlikely conversation, himself leading, speaking the truth as he saw it. He even recited poetry. 'I have an inkling it was done with the best intentions.'

'The road to Hell is paved with them, so they say.'

'What did you give us?'

'Peyote.' The doctor winced, as though his own cheek had been stitched. 'I use it to make sad men talk.'

23

'Sex magick,' said William. 'You're an occultist.'

'What? Good grief, man, no.' Dr Moon coughed; flecks of ham and bread hit the kitchen table. 'That's not what we were up to.'

'The phrase flew into my head like a moth.' The light from the oil lamp radiated golden across the kitchen table. William placed his hand before the beam, and it too shone yellow. 'It's fluttering about there now, looking for light.'

'There is no magic at Red Hollow,' said Dr Moon. 'And very little sex.'

'No magic? Surely you can't say that.'

'Magic, like ghosts and mermaids, does not exist.'

Ghosts don't exist, but we all tell stories about our dead. Magic is nothing but smoke and mirrors, but we all cross our fingers and wish for good luck. William's moth still fluttered. 'You believe alright. Why lie?' Then with sudden insight, he looked the doctor straight in the eye. 'I remember that first day. I'm not daft. Why did you shoot a full round of ammunition into the mermaid's pool?'

'My subconscious mind at work.' The doctor shrugged. 'I may not believe in the mermaid, but I still see her as a threat.' The doctor took another sip of coffee. 'She is a threat. Her vile story killed poor Tom.'

'Why, up here –' William tapped at his skull – 'do I associate peyote with magic?'

'This is beginning to feel rather like a police interrogation.'

'I'm doing my best, considering.'

'Alright.' The doctor sighed. 'We talked about Crowley when we first met. Perhaps you'd read about his drug use?'

'Yes, probably. I'm a big reader.' In his mind's eye, William saw a glittering cobweb of endless bohemian connections. Poets and occultists and artists and psychiatrists, their thoughts and behaviours flowing into the mainstream, forcing upper lips to unstiffen.

'Crowley uses mescaline, a tincture of the cacti, in his rituals. It is prized amongst his type because of the visions it induces.' The doctor poured coffee, and carved huge hunks of ham, pushing the plate towards William. 'Peyote has opened your mind to the possibilities of your prior knowledge, but I repeat: I am not an occultist, I am a man of science.'

'A man of science, yes.' There came a familiar soft thud above William's left eyebrow. Panic and fear pricked at the edge of his consciousness. Dr Moon was obfuscating, and his reaction to Tom's death seemed oddly resigned. 'Then tell me about your work here.'

'The work is experimental but scientific. I was privileged to witness religious use of the cacti in the Southwestern United States after I left Seale-Hayne, and I was struck by how useful it would be in the treatment of neurasthenia.' William's mind drifted to the conservatory, to Dr Moon's prized botanicals, and to Tom's poor, broken body. 'My own use of the drug is an adaptation of the practice of the Mescalero peoples. I grow the cacti and distil the tincture myself. Our use, in Red Hollow, is meditative, and with an emphasis on brotherly love, self-knowledge and the avoidance of alcohol. So far, few scientific papers have been written on its efficacy.' As the doctor stirred his coffee, the spoon's blurred edges glowed at the periphery of William's vision. 'I'm writing a paper, of course. *Peyote in the Treatment of Trauma, Alcoholism and Social Dislocation in the Male Subject.*'

'I had no idea I was a male subject.'

'Mr Garrett, don't you realise? None of the patients here knew they were under the influence. I made a foolish, and unethical, clinical decision early on not to tell the men.' He was straightforward, sympathetic, and yet, fundamentally broken. Dr Moon had the eyes of a man who'd seen a vision of his own disgrace. '*Pride goeth before destruction.* That's my sin; that's my secret, not occultism, not murder.' The doctor glanced at the kitchen clock and counted on his fingers. 'We'll be under the influence for a few hours yet. You may see and hear strange things, but I hope you may simply have a more heightened sense of colour and sound.' He frowned. 'You have vomited, and the coffee will help.' He gestured to the pot. 'It was a small dose, Mr Garrett.'

'*Tea and sympathy.*' English tea laced with New Mexican cacti, and all designed to make sad men talk. He shuddered. 'Small dose, my arse. I guzzled that Tommy's brew you made us last night.'

'The peyote is bitter, so I make black tea with plenty of milk and sugar. It's quite comforting.'

'*The cup that cheers, but not inebriates.*' William saw the men cross-legged like children before the fireplace; heard the background hum of the storm, and a propulsion of confessions. 'We were telling each other about our fathers.'

'The drug assists the talking therapy,' said Dr Moon. 'Visions and revelations also help the recovering addict find purpose. It's a safe and brotherly practice when done under supervision. I have had great successes. Freddy has made a remarkable recovery – and Tom, too.'

'You're fluffing your feathers. Tom's dead. Murdered and mutilated.'

'You're quite correct. I have no right to preen.' He stopped stirring the coffee, tapping the spoon against the side of his cup. To William, the clatter seemed unbearably loud.

'Mr Brooke knew,' said William.

'Good grief, man, no. I kept the peyote especially secret from him.'

'But he knew, nonetheless.' The vials of white liquid in the attic weren't morphine, after all. 'Did you know he was an occultist?'

'No.' Dr Moon reached into his jacket pocket and found his pipe. 'Absolutely not. I had no idea of this house's rather unsavoury history until quite recently.'

'Would he have guessed what you were up to? Did Brooke know enough about modern medicine to put two and two together?' William was tweezing out information like glass from skin, shard by painful shard.

'Mr Brooke was a reader of Havelock Ellis, the eugenicist and sexologist. In his youth, Ellis was an early experimenter with the drug. And, as I said, Crowley uses it.' Moon tamped the bowl of his pipe with a twitching nervousness, struck a match, and then sucked hard, eyelids fluttering at the hit of tobacco. 'I'm suddenly worried about that cake, Mr Garrett. Terribly worried.'

'Persephone's birthday cake?'

'It could be a flash of paranoia, but I do think, in hindsight, the man had an unnatural interest in the child. All that talk of magic and thirteenth birthdays is giving me the horrors.'

Dr Moon let the words fall like bombs.

'You think Brooke drugged a child's birthday cake. Christ almighty, what is wrong with men?'

'Is that rhetorical?' Dr Moon poured coffee down to the dregs; they had finished the pot between them. 'Thank God the cake is intact in the refrigerator. For some reason, I fancy another fried egg.'

William turned his chair towards the pantry, watched the game swing slightly in an unknown breeze, and reached out as if to touch an earthenware dish of hardened salt, until it all became a sickening kaleidoscope of country brown. Secret rooms with moss-green doors; Pike men in Pike masks; poppets of maids nailed in the groin; the evil, big-bollocked monkey; a middle-aged woman gone mad in her grace-and-favour cottage; a mermaid frolicking in the Warwickshire Thick; and a drug that made William see God.

William got to his feet. Faint, shaking, he steadied himself on the kitchen table until his head no longer swam. Gathering himself, he focused on the attic room, and what Tom had told Freddy about Brooke's mother. 'Brooke's mother was raped by the squire. He's Sir Leofric's son, and Lady Pike's younger brother. Brooke was conceived on the anniversary of the mermaid's death. Oh God. Do you understand what I'm saying?' William's heart thumped hard in his chest; he glanced at Dr Moon – his unreadable face was veiled in pipe smoke. Beads of sweat rose on William's forehead and the back of his neck: he couldn't form his thoughts. 'The Reverend Andrews tried to prevent a ritual and was killed for his trouble.' William paused, and then spoke each word with a slow, conscious deliberation. 'What if Brooke never left Red Hollow? What if the ritual he had been working on had to be completed on Candlemas? We need first to see to Tom, give him his dignity, and then look at where the poor bastard fell from.'

24

Tom's body lay eerie in the glassy light.

'Oh Jesus, what have I done? I'm not sure I can bear it.'
Dr Moon held an oil lamp aloft. It spread a broad glare over
Tom, illuminating the sleet, which fell through the shattered
conservatory roof and landed, glistening, onto Tom's white
body. Arched on the lap of Pan, like a pagan Pietà, and just as
dolorous. 'It all seems so much worse, now. Oh, good God,
poor Tom.' Dr Moon placed his lamp on the floor and bent
double, head forward, hands on thighs, chest rising and
falling.

William didn't comfort the doctor with platitudes, but
placed his hand on the weeping man's shoulder and watched
the weather. All about them, the sleet dampened hair and skin,
and formed cold puddles on the uneven tile floor. Only the
monkey remained safe from the rain, his balding pate dry as a
bone under his black silk parasol.

'When the sun comes up, the whole bloody world will see
him like this. I don't like it. I don't like how the body is so
exposed. Christ, it's freezing.' William drew the tablecloth
about his shoulders and removed the taxidermy from Tom's
torso. 'I won't have that bastard monkey sit there. It's a dese-
cration.' He held it at arm's length, as if the creature were
prone to biting, and then pushed it behind the nearest cactus,

catching the monkey's ratted fur on the spines. The creature gave out a wretched, indignant squeal. 'Quit your yowling.' William drove the monkey down with force, ruining the parasol, but the creature fought back, catching William's finger with his stinking little paw. 'Don't you try anything on with me, you fucker.' He shoved at the thing with the toe of his shoe until the monkey, with his big brown eyes and his big brown bollocks, was safely out of sight – and mind. 'Job done.'

The doctor straightened and wiped the tears from his eyes with the back of his sleeve as would a child. 'Are you hallucinating, Mr Garrett?'

'I hate that monkey shitbag.'

'Well, you can't argue with that. Where on earth did it come from?'

'From the heavens. The bastard thing is the angel of death.' William pointed to the shattered roof. 'Do you have any idea how Tom died?'

'No, I'd need to move him to find out, but I don't think it's wise. That's a job for a police surgeon.'

William shook his head slowly. 'He must be moved. We need to give the man some dignity.' He waved his arm as if to indicate the vast exposure of glass. 'He's in a greenhouse. Emasculated for all to see, for Christ's sake.'

Dr Moon took a deep intake of breath. 'Alright,' he said. 'We'll take him to the sofa in the patients' sitting room.'

'Grab his shoulders, and I'll take the feet. We'll lift on three.' William placed his hands underneath Tom's thighs, grasping the dead man's flesh. The man's body was supple, and not stiffened in death, so that upon lifting, William was at once confronted with the vulnerable humanity of Tom's flesh. He turned his face away from the bloodied humiliation of the empty groin, and a cry welled in his chest, but did not develop into sound. 'Would a large dose of peyote make someone mad enough to do this kind of murder?'

'It could bring on a state of psychosis, but I don't believe a man would do anything under the influence contrary to his essential nature.'

'We're all trained to kill, Dr Moon.' Tom was a weight, heavier and bloodier than the Reverend Andrews: his death a barbarity. 'A whole generation of us trained to kill, and now out in civvy street and all handy with a pistol or a bayonet.'

'Are you coming to your senses? You're beginning to sound more like yourself.'

'I'm not sure. But I do know this is real, God help us.'

They shuffled along the glass-scattered floor of the conservatory into the strange half-warmth of the patients' sitting room and placed the body on the sofa. Dr Moon left the room for a moment, and returned with the oil lamp, giving it to William, who held the light, at first, above Tom's handsome, heavy face, but then stepped back so all the body was illuminated. Dr Moon took the electric torch from his pocket and knelt beside the sofa, inspecting Tom's wounds, poring tenderly over each bloody outrage. 'I don't think this was done with a bayonet, if that's what you're thinking. In fact, I'm quite sure of it. Hold the light steady.'

William did as he was told. 'Was he mutilated before or after death?'

'Soon after death, or just before, I can't tell. Wherever he was killed, we'll find blood. If there's a lot, then the mutilations were done while Tom was still alive.' The doctor rested back on his knees for a moment. 'We can only hope that Tom did not know.' His voice trailed off as he leant forward once more, holding the torch steady over Tom's gore-matted groin. 'The cuts are strange . . . curved, perhaps.'

'Curved like the carving knife.' It lay on the kitchen table, blade sharpened into a soft arc through decades of use, next to the half-eaten ham, chunks of which swam amongst the coffee grounds in William's tender stomach.

'A smaller weapon with a more pronounced curve would be my guess. But I'm a psychiatrist, not a pathologist, and there's only so much I can tell from a cursory examination. Help me turn Tom's body on his side.'

William did as he was told. The doctor leant forward, guiding the beam of his torch to a depression on the back of Tom's head. Dr Moon rose and rubbed his legs, stretched out his back. 'The blow to the skull is heavy enough to have stunned him, if not killed him, before the mutilations happened. It's a similar head wound to Phyll's, and almost identical to the Reverend Andrews' injury. I shall tell the police to look for a heavy, metal object. Perhaps a golf club or the butt of a rifle.'

'Or the pommel of a sword.' William stared out of the window, attempting, in his addled state, to think clearly, and act as a normal man would act. 'Why did Brooke throw Tom out of the window?'

'Some cock-eyed idea that his body would land in the floodwater, I should think. Perhaps for symbolic reasons, considering Red Hollow's history, and your theory about Tom's murder being ritual. It's very similar to how you found both the Reverend Andrews and poor Phyll.' The doctor paused in thought. 'However, the murderer might be of a more practical bent. Throwing the body from the window would've been a quick way of disposing of Tom. The body may have remained hidden in the flood for days if it'd worked. Water is a very effective means of destroying evidence, Mr Garrett.'

'Don't I know it,' William blurted, stopping his mouth with the crook of his arm like a child. He breathed steadily and unmuffled himself. 'I'm not sure if that makes much sense. Unless Brooke believed himself to have the strength of ten, he'd know the body would land on, if not through, the conservatory roof.'

'You seem very sure this is Brooke's doing?'

'The murder and emasculation are part of some magical ritual, surely? The only other magician in the house is Percy. And it can't be her, for God's sake. She's just a child. Besides, Tom's quite a weight. A girl, or even a woman, could never have thrown him from the window.'

'Two women could've done it.' Dr Moon stepped away from the body. 'The emasculation is peculiarly humiliating, and there are obvious links to the mermaid story ...' The doctor's voice trailed out into the strange, early morning air. 'I would suggest the disposal of the body is an assertion of power. A showing-off, if you will.' Dr Moon reached for his pipe, and, moving to the fireplace, tapped out the bowl until a clump of tobacco fell and sizzled in the embers. 'The conservatory is my home in Red Hollow. The murderer is claiming that space and, of course, control of the house. A disturbed mind's idea of an offensive manoeuvre.' He paused for a moment, filling and lighting his pipe, suck-suck-sucking. 'Of course, they hated poor Tom. The murderer wants us to see the humiliating mutilation. The murderer is proud of their work. Anyway, it's all moot now.'

William turned, frustrated. 'What does that mean?'

'It simply means we can't bring Tom back. We must look that fact quite squarely in the face, and I must accept my own shortcomings. I have failed poor Tom, as I have failed all the other men who sought respite at Red Hollow. I'm quite culpable, Mr Garrett. Quite culpable.'

'Don't wallow. You've been a fool, and God knows you seem to have made one bad decision after another, but this madness isn't your work.' William removed the tablecloth cloak from his shoulders and laid it across Tom's bloodied body as a makeshift shroud, a modesty. Then he placed the blanket, which had covered Phyll only a few hours before, on top of Tom, muffling the horror. 'Unless you held the knife yourself.'

It was a half-arsed accusation, and Dr Moon didn't protest. 'You think I killed him?'

'You came to my aid pretty quickly.'

'I took the peyote. It can make you sleepless. I gave you Veronal to counteract the insomnia. Phyll and Queenie, too. You were all exhausted and needed rest.' He paused and winced. 'Irwell, too, obviously. Oh my God, I shall get struck off.'

'No doubt about it. You dish out the good stuff like sweet-ies. No wonder the addicts like you. No wonder I like you.' William whistled through his teeth. 'But the General Medical Council will take a dim view. Then, there's all the patients getting murdered on your manor. It ain't healthy.'

'I'm rather glad you like me, Mr Garrett. It's a consolation.' Dr Moon drew hard once more on his pipe. 'Is murder a culmination of a chain of events, do you think? A bloody full stop to a series of blunders, insults, cruelties?'

William shrugged. 'Perhaps,' he said. 'I suppose what's worrying me is Tom's murder isn't a full stop, but just another link in the chain.'

'Oh my God. You mean the murderer might strike again? But where do we even start with a thing like this? Good grief, man. What do we do?'

'We see where Tom fell from.'

'But where is that?'

'There's an attic room where Brooke keeps the old squire's God-awful magical collection. Did you know?'

The doctor shook his head once more, doleful. 'I feel I hardly know this place at all.'

William waved the oil lamp towards the conservatory. Yellow pools of light glowed on the shadowy vegetation, illuminating a pair of wide, brown eyes which may, or may not, have been peeking out between the wicked spines of a cactus. 'It's where our friend the monkey lives.'

25

Red Hollow Hall was country dark and hushed with water and winter weather. William led the way towards the attics, brandishing the oil lamp as steady as his shaking hand would allow. Dr Moon followed with the colder, pointed glare of the electric torch. Through the maze of doors and corridors they went, up the dizzying spirals of stairs until they reached the door to the maids' room.

William placed his finger to his lips, like an actor in a silent film. Dr Moon obliged and remained mute as he entered. Inside, nothing had been disturbed. All was as it was when William had left it earlier that night: the twin beds, their ticking mattresses stained with menstrual blood; the stoneware Britannia, battered and worse for wear; the Georgian mirror, blotched and disfigured with damp.

Only the open doorway to the attic stairs offered a clue to the room's recent use, for although William had not locked it as he left, he was sure that he had shut it. He stood before it as a Greek hero might before a cave, knowing there was a test to come, and touched Dr Moon on the arm, motioning with his oil lamp to the staircase, and indicating a need for caution. Then they climbed, William leading the way in an eerie echo of the journey he'd taken with Freddy and Queenie.

William took a deep, preparatory breath and opened the door at the top of the stairs. There came a gust of sleet-heavy wind, and a chill so fierce he believed the whole attic room to have disappeared; sliced from the top of the house in some vindictive, magical act of destruction, so that if he were to step over the threshold he might fall, tumble and spin in the cold night air, and land, like Tom, in the conservatory below.

But William and Dr Moon were alive and warm, and the sleet soon melted into mist at their body heat and the lamp-light. William squinted into the room, and at first he thought himself the victim of some elaborate prank, for what he saw reminded him of a haunted house at the fair. Slumped and swaying before the mahogany wardrobe, and in the far centre of the room, was a palely shrouded shape. Prettily rimed with a glittering halo of sleet, the figure wore the fish-head mask – but slightly askew, so the man's chin stuck out from beneath a gilded gill. His pointed toes peeped from beneath the hem of well-starched white robes, and caressed the bare floorboards in a slow, pendulum-like motion; the body had heft.

William held his light aloft to see the heavy pull of a noose about the figure's neck. The rope, slung over a broad oak beam in the ceiling, was dirty green, tarred at the edges, and perhaps once used to moor a boat. Dizzied by the body's circling motion, William steadied himself on the door jamb with his free hand, turned to Dr Moon, and whispered, 'Am I seeing things? More ghosts and monkeys?'

'Oh God. Oh Jesus Christ.'

The inarticulate horror of Dr Moon's outburst was a strange comfort to William. Now the hanging man was real, William wasn't alone in his terror.

The doctor shone his torch over William's shoulder, spot-lighting rough hemp rope, then the pale hanging beauty of the robe, and finally the hideous fists, clenched in death. 'What in God's name has happened here?' He made to step into the room, but William held out a restraining arm.

'Don't go in just yet,' said William. 'There's too much clutter, strangeness. Weird stuff all over the place. We can't just bluster in without decent light. We'll have to be cautious.' He squeezed the doctor's shoulder. 'Catch your breath for a bit.' William waved the oil lamp in a slow arc, lighting the attic in sepia fragments. With nothing properly illuminated, objects glowed momentarily and then blurred into shadow. William pointed to a corner. 'Shine your torch there, please, Dr Moon.' The doctor obliged, and William saw, shifted upright, and slumped besides the wardrobe, the tiger-skin rug, rolled in such a way the animal's black nose and glass eyes peeped out of its own hide. 'And now the floorboards.'

Dr Moon's torch shone on a portion of floor painting. A five-pointed star intersected with the arc of a circle, all drawn with remarkable accuracy. William knelt, and placed his oil lamp on the floor an inch or two past the threshold. Its yellow light contrasted with the surrounding shadows and the cold, white glare of Dr Moon's torch. But all, now, became illuminated. The star was one of five. Its mother was big and cosy in a perfect circle, her four children nudging across the circumference, each placed as a cardinal sign on a compass.

William squinted. 'Sinister left.' He directed his lamp towards a sticky black pool, shimmering like spilt oil across the south-western point of the pentagram. No, not black, but dark red, like cheap port. The size of a cartwheel, it began near the door, but moved further to the left in smeared drag lines which ended at the desk and the open window. 'We can go in, but for God's sake, don't tread in the blood.'

'Do you think it's Tom's?'

'I'd hate it to be someone else's.'

William leapt over the threshold and landed a foot or two away from the blood, rattling the glass doors on the cabinet of esoterica. A glass vial scooted across the floor and spun like a top, stopping at the edge of Tom's blood. William reached for his handkerchief, and covering his fingers with the cloth, gently picked up the bottle of liquid and handed it to Dr Moon. 'Is this yours?'

Dr Moon followed William's lead and used a handkerchief to hold the bottle. 'Mescaline. The distillation of the peyote plant.' He uncorked the vial, examined it, and placed it in his pocket. 'It's all gone. Is there liquid on the floor?'

William sat on his haunches, fingertips gently hovering over the floorboards. 'Nothing on here but blood and puddles of sleet. But if it's not been spilt, it must've been used.' He stood and faced the doctor. 'Is that a problem?'

'There are days of dosage in one bottle, Mr Garrett. Overuse of any drug is never a good thing.' Dr Moon let the words drift.

'Have you checked your supplies recently?'

'No. The peyote we used tonight was a ground powder from the dried tops of cacti. A milder version of the drug. This is from the cabinet in my private rooms.'

'I saw at least three vials earlier today when Queenie and I searched the house with Freddy.'

The swaying noose let out a plaintive creak, and William turned his attention to the hanging man. Further along the room, and in the partial shadow of the body, stood an oblong stool. Draped in purple plush velvet, it held a silver chalice and salver, both covered in a starched white cloth as if prepared for a eucharist. A makeshift altar, with no candles, a sacrament without light.

William uncovered the chalice, and shuddered: it was filled to the brim with a bright, red substance. He sniffed at it like a dog. 'It's alright. I thought it was blood for a second, but it's alright. Just wine, I think.' William handed the chalice to Dr Moon.

'Most definitely wine,' said Dr Moon. 'If it's been laced with mescaline, wine would disguise the drug's bitter taste.' The doctor, too, bent on his haunches. 'What's on the salver?'

'I wish I had a knife.' William was face to face with the masked figure. 'It'd be the decent thing to cut him down, but at least we can try to remove the mask.' He turned to Dr Moon, who now stood at his side. 'Aren't you in the least bit curious to see who it is?'

'Moot,' said Dr Moon. 'The damage is done.'

'I wish you would stop saying that.' William once knew an officer at the front who blew his brains out after misreading a map and sending an entire battalion to their deaths. Dr Moon reminded William of that officer. It was the apparent numbness to horrific realities. Another symptom of shell-shock. 'It does you no good, you must know that.'

Nonetheless, it was the doctor who fiddled with the mask, prising his fingers beneath the rope, tugging at the blonde wig, and exposing the dead man's face with a strange showman's flourish. William didn't recognise him, but few would. The head had slumped to the side like a rag doll; his mouth was softly open, and the tongue lolled as a purpling grotesque; his eyes bulged hard, so that the whites, bloodshot and jaundiced, protruted unnaturally.

'Mr Brooke, as expected.'

'You knew it was him.'

'You told me.' The makeshift noose, a Boy Scout hitch knot, seemed starker without the mask. 'Will you take some of the weight, Mr Garrett, while I look at these markings?'

William placed his oil lamp on the floor and knelt before the hanging Brooke. Grabbing at his calves, he pushed the body slightly upwards while Moon inspected Brooke's neck by the light of his electric torch.

William didn't need the doctor to tell him the dead man was stiff with rigor.

'The ropes have cut into the neck. Sometimes these chaps decapitate themselves, you know. Death by hanging calls for a more careful calculation than one realises.' He looked down on William, cheek against Brooke's knees, and added, by way of explanation. 'We learnt about it in medical school.'

William's skin pricked. Potential shell-shock or not, it was an odd thing to say; macabre, even in these circumstances. William remembered Queenie's warning: he liked Dr Moon too much. He had form for misjudging character, blind to the obvious faults of his friends – Queenie, Ronnie and now Dr Moon. He shook away the thought, and all its implications, from his still-swimming head. 'Are there any other injuries?'

'None. Let the poor man go, Mr Garrett.'

As William released and stood, stiffly, Brooke resumed his pendulum-like swing. Sleet drifted with a horizontal force, pricking at William's cheeks. He marvelled at the whirling glitter, privy now to see, not feel, the direction of the breeze. 'Why not shut the window? Why not practise your nonsense in comfort? If you could ever be comfortable in such a place.'

He moved to the open window. The once-tidy desk, with its typewriter and ream of paper, was in disorder and sharply askew; shifted, just enough, so that a man might have room to shove a dead body out into the freezing air. Outside, and immediately below the window, was a narrow strip of lead-lined walkway, bordered by low crenellations, beneath which was the glass roof of the conservatory. It would take some strength, let alone determination, to get Tom out there.

William returned his attention to the desk, remembering the candelabra which once stood there. Where was it? Without a lamp, torch or electric light, it would be nigh-on impossible to conduct any complex ritual in the black of night. Brooke had not been alone, and whoever his friend was, he'd left him swinging in the dark.

Three or four sheets of paper escaped from the ream. Fluttering in the breeze, they floated upwards, and then drifted prettily down into the centre of the magic circle. William bent and gathered up the paper before it landed in the blood. Returning to the desk, he noticed, for the first time, another sheet still in the roller of the typewriter. Flapping in the wind, it was dampened by sleeting rain, but held firmly in place, not just by the mechanism, but by a card. Shoved halfway into the roller, William knew it to be The Hanged Man of his mother's beloved tarot, and he interpreted the card aloud as if it were a personal message to him. 'The wisdom of a new perspective. A trial ahead. Use your intuition.'

'Take it out of the machine,' said Dr Moon.

'The card?'

'Well, yes, but also the letter behind it.'

William had not noticed the closely written paragraph of typeface behind the tarot card. He rolled the wet paper upwards, not tugging, but patiently allowing the machine to do its work. Soon, both the letter and card were safe in his hands. 'Do you want me to read it?'

'Yes, please do so.' William half-expected Dr Moon to light his pipe, but instead he simply shone his torch on the type-script. William began:

'*The final statement of John Brooke. On the night of her death, I cast the circle, lit the flame and called her by her name. She came but not alone. With her, she brought a pilgrim. One who would open the door wide. She whispered in my ear and guided me all the way, her hand on mine. Together we took what was her due. The remnant we threw to the elements, the howling wind and all-consuming rain. But the next instant, she left me like a fickle goddess, casting me, her true acolyte, aside, despite my long toil and sacrifices to bring her forth and give her corporeality. Now I am forsaken. Frozen, my hands mottled with blood. But the sacrifice has brought me no redemption. In the circle, I spread my tarot, and read the dreadful future she has ordained for me: The Hanged Man.*'

'Is there any blood on Brooke's hands?' asked Dr Moon.

'I don't know.' William folded the letter around the card and placed it in his inside pocket.

'I shall look.' Dr Moon moved with his torch towards Brooke's body, hunkered down and examined the hanging man's clenched fists. 'It's difficult to see. I don't want to break the finger joints.'

'It's all nothing but bullshit, isn't it?' William squinted confusedly about the room. 'It's all nonsense. Pull back the curtain, and you'll see nothing but smoke and mirrors, a stage set designed to give you the creeps. It's not what The Hanged Man means. This devotee of the Crowley religion –' William motioned to Brooke with his thumb – 'hasn't got a clue about reading the major arcana.'

The doctor straightened, rubbing ferociously at his gammy leg. 'More importantly, the fellow is as stiff as a board, and Tom is not. I'm not a police surgeon, but I would bet my pipe Brooke died first. The letter seems to imply he killed Tom in some bizarre ritual and then committed suicide.'

'And the blood on the floor?'

'If it's Tom's blood, the emasculation happened when Tom was alive. My guess, and it is a guess, is that the killer hit Tom over the back of the head so that he was unconscious, mutilated Tom's groin, and then threw him from the window.'

William sighed in relief. If Dr Moon was responsible for the fakery, then why would he debunk the staged murder-suicide? 'And Brooke?'

'As I said, dead before Tom, but there's nothing to indicate it wasn't from suicide, but it's difficult to tell without cutting him down and giving the poor fellow a proper examination. We can't rule out murder.'

'It was murder alright, and done by someone who thinks we're both a bit thick.' William looked out onto the early hours. 'I was once told that the bearded lady at the fair was a strategically shaved bear. A doped-up bear in a frock – I ask you.' The mermaid weathervane glimmered in the bruised sky. Below, the black flood lay glassy and thick. *Don't go near the water, my babby.* 'We're being flimflammed, Dr Moon. This room has the con man's touch of bad lighting and shock value.'

But, of course, the room was outraged at William's accusation. It was not party to some tawdry bamboozle. And so, as William bent once more to find his oil lamp, which had been placed at the feet of the hanging man, the mahogany wardrobe began to pulsate, like a huge and vital human heart.

26

Bur-dum. Bur-dum. Bur-dum.

William held the light towards the wardrobe. The red-brown wood groaned, undulating back and forth in a slow, rhythmic thump. It had become a pregnant belly, the child inside kicking and squirming. 'Do you hear it?'

'Open the door, Mr Garrett,' said Dr Moon.

'For God's sake, no. The thing is alive.' Unlocking the wardrobe would be like opening a sluice gate on wicked-ness, for the wardrobe, William knew, was the heart of Red Hollow Hall. The repository for all the rape, murder, injust-ice and hatred associated with the house. 'This whole place is alive, and it's evil.' William pointed towards the pulsating mahogany. 'This is the beating heart. This is the heart of the house.'

'Mr Garrett,' Dr Moon said, placing his hand on William's shoulder in a reassuring grip of tangible reality. 'I do believe you are experiencing another hallucination.'

William looked at the wardrobe's heavy, muscular pulse, and frowned. 'I hate the fuckin' monkey.'

'You have every right to.' The doctor gently manoeuvred William away from the wardrobe. 'I imagine what you're seeing is unsettling, but you must know it's not real. Now, I'm going to open the wardrobe door because I can hear a knocking. Someone or something is in there.' The doctor spotlighted the doorknob with his torch and called out, 'Hello? I say. Is anyone there?'

'Oh God, no.' William placed his head in his arms, like a terrified child, crying, 'Please don't do it.'

Dr Moon ignored William's desperate pleas and opened the wardrobe door.

William peeped through his fingers. The mahogany had stiffened into normality. He sighed in relief. 'It'll be the cat,' he said. 'She's done it before, given me a fright.'

But it wasn't Rossetti, for there, hunched amongst the dangling robes, was Freddy. Eyes clenched shut, right hand tapping a woody, reverberant SOS, and, clenched in his left, the Hand of Glory from the cabinet of esoterica. Freddy had used it as a ghoulish candelabra, as wedged between the knotted knuckles of the wizened hand was a flickering candle stub. Its flame caressed the swaying linen, dangerously. Dr Moon bent forward and blew out the candle, and as he did so, Freddy opened his eyes, wide. 'I thought I heard you fellows. Save Our Souls.'

'Why have you got this, Freddy?' William nodded towards the Hand of Glory.

'It's the only light there was.'

'May I have it?'

'It makes one invisible to one's enemies.' Freddy shook it at William. 'It says so on the label.'

'We can see you, Freddy,' said William, shuddering in a cold sweat as if waking from a nightmare. 'Therefore, we must be—'

'Friends.'

'Will you come out?' asked Dr Moon.

'I think not. I'm quite safe here.'

'My dear chap, no. You're much better off out here with us.' Dr Moon nodded to the Hand of Glory. 'Do give me whatever that dreadful thing is, and come with me and William.'

Freddy shook his head. 'I was intent on pinching things, you see, and I heard them coming, and I got the wind up.' Freddy crooked his finger, drawing the two men in closer. 'I hid in the wardrobe. The sound of raised voices, and then she came. A heavy creature, dragging her tail about like a sack of fish.'

'You heard the murderer dragging Tom's body,' said William. 'The mermaid is just a vision. A creation of the mind.'

Freddy shook his head, resolute. 'I knew she'd come, of course, because of the disorder. This is a disorderly house. There's been a fissure, a crack. Deep, deep beneath the house, beneath the clay, it's the mining, you see, it's angered her.' He looked down at the Hand of Glory as if seeing it for the first time, and screwed his face, disgusted.

'I'll take that from you, I think,' said Dr Moon.

Freddy nodded and obliged. 'Each river, each hill, each tree has its genius, Dr Moon,' Freddy continued in a low, urgent whisper. 'Each given a god, or a part of a god, or an atom of a god – don't you see? Because the world and everything in it is holy. But what if holy things are to be feared?' He nodded to his audience, as if his rhetoric had hit home. 'At Red Hollow, we have the mermaid. She is a saint, a water sprite, and an old goddess. She is the beheaded St Winifred. She is the drowned bastard child, Sabrina of the Severn. Moreover, she is Coventina, the goddess of the watershed. Don't you see? There is power in this place, this watershed of England. We must fear this holy place. But we haven't, and now we must rue the day. It's quite simple, really.'

Dr Moon slumped into silence and shot William an imploring glance. This was the doctor's true moment of defeat. Not the murder of Tom, but the madness of Freddy.

'Yes, I do see that, but now we have Phyll to consider,' said William. 'I have work to do, and I need you to go to Phyll. She's had a horrible rough go of things.'

Freddy looked at William, a little open-mouthed. 'Darling Phyll.'

'Come out of the wardrobe,' said William.

After a moment's consideration, Freddy shook his head. 'I think not. Miss Maggs will take care of Phyll. She has her Derringer.'

'Freddy, old son, listen to me. There are much better wardrobes in this godforsaken hole than the one you're in.' William motioned with his thumb to the swinging Brooke, the swirling cold of the sleeting rain. 'The one in Phyll's room is like a mansion compared to this one. It's big, and warm, and there are no dead bodies. Importantly, you'll have two women ready to wait on you hand and foot, rather than this poor, hanging bastard to keep you company. It's the fuckin' Ritz of wardrobes down there. Use your common sense.'

'Do you think I'm mad?'

'You're no madder than me.'

'Will you hold my hand?'

'Alright, but will you hold mine?' He offered his hand to Freddy, who took it and smiled, and then William hauled his friend from the bottom of the wardrobe.

Freddy unfurled himself like a dormouse and stood before William, stiffly. 'Will I be alright?' he asked.

William smiled, and brought Freddy's ice-cold body into his own in a brief embrace. 'You'll be fine, old pal. Just stick with me.' He slapped at Freddy's back and then grabbed his hand. 'Let's get out of here and try not to tread in the blood.'

'Well done, William,' said Dr Moon. 'Brotherly compassion at its finest.' He too patted Freddy on the back. 'You did splendidly, Freddy. We have been experiencing the most traumatic circumstances. Quite awful, for any mind to endure, and you have done remarkably well.'

To Dr Moon, Freddy's emergence from the wardrobe was akin to a nature lover hearing the first cuckoo of spring, and his pleasure was contagious. For a second, they were all quite jolly. Until someone nudged Brooke, so that the dead man creaked and swayed, unbearably fast and rhythmic, his pointed toes toppling the contents of the small altar.

Down fell the chalice. It did not clink – the silver was too ancient and heavy – but thudded and rolled. Wine and mescaline spilt across the floor, mingling with Tom's blood. Then the salver, with its chaste covering of stiff white linen, teetered on the brink of the altar and fell.

A short knife with a pronounced curved blade scudded across the floor.

'My favourite wood-carving knife,' said Freddy. 'Goes through wood like butter.'

Freddy's favourite knife was gored with blood. From the metal tip to the end of the wooden handle, it was smeared with the prints of the man who held it.

William released Freddy's hand, bent and wrapped the knife in his pocket handkerchief with a swiftness that surprised him. 'Then we should take it with us,' he said. He rose, and once more took Freddy's hand, guiding him away from the smears of blood. 'I think you should be the one to hold the lamp,' he said. 'You can go first down the stairs. You're more used to them. They're so steep.'

William maintained a nervous, friendly prattle. But he didn't lie. The stairs were near vertiginous, and Freddy was used to clambering about church roofs, bell towers, the high places of the manor.

'Mr Garrett, please come back.'

It was only then William realised Dr Moon had not followed him and Freddy out of the attic room. He turned in the doorway to see the doctor hunched at the feet of the still-swinging Brooke, transfixed. 'Stay here, Freddy,' he said. 'Don't move.'

'I think not,' said Freddy.

And so, hand in hand, the two men picked their way over the blood, and the wine, and the ream of drifting paper, and the puddles of sleet, back where they came from, to Brooke and Moon and the toppled sacrament.

William thought it was a dead rat. A young pink rat, mauled by a cat, so that he nearly said, *Oh, this is Rossetti's work. She's a born mouser.* The dead thing lay on top of the folded cloth, its blood soaking through the white linen, so that he was reminded of a woman's monthly rag. It had been on the salver all this time, with Freddy's knife, and next to the chalice of mescaline-laced wine. William made to kick it with his shoe, by way of further examination, but the crouched doctor held his leg, stopped him, forcing William to bend down and see it, properly, for himself. The dead thing seemed familiar, as though he were looking at something commonplace but from an unusual angle. The bloodied top half was fleshy, wrinkled and tan, sparsely hairy, becoming slimmer and pinker along its short, smooth trunk. At the end, was the creature's one eye.

'What the fuckin' hell.' William jumped backwards.

'What should we do with it?' asked Dr Moon.

'Throw it in the bin,' said Freddy. 'What use is it now?'

'We can't take it with us,' said William.

'We've taken everything else.' Dr Moon patted the vial of mescaline in his pocket and nodded to the knife wrapped in William's handkerchief.

'Cover it with the cloth. When we get downstairs, we'll lock the door to the attic room and keep the key with us. I don't want anyone tampering with the room.' Oh God, he meant he didn't want the cat getting at it. 'Freddy, is the key still underneath the Britannia ornament?'

'The door was open when I came.' Freddy shrugged. 'I couldn't sleep. Tonight's tea was too strong, and I had the urge to pinch things.'

'What things, Freddy?' asked Dr Moon.

'I came for the mermaid.'

'Oh Christ, Freddy.'

'Look at her.' Freddy released William's hand and fiddled with his jacket pocket, pulling out an ancient, carved roundel, about the size of a saucer. 'She belongs in the church, not up here with all this muck. She was hewn from good oak over seven hundred years ago, Billy. Carved and painted for the glory of God, by a man who loved and feared Him and used his talent for His glorification.' Freddy caressed the sinuous curve of the mermaid's sweeping, fishy femininity. Even in the dark of night, the remnants of gilding on her yellow hair glinted to spectacular effect. 'Quite wrong for her to be up here, yes?'

Freddy wanted validation. He needed permission to take the boss and return it to the church. The man was so essentially moral, William believed, that even theft in the name of Almighty God was, for Freddy, still theft. William sighed in relief and smiled. 'I'm glad you took the carving, Freddy.' He looked at his friend straight, pushing the drooping blond hair away from his eyes. 'I think you've done right by the men who made her. Pop it in your pocket now. You can take it back to St Chad's in the morning.'

'She's so incredibly beautiful.' Freddy nodded, sane and solemn. 'It's an awful shame she came last night and bit off Tom's cock and balls.'

27

William's body crowded out the narrow stairwell. He thought suddenly of Phyll, worn down by the burden of Freddy's illness, and a strong drag of vertigo unsteadied him. And he knew, in that moment, he would help her carry it.

'Hold William's lamp now, Freddy. I think you should lead the way.' Dr Moon, behind them, closed the door on Brooke, and all the aberrant horror of the attic room. 'By the way, how many cups of tea did you drink last night?'

'More than usual, but it had been a trying day.' Freddy, lamp in hand, squeezed beside William, took two steps down and then turned. 'I downed the stuff. Billy and I drank Tom's too. Is gluttony really so much of a sin, do you think?'

'Freddy hasn't vomited.' There was a note of hope in Dr Moon's voice. 'And he has taken a good deal of peyote. It's very much in his system.'

'The night is still young,' said Freddy. 'I may vomit any minute.' William saw the open doorway to the maids' room as a rectangle of shimmering grey light. Freddy, a few steps ahead, halted, reluctant to pass over the threshold. William, sandwiched between the two men, sensed the rise and fall of their chests, their wheezing pulls for breath, the tremor of Freddy's shoulders, and suppressed a memory of whistles, panic and barbed wire. 'What's peyote?' Freddy stepped into the room, circling his lamp to illuminate the shadowy corners. 'All is well, men. The mermaid does not lurk poised to snap.'

William and Dr Moon followed stumblingly behind Freddy. A shifting, silver flash shimmered in the corner of William's vision. He turned, skin pricking, and was confronted by his own patchy reflection in the Georgian mirror. William squinted into it, his face eerily disfigured. The silver backing had lifted in huge portions, so that his cheek, chunks of chin, an eye, all disappeared into a terrifying black absence. 'We must find a way to make the room secure.' He moved away from the looking glass. 'Everything in the attic needs to remain untouched so the police can do a proper investigation.' William's fingertips grazed the handkerchief-wrapped knife in his jacket pocket. He thought once more of Phyll. Two seconds' work, he knew, would obliterate the bloodied prints on the handle. William resisted the urge. Dr Moon said peyote couldn't change a man's essential nature, and surely Freddy was good, like his sister? Yes, there were nastier bastards than Freddy on the premises.

'God only knows where the key is,' said the doctor. 'I suppose it could be in Brooke's pockets. Did anyone think to check?'

'God is not omnipotent, Dr Moon, but He might be omniscient and know where the key is,' said Freddy. 'We are in a constant battle between the light and the dark, between good and evil, because the devil is not defeated. It's a heresy, but it's the truth. We could try prayer. Pray so that God might reveal the key to the devil's room.'

'Let's hope St Anthony of Padua takes an interest in old keys,' said William.

'Are you High Church?' asked Freddy. 'On consideration, I believe you're of Irish Roman Catholic descent.'

'No, I'm just a common-or-garden gypsy, and I've got the itch to get travelling.' William peeked beneath Britannia's skirts, and then thanked St Anthony of Padua, for the key was there. It was a small mercy, on such a night, not to have to check a hanged man's pockets, but William was grateful for it. He turned the key in the lock to the staircase door, so that it once more became camouflaged in sprigged wallpaper, and breathed a sigh of relief. William tugged at Freddy's hand as one would a recalcitrant child. 'Let's get the fuck out of here, shall we?'

'When did Brooke return to the house, I wonder?' Dr Moon moved ahead, shining his torch along the corridor with its awkward canted roof. 'And what the hell was the man up to? All this business with Persephone worries me. She knows about that room. Brooke seemed intent on thinking the contents were part of some inheritance.'

'He never left us,' said William. 'You know that. He wanted to finish what he'd started.'

At the servants' staircase, moonlight streamed through the frosted window in a magnified light, hitting the green baize door in a gentle roundel, and prettifying the stone steps into a smooth sheen.

'Wise words, Billy. Brooke would've stayed to complete the ritual Phyll interrupted.' Freddy stopped, and gestured with his oil lamp towards the heavens, or the attics. 'Times, dates, the waxing and waning of the moon, these things would've been important to him. And wasn't he found dressed up to the nines in mask and robes? Not alive, but definitely kicking.'

'Freddy, my dear chap.'

'Too dark, Dr Moon?'

'A tad.'

'I'm just glad someone finally appreciates my wisdom.' They had reached the newel posts of the main staircase. No one, real or imaginary, had been impaled here. William caressed the point of the pyramid with his free hand and sighed with relief. 'And I agree. Brooke was here secretly because what he needed to do depended on both time and place. I can't help but feel his mucking about in the crypt has something to do with his death. How Tom Sherbourne fits in, Christ only knows.'

'The mermaid killed Tom. But nonetheless, it's puzzling because the attack seems contrary to the mermaid's essential nature. In times of peace, she eats the poor minnow, the roach, and the silver bream. When she polishes her scales and prepares for war, she is hungry for male flesh. However, there are worse men in Red Hollow than good, dear Tom to feast on. Why not emasculate Brooke? Why not nibble on Irwell's, no doubt scanty, manhood?' Freddy halted before the portraits of bosomy Pikes of old, who stared down at their weak-chinned husbands and sons through heavy, disapproving eyelids. 'I've always found these family portraits so interesting. The few pictures of the barons show them as either insipid or dissolute.' He shuddered as if in receipt of a revelation. 'I prefer the women. They have strength and dignity, but the old girls don't much like us here, you know. We're traipsing all over their nice matriarchy with our dirty boots.'

William looked down at his feet and the plush, blue carpet. Freddy had cracked. He only hoped it wasn't permanent. But God, so what if it was? Freddy was his friend now. He took the man's hand once more and moved forwards. 'I can't help but think of Phyll's description of

Brooke sliding down the bloody banister. There's a certain joy, a naughty glee, in that action. What the fuck was he up to? It's itching at me.'

'You're a very perceptive fellow, William,' said Dr Moon. 'Either the ritual, or the results of the ritual, gave the man pleasure. The sliding down the banister was done by way of a celebration.'

'Men like Brooke claim to be seekers of esoteric knowledge,' said Freddy. 'But when you strip their faith down to the essentials, all they want is money, power and sex. Crowley-type manifestation is just prayer done by disaffected capitalists. Had his prayers been answered, one wonders?'

'Money, power and sex,' said William. 'Magic is a blind. Just because a man believes in magic doesn't mean it exists. Men do murder for money, power and sex, too.'

'And love,' said Dr Moon. 'A man might kill for love.'

'It depends on how you define love,' said Freddy.

And now they were at Phyll's door. No more than a few hours earlier, it had been empty of Phyll, but he had found her, as promised — even if she was neither safe nor sound. William didn't speak but released Freddy's hand and knocked.

Another dark heartbeat sound. A sound no one wanted to hear on a rain-soaked night.

William pounded at the door once more.

'Good grief, Billy.' Queenie opened the door blinking and bleary, stupid with sleep. 'What is it?' She held a nightlight up towards William's face and squinted. 'What the bloody hell happened to you?'

'No, Miss Maggs. When someone knocks, you must say: who's there?'

'Freddy? Is that you?' Phyll's voice called softly from the bedroom.

'Do not say another word until I say so.' William waved a warning finger at Freddy. 'You're all bloody chaos tonight, and you'll confuse Queenie and Phyll.'

Freddy put his free finger to his lips and nodded solemnly.

'I was cut with some glass and Dr Moon had to stitch me up. It's nothing to worry about. It doesn't hurt.' This was a lie. His heartbeat throbbed in his face. 'And at least I still have my boyish good looks.'

'That's debatable,' said Queenie.

'I do not want to alarm you, ladies, but there has been an unfortunate incident.' Dr Moon's natural inclination was to take charge, but he lacked the ability to explain the unexplainable; he had run out of steam. He looked at William in wide-eyed desperation. 'William and I wondered if Freddy might spend the rest of the evening with you.'

Freddy removed his finger from his lips with a flourish.

'We found Brooke murdered in that rotten attic room.' He pointed skywards and made a pantomime of hanging. 'I heard the mermaid kill poor Tom when I was hiding in the wardrobe.' Freddy paused in consideration. 'However, I have been more frightened, pretty Miss Maggs. I have seen more death, and I've felt more alone.'

'Well said, Freddy.'

'You may think so, Dr Moon, but some bugger needs to translate Freddy's little speech because I still don't have a bloody clue what's going on.'

'Queenie love, can we come in?' asked William. 'I don't want to talk out here. I've got the wind up.'

'Never invite me for a day out in the country again.' Queenie flung the door open wide. She wore a pair of striped men's pyjamas. Bed-flattened curls, her good skin plain of make-up, she'd never been more beautiful.

Freddy eyed her unashamedly. 'I say, Queenie, you do look nice in my pyjamas.'

'I thought I heard Freddy.' Phyll threw back the bedclothes and swung her legs from the bed. Reaching for the dressing gown which hung from the bedpost, she quickly covered her pyjamas and placed a loving arm about her brother. 'Are you alright?' She looked towards Dr Moon. 'Is he alright?'

'Freddy, William and I have taken a preparation of the peyote cactus.' Dr Moon reached into his jacket pocket for his pipe but did not bother to light it. 'Freddy is remarkably unselfconscious despite enduring real terror and moments of disorientation. William's hallucinations are of the most vivid and disturbing quality.' He extended his arm to bang the bowl of the pipe against the fireplace. 'We use peyote in Red Hollow as a treatment for the traumatised male subject.'

'He's like the fuckin' King.' William paused and sighed. 'We're all his subjects.'

'Freddy's been doped?' Phyll hastily flattened a few blankets and sat Freddy down on the bed. 'As part of his treatment?'

'Tea and sympathy, I believe.' Freddy nodded sagely. 'From what I gather, we spend much of our time here off our heads. I've had my suspicions for some time. Six impossible things before breakfast, don't you know.'

William brought his hand to his lips once more in a gesture of warning to Freddy. Quoting *Alice's Adventures in Wonderland* was out of order. A sudden pang of conscience about the evening's dark humour overwhelmed him. There was nothing to laugh about, for it was all horrific. William had sobered up. 'More importantly, Tom Sherbourne and Mr Brooke have been murdered. Tom is in the conservatory, head staved in and emasculated, and Brooke is in the

223

attic room, hanging. It was made to look like suicide after he'd done some ritual or other.'

'And the patients at Red Hollow are regularly given a drug that makes them hallucinate?' Queenie lit a cigarette and handed it to William. He took a much needed hit of tobacco, and knew he'd never loved her more. 'Well, that explains the bloke seeing the fang-cunted mermaid in the bath, don't you think? Not to mention dead vicars, hysterical lads waving pistols about, and grim, bloody murder committed in the small hours.' She turned and wagged a finger at Dr Moon. 'Don't you dare gasp at my foul language, pal. You must've known this peyote stuff was partly responsible for what was going on here long before you called in Phyll and Billy. Tut, tut, fucking tut.'

'Yes, Miss Maggs, it was wrong of me to administer the drug without the men's consent, but I had no idea Mr Trent had been hallucinating in his bath until Percy told us last night. I do understand how culpable I am.' The doctor sucked on his pipe with worried concentration. 'But, as I've told William, a man under the influence of peyote would do nothing contrary to his essential nature.'

'I think that might be Queenie's point, Dr Moon.' Phyll fussed over Freddy, covering him with blankets, offering water. 'Was Brooke taking the drug?'

'We believe so, yes,' said William.

'And do you still think he murdered the Reverend Andrews?' asked Phyll.

'I do.'

'So, there may be another man amongst us whose essential nature is murderous,' she said.

'Money, sex and power.' William cupped his hands against the windowpane and peered out onto the storm. Sleet, and no sign of life. 'Those are our motives.'

Queenie moved to the window and clicked her fingers before William's passive face. 'Billy has a chief suspect, but he ain't telling.'

'Who at Red Hollow wants sex and power?'

William counted three full seconds before Queenie spoke. 'Oh, no.'

William shrugged.

'But Irwell's sedated,' said Queenie.

'So were you,' said William. 'But you woke up when Freddy banged on the door. You're too used to the stuff.'

'Good grief, Dr Moon. I feel sick,' said Phyll. 'Irwell isn't a Veronal addict, is he?'

'He's here for nervous exhaustion, like Freddy.'

'Let's see if I can find the Ritz.' William moved from his window sentry post and checked inside the wardrobe. It was a large and perfectly empty space. 'How safe are you feeling, Freddy? In need of the wardrobe?'

'No, I think not, Billy, for I have made a breakthrough. Dr Moon, I am surrounded by love.' Freddy lay on the bed, and closed his eyes, adopting a smiling, almost beatific expression. William worried it wouldn't last long. *Excess of sorrow laughs, excess of joy weeps.*

Phyll tucked her brother in tight; kissed both eyelids. 'You did lock Mr Irwell in his room after the incident with Percy, didn't you, Dr Moon?'

'My dear Phyll, of course.'

Queenie let out a bark-like laugh. 'Forgive me for wanting to check up on your work, but I reckon we need to go down-stairs and make sure he's still in the land of Nod.'

'If Irwell killed Tom and Brooke,' said Phyll, 'what on earth do you think he has planned for Percy?'

'Mr Irwell is deeply neurotic, but he's shown no actual tendency towards violence.' The doctor chewed on his pipe with the corner of his mouth. 'Tonight's unfortunate incident was a cry for attention. He is, I'm afraid, a very immature young man.'

'Oh, for God's sake, Dr Moon.' Phyll's voice held a note of irritated panic. 'You are a kind man, but you are hopelessly naive. Decent, emotionally mature men don't hurt women. Irwell is just the type to harm a young girl. He is absolutely the type.'

'Christ, I hope Phyll's wrong. I hope we're both wrong.' William looked out onto the night and trembled hard at the oozing black of the pasture, seeping onwards along the lane and to the ford, and then to Watling Street. Would the road be passable? Could he cadge a lift to the nearest cop shop? He turned to Dr Moon. 'We'll go down and check on him now. Freddy is safe here with Queenie and Phyll. If Irwell is in his room, then someone else is responsible for this bloody mess. Either way, come dawn, I'll go for help. Do you have your Webley?'

'Yes.'

'Hand it over.'

Dr Moon fumbled in his pocket and produced his pistol. 'William, I think I had a sergeant like you during the war.'

William smiled, flicked his cigarette butt into the fireplace and winked. 'Henry, my friend. You're still alive, so it's very likely you did.'

'Lock the door behind us, Phyll.' Queenie was half-dressed, buttoning her blouse askew, forcing bare feet into damp rubber boots. 'I'd like to keep my Derringer with me, but I'll leave it with you if you prefer.'

Dr Moon stared open-mouthed at Queenie's muscling in but said nothing.

'We shall lock the door behind you, and Phyll will hit Mr Irwell over the head with a candlestick if he dares to come anywhere near,' Freddy called out from his bed. 'And Miss Maggs, if you're going downstairs with Billy and Dr Moon, would you mind awfully bringing me back a Horlicks?'

28

The psychological effects of the drug had worn off, William knew, but the clumsiness, the palpitations, the sense of not quite being in his own body remained. So, when Dr Moon halted before a bedroom door with sudden abruptness, the floor rolled dizzyingly beneath William's feet, and, as he reached out to steady himself against the wall, the wainscoting eddied as though some monster moved behind the ancient wood. The permanent feeling of dread which hung heavy in his gut had disappeared when William was drunk on peyote. With his coming sobriety, he realised, the sense of doom had returned.

William held his oil lamp aloft, assessing Mr Irwell's bedroom door. It was shut.

'We should knock,' whispered Dr Moon.

'And give the little bastard a chance to prepare himself?' said Queenie. 'No fear.'

They turned their grim, expectant faces towards William, awaiting his decision. This was his show. Even Queenie was prepared to follow William's lead, at least for as long as it suited her.

'Give me the key to the room, Dr Moon. We won't knock, but we'll go in quietly.' The doctor rummaged in his trouser pocket. 'Take my oil lamp, Queenie. Hold it steady as I go in.' Dr Moon fumbled with a huge fob, and William, on instinct, turned the handle on Irwell's door. It opened, just an inch, and with a hushed click. William slow-blinked against Dr Moon's dumbfounded face, and took a steadying breath, pulling the Webley from his pocket. 'Both of you keep to my right and against the wall. Do not enter the room until I give the all-clear.' Dr Moon's face fell into grave lines. 'Not until I give the all-clear. I'm talking to you, Queenie.'

'Yes, Billy, yes.' She nodded, a solemn good soldier in the lamplight. 'The all-clear.'

William shoved the door with the toe of his shoe. It swung open with ease and without a sound. William entered and sensed, even before his eyes adjusted to the gloom of the room, that it was empty. The single bed, pushed against the wall to his left, was askew: counterpane rucked; striped pyjamas on the head-dented pillow; an ashtray upended on the tangled sheets. Crumpled pulp and horror magazines lay on the floor, next to a few dusty odd socks. The room reeked of sweat, and fags, and cheap eau de cologne. The window was shut, and the curtains drawn. He walked over and looked out. Sleet had become so ubiquitous it filled the night air with dancing water.

William moved to put his hand under the bedclothes. Still warm; wherever Irwell was, he wasn't far away. The whole scene seemed strangely anti-climactic in its ordinariness. But what had he expected to find in the room: a disembowelment; a portal to an unknown realm; an opium den? Nothing would surprise him in this godforsaken hole.

He knelt to check under the bed – Christ, the kid's used underwear, and nothing else. The wardrobe rattled as he rose to his feet. He checked it: good navy suit and city shoes, no overcoat or brogues. Tallboy drawers, partially open, held the detritus of a young man's life: a tin of Germolene; an empty canister of toothpowder; a dandruff-encrusted comb; a garish American-style tie; but William could see neither Irwell's watch nor wallet nor cigarettes.

'He's scarpered. Bring the lamp in, Queenie,' he called. There came no answer from the hallway. Christ, Dr Moon was waiting for the formal all-clear. 'All clear, Dr Moon.'

The doctor entered first and switched on his electric torch. William blinked in its hard white glare. Now spotlit, the room appeared even more sordid. 'He's scarpered,' William repeated. 'And it looks like there are signs of a struggle.'

'What makes you say that?' asked Dr Moon.

William waved his hand in a wide, encompassing gesture. 'Just look at the place.'

'I'm afraid Irwell's room was often in a state. Our chars complained that it was impossible to clean.'

'Dirty little bugger.' Queenie, for whom cleanliness was next to godliness, huffed sanctimoniously and placed the oil lamp on the dresser.

'His coat, watch, shoes and wallet have gone. Wherever he is, he's left in a hurry. Everything else is here – suitcase, good suit, everything. And wherever he is, he's not far, his bed's still warm.'

'Should we go after him?' asked Dr Moon. 'Could he still be in the house?'

'He could be anywhere. He took his essential stuff with him. Although it would take the equivalent of a bomb going off to get that lad outside in the flood.' William shook his head slowly. 'He's one of your true believers, Dr Moon. He thinks the mermaid is real and is out to get him. What was that little bastard up to in civvy street, I wonder?'

'Christ, this place stinks.' Queenie moved to open a window. 'Sedated, my arse.'

'He was sedated at six o'clock yesterday evening. It's now four o'clock in the morning.' As if on cue, the church clock struck. Dr Moon waited politely for the sonorous chimes to end before he continued. 'Veronal doesn't necessarily knock a patient out but puts him gently to sleep. He was sleeping when I left him. And, yes, I locked the door behind me.'

'But you've lost the key.'

'No, Miss Maggs, I found it.' Dr Moon patted his jacket. 'It was on my fob as expected.'

'I can't work out if you're plain incompetent or an actual villain.' Queenie gestured to William with her thumb. 'He's too fuckin' trusting. I ain't.'

'Think, Dr Moon, would Irwell have a tolerance to barbiturates?' asked William, ignoring Queenie playing the battle-axe. 'A man can soon get used to Veronal, and if you're determined enough, you can even fight against its effects.' William twitched and shivered. Pavlov's dog once more, because, in truth, he needed a cachet of Veronal. He still had the habit, and it had been a rough night.

'I shall repeat, for the benefit of Miss Maggs. Mr Irwell was admitted by his brother in November for a spell of rest due to nervous exhaustion. He was not an addict.'

William shook his head. 'He's not just some scruffy, woman-hating little sod with the wind up, Dr Moon. I don't think, for all your treatment, you ever discovered the real reason why Irwell was here.'

'Do you still think Irwell killed Tom Sherbourne and Brooke?' The doctor waved his arm about the adolescent chaos of the room.

'The timings are out. The boy's bed is still warm. Why sadistically kill two men, then come back to bed for a couple of hours' kip?'

'Could he have witnessed something?' asked Queenie.

William shrugged. Irwell had been wound tight all night; it would take a gust of wind blowing the wrong way to throw him into panic. But Queenie had a point. William was surprised, despite Dr Moon's free hand in sedating his guests, that no one else had heard Tom crash through the conservatory roof. And wasn't Irwell's bedroom down the corridor from Tom's? 'The lad's either dead, scarpered or he's a maniac and he's on the loose. At the moment, I'm less sure what's gone on here than when I walked into the room. The warm bed is bothering me.'

'What do you have there, Miss Maggs?' asked Dr Moon.

Queenie stood by the open window surrounded by specks of dancing rain. In her hand was a heart-shaped box. Blood-red leather, flattish and about the size of a dinner plate, the gold, tooled border shimmered in the light of the doctor's torch.

'It's nothing. It's empty. I found it underneath the kid's pillow.'

'An odd thing for a young man to have in his room, don't you think?' said Dr Moon.

'Hand it over, Queenie.' William only imagined her biting her bottom lip, he was sure of it. Nonetheless, she complied with a grudging silence. 'It's for a necklace. Even if Irwell was inclined to buy his best girl nice things, which I doubt, the lad could never afford whatever was in this box.' He opened it. Empty, like Queenie had said; the interior was lined with a pearlescent silk, and inscribed in gold lettering: *Cartier, Paris, Rue de la Paix*. 'Fuck me. Cartier. Worth a fortune. Double stranded, judging by the box.'

Strands. Pearlescent. Pearls. William's adrenaline surged. He thought of the day he and Phyll trawled through the newspapers. He thought of the nudists and the bank job in Stoke-on-Trent and the call from Dr Moon. He snapped the box shut and threw it on the bed as if it might turn on him and bite.

Dr Moon bent down, picked up the horror magazine and folded it flat, considered the cover, handed it to William, and said, 'What do you think of this?'

It was top-shelf, American pulp horror and luridly illustrated. A near-naked strawberry blonde was surrounded by men sporting monk's robes and evil intent. They were forcing the girl to take some kind of potion. Behind her, in glass coffins, a series of fair-haired, pale-shouldered women lay comatose, or dead. William wasn't sure which story was depicted on the front cover. Was it *Brides for Murdered Men*, or *The Corpse Surgeon*? On reflection, it was *Girls for the Coffin Syndicate*. 'Are you thinking this is where our murderer got his information on the esoteric, Dr Moon?'

The doctor shrugged. 'There was a touch of the penny dreadful about that attic room. You said so yourself.'

'There's a touch of the penny dreadful about this whole bloody place.'

'Including under the bed,' said Queenie.

'What? Did you find the kid's dirty underwear?'

'No, this little lot.' She had moved the mattress from the bedstead and shone the oil lamp towards the shadowy far corner of the room. There, beneath the slats, loosely wrapped in canvas, lay a claw hammer, a spanner, a knife and a length of stout twine. 'Mr Irwell didn't strike me as much of a handyman.'

Dr Moon bent forward and picked up the hammer. He passed it to William, pointing to the initials etched and inked in its wooden handle. '*F. H.* Freddy Hall. These are Freddy's carpentry tools.'

'Or Mr Irwell's arsenal.' William stretched out his back, cricking the vertebrae in his neck. His muscles spasmed, and he needed a piss. When would this fucking night end? 'I want to know what's missing from this stash. I want to know very much what he still has on him. Christ, at least they're clean.' William touched the knife, protected by the handkerchief, still in his pocket, and was suddenly thankful he hadn't succumbed to the temptation of obliterating the fingerprints. 'Did Freddy say anything about missing his tools?'

'Not to me,' said Dr Moon. 'But he has so many. Would he have missed these few?'

William's father had been a craftsman, a gunmaker, and his tools were his most precious possession. Would a man of Freddy's class, whose livelihood did not depend on his hands, be more careless?

He looked once more about the room. 'Come on, let's get back to Phyll and Freddy. In the morning, I'll go for the coppers, but until then, I don't want anyone wandering about this house alone. We're safer in numbers.'

They left the room, closing the door on Irwell's mess, and trudged in solemn procession along the corridor.

'Shouldn't we check on the Pikes? The tower is meant to be impenetrable, but, as you fellows say, I have the wind up about Percy. If Irwell is unwell, then Percy is in danger, and I feel I have something of a responsibility to the child. After all, I brought these men into her home.' There was a plaintive note to the doctor's little speech. 'Should I go alone and meet you both upstairs once I know they're alright?'

William's head spun. He began to panic; he was Sergeant Garrett again, up to his knees in muck and blood, and once more his men needed answers. *Billy can't make decisions, not really, not since the war.* Leadership and heroism had been thrust upon him; why had he been forced to take the responsibility?

'Or perhaps we should go together. William, what do you want me to do?'

Queenie suddenly halted, causing a comic pile-up in the corridor akin to the Keystone Cops, but she always reminded him of the glorious Mabel Normand. He thanked God for her, and the distraction she caused. She turned to him and said, 'Do you think I should make Freddy a Horlicks?'

'No, Little Lord Fauntleroy can fucking well do without.' The muscle-relaxing relief of a question he was qualified to answer. 'Cheeky sod.'

'I dunno. Perhaps I should get a kettle on the boil.'

'Why in heaven, woman?' William sighed. 'Is someone having a baby?'

'No, but if we're going to be stuck in that bedroom until dawn, then we'll need tea and perhaps something to eat. Besides, I did promise Freddy a Horlicks.'

'It's not such a bad idea. Tea, food, milky drinks will see us through the night,' said Dr Moon. 'And I should like my doctor's bag. I left it on the table after I stitched your face. I'll check on the Pikes and then meet you in the kitchen.'

William's simple plan to stick together and stick it out until dawn had fallen at the first hurdle. And yet, he marvelled at humanity. Trapped in a manor house with three dead bodies and possibly a murderer on the loose, his friends' minds turned to the practical business of sweet tea for shock and milky drinks to keep their strength up. However, William had seen enough suffering to know true terror happened alongside the commonplace. The five-nines always came when a man began to brew up for his mates, and loss could be counted in undrunk mugs of cocoa.

The gnawing pain which had returned to his gut sang, but William had decided. He handed the Webley to Dr Moon, and said, 'Use it if you must. I'll stay with Queenie and make Horlicks. Meet us in the kitchen once you know that Percy is safe.'

29

The green baize door shut softly behind them. Queenie placed her oil lamp on the kitchen table, but it did little to dispel the subterranean chill of the kitchen. If the attic room was the heart of Red Hollow Hall, then this room was its bowels. William glanced at the hacked-about ham, the yellowing butter, the dregs of coffee, and then grimaced at his own analogy. Dr Moon's bag was where he left it, along with a saucerful of bloodied, broken glass, as pretty as uncut rubies.

Up leapt Rossetti, coal black and as lithe as an eel. She didn't shock William, for by now he was used to her tricks. Arching her back, she nudged at the butter dish, her pink tongue darting out in dainty licks. Queenie grabbed Rossetti, holding her to her bosom like a child, and kissed the top of her head, stroking the cat's upturned nose. 'She gets everywhere, don't she? I like her. People used to worship cats in Egypt. I read it in a magazine. It said they were mummified in King Tutankhamen's tomb. The Pharaohs adorned their favourite cats with gold and precious jewels. Turquoise, lapis lazuli, jasper, they thought the stones protected them from evil or disease.'

William knew there would've been some point, back in the 1920s, and in the heyday of Egyptomania, when the young

Queenie considered tomb raiding. Even now she seemed to have treasure on the brain.

'Alright,' he said. 'Spill it.'

She let go of Rossetti, the black cat disappearing into the black shadows, then filled the kettle and put it on the range. 'What do you reckon, about five minutes to boil?'

'I'm too tired to play this game.' William sat at the table and held his thumping face in his hands. Reaching for the doctor's bag, he found, and then discounted, the morphine and the Veronal, and opted for two aspirin. He crunched at them, too lazy to fetch water, and allowed the bitter grittiness to dissolve in the spittle at the back of his throat. 'Why do you always have to do it, anyway? This weird, domestic hedging you play at before you want me to do something. It's exhausting, and Dr Moon's happy drugs have worn off. Ask me what you want.'

'Where's the Horlicks?'

'If that's what you really want, then fine. Here's my answer. I didn't do an inventory of the kitchen cupboards after I found Tom Sherbourne murdered and emasculated, so how the fuck would I know where the Horlicks is.'

'Be nice.'

'I told you to come right out with it. You're trying my patience.'

'Alright, have it your way.' Queenie chose a Willow Pattern teapot from the dresser. 'I want you to leave the doctor with Freddy and Phyll so you and I can hunt down Irwell alone. I need to find the little bastard.'

'You can fuck right off.'

'This is very important to me, Billy.' She piled the rest of the Willow Pattern tea service on the table. 'Can you see a tray?' William found a huge, brass-banded mahogany tray and held it before him like a butler in a play. 'Ooh, that's a nice one, ain't it? This place is full of nice things. Pop it down.' She sniffed at the milk, returned to the range and poured some in an enamel pan. 'You see, the kid has something I want.'

'I'm just surprised you're not already hiding that Cartier necklace down your knickers.'

'Christ, you don't miss a trick.' Queenie looked at him darkly through her claggy lashes, mascara clumped like oil on old machinery. 'This is why I love you and need you. You're the cleverest man I know. Not many men can match me for brains, and, in truth, it gets on my tits. We find the kid; we get the necklace; we deal with Irwell. Come dawn, you go and fetch the coppers like you planned. Tell the police Brooke murdered the Reverend Andrews and Tom Sherbourne. Then, say Brooke topped himself in remorse. If they ask, say Irwell has run off scared, and leave it at that.'

'I repeat. You can fuck right off. I won't find the necklace for you, and I won't deal with Irwell, whatever that means, you sinister fucker.' William snatched the tea canister from in front of Queenie's nose and shovelled six or seven spoons in the pot. He thought of Tom Sherbourne, not a perfect man, but a decent man, murdered and mutilated. 'I won't play up the murder–suicide angle to the coppers either. I owe justice to the dead. So, you can get that notion out of your wicked little head.'

'I honestly don't know why you're so angry with me.'

William screwed his face tight, and hoped the kettle might boil.

'It ain't like you.' She filled the sugar bowl with tinkling cubes. 'What exactly do you think you know, Billy?'

Until that moment, William knew nothing. It had all been guesswork. He closed his eyes and steadied himself against the kitchen table. Yew berries on white frost like drops of blood. Yew berries like red stones. The flat black flood of the crypt, and a flicker of a fish tail – and she emerged from her watery lair draped in rubies and pearls. Scales like dulled armour surrounded a respectable prettiness. She had been saving up to get married, the newspapers had said. Her fiancé was a history teacher from the grammar school. The mermaid turned her head to show William the gored depression above the blackened eye; the dark blood trickling from her ear; the fishy pout of a fat lip. William nodded acknowledgement. He saw her, and he understood. Then the bank clerk from the Stoke-on-Trent branch of the National and Provincial swam away.

'The man is young, twitchy and can take a punch. He likes to go around tooled up. Literally. There's a whiff of the dark satanic mill about his accent, and I doubt his real name is Irwell.' William paused, took a great gathering breath, and let her have it. 'This whole mess has all been about the contents of a few safe deposit boxes blagged from the National and Provincial up in Stoke. Am I hot or cold, Queenie?'

'Hot.'

'Irwell pulled that northern bank job back in November with Sammy the Manc. And, using my limited experience of that foul little bastard, I reckon he's the one who raped and murdered the bank clerk they took hostage. You've been hiding him out here as a favour to that big fucker. Irwell is Sammy's little brother, ain't he?' Queenie gave him a slow and silent nod. There came a sound, like an indistinct, muffled male voice. William stopped dead, fizzing with fear. Not sure where the noise came from, he listened, twitchy. Placing a warning finger to his lips, he fixed Queenie with a wide-eyed stare. What did he hear? Only those uncanny, early morning sounds: the slow heavy tick of a clock; the rattle of a pan of milk coming to the boil; the gentle hum of breeze-blown servants' bells. However, he could not shake the overwhelming worry that they were being spied on. He nodded towards the pantry window and lowered his voice. 'There's someone out there. At the back of the house.'

'You're paranoid.' Yet she matched the pitch of her voice to his. 'Dr Moon's dope has given you the creeps.'

'Maybe. Maybe not.' William walked down to the pantry. At the water's edge, the flood had become so black, and still it was a mirror, reflecting his five o'clock shadow, the dark circles beneath his eyes, his right cheek fat with bandages. William blinked at the unfamiliar man, and the unfamiliar man blinked back. He took off his shoes and rolled his trouser legs. Wincing with cold as he waded into the flood, he pushed through the dangling game, and peeped out of the small window. Not a living soul; nothing but a vast shimmering blackness pricked by needles of icy sleet.

Queenie waited for him, sitting at the top of the pantry steps with a tea towel in her hand. She handed it to him as he rose from the water, and he sat with her, in silence, rubbing at his feet and ankles. 'Sammy says they didn't mean to do it,' she said, finally.

'What? Rape and murder the bank clerk?'

'No, the little shitbag meant to do that. I'm referring to the necklace. Twenty thousand pounds' worth of pearls and rubies, Billy love.' William couldn't help but whistle. 'The brothers didn't realise they had such a big haul. They were in it for a couple of thousand-worth of gold sovereigns in the safe deposit boxes. Sammy is nothing but muscle and vanity. His little brother has got him in hot water, and he came to me to provide a solution because he don't have the brains or connections to do it for himself.'

'I thought you didn't care for rapists, Queenie. I remember the good old days when you used to dangle them off canal bridges by their ankles.'

'Still do. But there's a time and a place for rough justice. Once I've got my pearls and rubies, Mr Irwell will get his comeuppance.'

'Your pearls and rubies?'

'Finders keepers.'

'Your morals go out the window when it comes to a fortune in jewellery.'

'No, it's simply expedient that Mr Irwell receives his just deserts as soon as I get the necklace.'

'I won't murder Irwell.'

Queenie let out a sigh akin to the hiss of a cat.

'Have you always known the necklace was here?'

'No, Billy.' Queenie shook her head and looked at him straight. 'I didn't have a clue until we searched the kid's room, honestly. Then the penny dropped. It's just the stupid kind of thing those brothers would do. Hide the necklace here. It's the reason you and Phyll were called to Red Hollow in the first place, ain't it? The intruder wasn't the mermaid, it was some-one looking for the necklace in the middle of the night. I reckon Irwell, probably when on the peyote, let slip he'd hidden the jewels somewhere in the house, and there's been a treasure hunt going on ever since.'

'He told Mr Brooke,' said William. 'Summoning mermaids on Candlemas has got nothing to do with the murders. It's all about the necklace. Freddy said the old alchemists did magic to find treasure.'

'Brooke's dead.'

'Don't I know it, but it's a chain of events. Brooke hunts for the jewellery and even tries a magical ritual in the crypt. Phyll witnesses his nonsense, and Brooke clunks her on the head, leaves her for dead. The Reverend Andrews arrives at the church because he suspects Brooke is committing some unholy hocus-pocus on the premises. He gets clunked. We return in search of Phyll and inadvertently give him the opportunity to finish his search for the jewels. More murders happen. Ad infinitum until none of us are left.' William glanced at the steep pantry steps. 'This necklace ain't like those ancient Egyptian jewels you were talking about. It don't protect you from evil; it attracts it like a magnet.'

'It ain't a curse, Billy. It's just bad bastardy.'

'That's the definition of a curse, Queenie love. You know that.'

'Irwell don't know who I am, you know. We never met. Arthur Stokes did all the legwork. I knew about Red Hollow because Phyll told me about Freddy. We sorted false papers, and Arthur settled him in, signing the relevant documents, pretending to be a relative, and paying for three months up front.' Queenie took the tea towel from William and balled it up in her hand. 'Your new pal, Dr Moon, ain't the brightest spark.'

William put on his shoes. He stood, and as he straightened, blood rushed to his injured face with a dizzying surge. As did his anger. 'You fucker, Queenie.' He touched his cheek, testing the power of the pulsing throb. 'You thought Phyll's disappearance had something to do with Sammy's brother. That's why you came with me, and that's why you dropped everything. Not because you were worried about Phyll or wanted to help me, but because you wanted to keep Irwell's identity under wraps.'

'It was all of those reasons, Billy. I'm fond of Phyll, and I was worried that she'd come to harm.'

'Fond.' William shook his giddy head, praying the aspirin would kick in soon. 'You're a bad bastard, Queenie. This place was Freddy's home. You brought Sammy the Manc's murdering kid brother into Freddy's home. You're just like your old man, a right fuckin' user. Phyll deserved better than the likes of Ronnie for a pal, and she deserves better than the likes of you.'

'You're right. She does deserve better than me.' Queenie ran her fingers through her dark curls, and William readied himself for battle. 'God knows I ain't got much morality. I weren't ever taught to treat people proper, Billy, and I'd do anything not to be fuckin' poor, and you're right, it's made me a bad bastard.'

Then, Queenie cried. Her make-up ran in sludgy trails down her cheeks, kohl and mascara mingling with the natural traces of exhaustion beneath her eyes. She was done in, but in that moment looked so like her brother that William turned his back on her. If you cannot see the ghost, the ghost cannot see you. He took a deep, belly-filling breath, and then exhaled slowly. 'How long has it been going on?' he asked.

'She don't know how I feel.' Queenie wiped away black tears with the sleeve of her blouse. 'I ain't told her. Don't tell her I put Freddy in danger, please, Billy. Don't tell her. She'll never forgive me. If we've ever been friends, if you've ever been a brother to me.'

'A brother? What the fuck are you talking about, woman?'

'You know what I mean. We're close. We're like blood, ain't we? You're a Maggs, really, ain't you?'

'Jesus, Queenie. What a thing to say.'

'I've fallen for her, Billy. Don't tell.' She whispered the words like a prayer. 'Please, I swear, I'll never put her in harm's way.'

Queenie never begged; she only called in favours as a cold calculation. Could it be that Queenie loved Phyll in a way she'd never loved William? Jealousy came and landed strangely, like a cat who'd lost its sure footing. Phyll was his best friend, and he didn't want to share her with a glutton like Queenie. 'Oh, fuck it, Queenie. I'll think about it, alright? I'll think about it.'

'Well, ain't that a touching moment.' The voice was a distinctive, Mancunian monotone, emotionless, nasal, deep, and it sounded out above the long, shrill whistle of the kettle. 'Ain't that sweet. Now, where the fuck is my necklace?'

30

The gold tooth glimmered in the soft lamplight. But Sammy the Manc was the one with the pistol, so he had every right to grin. He filled the kitchen doorway with his bulk; his suit crumpled, his shirt collarless, there were muddy shadows under his pale blue eyes, and he'd lost something of his princely bearing between Birmingham and Red Hollow. The man William knew as Irwell, a head shorter and two stone skinnier than his brother, hovered behind Sammy's left shoulder, fidgeting and grinning. With big brother at his side, Irwell had power, and he liked it. The brothers squeezed into the kitchen shoulder to shoulder. As an added surprise, Arthur Stokes – turncoat – followed, dragging Dr Moon by the humiliating scruff. The doctor was the worse for wear. More than the obvious signs of a beating, there was a look of pitiable bewilderment on the man's face. All three men stank with the usual bravado of a well-armed bully.

Queenie squared her shoulders. 'I ain't got it,' she said, nodding to Irwell. 'No matter what junior says. It ain't in my possession.' Queenie moved to the range and removed the singing kettle. She returned to the kitchen table, and, for a second, William thought she might scald the brothers into submission. It would be a fitting move for a woman keen on both domesticity and violent retribution. She paused, kettle hovering over the Willow Pattern teapot, and considered the Judas. Arthur Stokes flushed pink but did not meet her gaze. 'If I had the necklace, I wouldn't have hung around here. I'm not stupid. And it seems to me, I've got more right to take umbrage with you than the other way around. I ain't been the one ballsing stuff up.'

'That's the bitch that hit me. I'm sure. That's her.' Irwell had a Thompson submachine gun slung over his shoulder. William had only ever seen them in the movies, and Irwell wore it like a toy. The kid was Jimmy Cagney. Gun crazy, a nice little thug, he would call them all 'yellow-bellied' soon, and say it in an American accent. 'Do something about it, Sam.'

Sammy shook his head, exhausted and indulgent, at the sour-faced Irwell.

'That's a nice big gun you have there, son,' said William.

'Birmingham Small Arms, fat man.' Irwell glanced at the ham on the kitchen table, turned his nose up and made for the refrigerator. 'I'm starving. I didn't have any tea.' He pulled out a cake tin and settled down at the kitchen table. Irwell was mother only to himself; he poured a cup of Queenie's brew, and drank it, slurping. William looked at Persephone's birthday cake, rich, fruity, and not yet iced, and silently prayed that Dr Moon would keep his theories on the cake's secret ingredient to himself: the mescaline, if it hit Irwell hard, might just work in their favour. Irwell clocked his interest. 'Keep your paws off, tubs.'

'Ignore him, Billy, you ain't that fat.'

'He is.' Irwell took the carving knife and sliced off a good hunk of fruitcake. He ate just like his big brother – with his mouth open.

William spoke to Sammy. 'Did you give him that Tommy gun for Christmas? He ain't big enough to play with it. I'm not even sure if he deserves it. From what I've heard the kid is a fuckin' liability.'

Irwell grinned and made a mime of peppering the kitchen with gunfire, circling the barrel around the assembled company, his brother included, in a mock execution. The display was punctuated by a triumphant 'Ha!' Then Irwell went back to his tea and cake.

'Why are you riling our Vince?' Sammy turned to William, perplexed. 'What's the point in getting him all mithered? Stay over there with the doctor and keep your big mouth shut.'

William did as he was told.

'I have no idea who these people are or what they want.' Dr Moon huddled in close to William; his words came as a plaintive jibber. 'What are they doing here?'

William breathed deeply. There was a metallic tang in the air, like the brewing of a summer storm, uncanny in this winter weather. 'They're after the stuff that nightmares are made on.'

'Shut the fuck up and sit down.' Arthur Stokes gestured to the kitchen chairs.

'What do you mean? Stuff of nightmares? Speak plainly, William.' The doctor slumped into the nearest kitchen chair and reached for his bag. Arthur shifted forward, snatched it from him, and wagged his finger. 'I simply want an aspirin.'

'Don't be a prick all your life, Arthur,' said William. 'Give the doctor his bag so he can have an aspirin. Anything in there is no match for two pistols and a Tommy gun.' Arthur, a well-trained and instinctive dog, glanced at Queenie for his orders. She let out a laugh like a curse. Then he looked at Sammy, who nodded. Finally, Arthur rummaged in the bag and then handed a bottle of tablets to Dr Moon. He wandered off to whisper in his new boss's ear, in front of a watchful Queenie; the man was both brazen and stupid. William took advantage and pulled up a chair next to the doctor, keeping his voice low as he spoke. 'What I mean is, they're the reason why Red Hollow has become a dangerous place to live. These men are the first link in your chain of events. They stole a necklace worth a fortune up north and killed a female bank clerk in the process. Irwell has been hiding out here under an assumed name. He brought the loot with him. Unfortunately, he's been a very careless and loose-lipped boy. Brooke was searching for the necklace these past few months, using his magic, and God knows what, and then probably feeding Irwell a few extra doses of mescaline to get him to talk. But Brooke is dead, and Irwell still doesn't have the loot. We're going to spend a long and fractious morning with these fuckers until they find that necklace. Do you understand?'

'Mr Irwell is a gangster?'

'Mr Irwell is a violent shitbag with a Tommy gun over his shoulder. His brother is a common criminal, ambitious but not bright. Miss Maggs is the gangster, ruthless and clever. Arthur is a knackered bull terrier who doesn't know who his master is. I'm who I've always been. This is all you need to know.'

'Do you have a plan?'

'I'm extemporising. I need to get a feel for how they work.' William shrugged. Planning might stop a man from getting killed, but it was no guarantee. 'But I reckon a fruitcake full of mescaline might help us out a bit.'

'Quit your whispering. Quit it. Conspiring bastard.' Irwell waved the cake-covered carving knife vaguely in William's direction.

'Vincent, shut it, will you.' Sammy reached for the aspirin and shook a few out onto his bear-like hand. 'I ain't got time for your temper tantrums now.' He turned to Arthur Stokes and, nodding to Queenie, said, 'Search her.'

'Search me, Arthur?' Queenie was faux outraged.

'It's nothing personal, Queenie.' Full of fearful bravado, Arthur pushed Queenie against the kitchen wall too hard. She braced herself, flat palms against the crumbling plaster-work, and licked her lips.

He patted her down. Starting at her ankles, his big, hard hands travelled up her legs until they reached her thighs. At that point, a flurry of hail clattered against the windowpanes. William turned, felt a gust of wind so cold it pricked his cheeks, but no window had opened. The flame guttered blue and white in the oil lamp. Arthur let go of Queenie's flesh and stood straight. Each man in the kitchen held his breath. Then, from the flooded depths of the pantry, came an echoing splash: a distinctive amniotic plop in the darkness which made William's tender stomach lurch.

Irwell jumped to his feet, alert, and fingered the trigger of his Tommy gun. Turning to his brother, he said, 'Oh Jesus Christ, didn't I tell you?'

'Mr Irwell, please be rational. A large hailstone must've fallen into the floodwater. The little window has swung open in the wind, I'm sure of it.' The doctor waved an exhausted arm in the general direction of the sound.

William rose, and moving with the oil lamp towards the pantry, he stepped down and faced the flood. He let the water eddy against the toes of his shoes and peered through the swaying game to the small window. If it was ever open, it was now closed. Through the glass, the hailstorm had that vivid silver quality of rain in a photograph. 'I haven't a clue what made the noise.' William returned to the kitchen, and, raising his lamp, he assessed Irwell's panicked face. 'Nothing is out of place as far as I can see. Whatever it was that made the splash has disappeared. But it was big because the floodwater is lapping against the steps like a wave.'

Despite the cold, a sheen of sweat appeared on Irwell's forehead. He swallowed hard, and wiped his face with the back of his sleeve. William smiled.

Arthur shrugged, and once more turned his attention to Queenie. 'I need to finish the search.' He ran his hands over her hips, but with no gratuitous lingering. Out came the Derringer from the pocket of Queenie's skirt. 'Like I said, it's nothing personal. It's just business. A better offer, you understand.'

'Business is personal, Arthur.' Queenie regarded Arthur steadily and kissed him on the cheek, her lips lingering near his earlobe. 'I'm in this game because I've taken all the bad cards dealt to me really fuckin' personally. I am who I am because everything that's ever happened to me, I've taken personally. I hold grudges, Arthur. I hold them so hard it hurts.'

Arthur, as impassive as a block of meat, released himself from Queenie's embrace. He didn't know he was a dead man walking. 'Just the Derringer,' he said to Sammy. 'A pop gun.'

'Search her fancy man.' Sammy grinned.

Arthur Stokes rolled his eyes.

William turned, acquiescent, his hands up like in a movie, and Arthur pushed him against the kitchen wall. 'Oh, Arthur, I didn't know you cared.' The frisk was quick and efficient, and Arthur found, as William knew he would, the gory wood-carving knife wrapped in his pocket handkerchief.

Arthur unrolled the bloodied knife from its swaddling. It thudded onto the kitchen table with a dramatic spin, slowly coming to a stop with the blade pointing towards Irwell. Sammy squinted at it as if it were some mysterious artefact. 'What's this?'

'It's a murder weapon. We've got three dead bodies on our hands, old son. Two of them killed tonight. Whoever did it is probably still on the premises. There's a madman on the loose. I'm surprised your brother didn't tell you,' said William.

'I only know about the dead vicar, Sammy. Honestly, I do.' Crumbs of cake, and a raisin, fell from the boy's mouth. 'If anyone else's dead, then the mermaid did it. Can you remember me telling you about the bloke who drowned in his bath?'

'Jesus, Vince, mermaids don't roam around the arse end of the Midlands doing murders. They live in the sea and fuck lonely sailors. In stories, our kid. In stories.' Sammy closed his eyes and rubbed his temples. 'I can't believe you lost the necklace in this madhouse. What have you got me into?' He winced and tousled his brother's hair. 'You worry me, you really do. Why can't you be more careful?'

'Your brother's a half-wit,' said William. 'What I want to know is if the two of you make up one full-wit. The jury's still out.'

'Shut your big fuckin' mouth.' Sammy waved Dr Moon's Webley towards William, but listlessly. 'Our Vincent went to the grammar school.'

'If you're searching for something as small as a necklace, you'll be here for a very long time. The house is large and then there's the church, stable block, barns and other outbuildings. You really could be here for weeks.' William caught the doctor's eye and shook his head, but Dr Moon didn't understand William's warning and kept talking. 'Don't you think it's best to cut your losses and leave before dawn?'

'I'm very tired, and I don't want no bother, but I said I'd give the necklace to my Violet, and I aim to do it.' Queenie twitched, and William bit his fist to stop himself from laughing. Gin-happy Violet, smothered in mangy fox fur, clarting about Moss Side or Hulme with twenty grand of rubies and pearls draped around her grubby neck.

'Did you give your brother the necklace when you divvied up the bank job?' asked William. 'But your Violet read in the newspapers how much it was worth, so she sent you down south to fetch it?'

'The divvy had to be fair. Violet's right about that.'

William nodded. 'So, you arranged to pick him up tonight, come hell or high water. Told him to fetch the necklace from where he'd hidden it, probably in the crypt, and wait in his bedroom until you arrive. But when you got there, the daft little bastard didn't have the jewels, just the empty case.'

'It needed to be tonight because Vince telephoned yesterday morning to say there were a couple of detectives sniffing about.' Sammy became wide-eyed as if in receipt of some marvellous revelation. 'That ain't you, is it? Just my fuckin' luck.' He let out a deep, chest-rattling sigh. 'The doctor is right. We can't search a place like this. We can only ask whoever has our property to return it. We'll use our best manners, of course.' He fingered the Webley with a look of weary resignation and turned to his brother. 'Vince, go and wake up the whole house. Everyone. Get them down here, and quick. Someone in this godforsaken hole knows where the jewels are. All we have to do is beat it out of them.'

Mr Irwell slurped his tea to the dregs, hitched the submachine gun over his shoulder, and left the kitchen. A second later, he returned. Eyeing William, he placed the lid back on the cake tin, and put the whole thing under his free arm. 'Can't leave it here with Billy Bunter,' he said. 'Fatty's not to be trusted with a cake.'

'Christ, the kid is really pissing me off now,' said William.

31

The hail came down like a salvo, clattering hard and with heavy regularity against the walls of the house. The doctor turned in his chair towards the direction of the noise. 'The weather has been so strange today. This hail is odd. It's as though the front of the house is bearing the brunt of the storm.' He craned his neck to look out of the kitchen window. 'It's uncanny. When you look outside, it's sleeting. It's almost making me believe in the supernatural. I know there's a rhyme about the weather and Candlemas day, but for the life of me, I can't remember it.'

Dr Moon's voice was a vague hum on the margins of William's consciousness; he was concentrating on that familiar, regular beat. It was the sound from an old nightmare, a hammering, distant bombardment that drummed on his nerves. 'That's not hail. That's machine-gun fire.' He turned to Sammy, and saw his own fear and exhaustion reflected in the man's face. 'Christ almighty, what the fuck is your brother up to?'

He didn't wait for an answer but sprinted out into the corridor. Pitch black without the lamplight, he wasn't sure of the way, and blindly ran towards the hallway with its vast oak door, his heavy feet pounding in time to the continuing splatter of gunfire. Behind him torchlight glimmered, shining a vague spotlight onto the wide floorboards. William turned momentarily to see Dr Moon at his heels, black bag in hand, and behind the doctor, he glimpsed a frantic Queenie.

'Turn left, William,' the doctor called out, and William obliged. 'Now, through the door to your right.'

He was in the entrance hall. William stopped, frozen in fear. The body of the Reverend Andrews lay like a sleeping wino in the open doorway. His makeshift mortuary slab, the refectory table, had somehow disappeared into the night. Sleeting rain dampened the flagstones in dark patches. And, although it was coming from outside, the gunfire seemed unbearably loud. A few stray bullets ricocheted off the stone floor, flew past the fat, black noses of taxidermy bulls' heads, and penetrated the wood panelling with a powerful thud. Sammy barged the motionless William out of the way, but soon retreated to the cover of the corridor. Arthur, at his new boss's tail, and avoiding Queenie's gaze like she, or he, hadn't been born, dropped to his haunches at the whizzing proximity of an erratic bullet.

'The Reverend Andrews cannot lie there. He's becoming riddled with bullets.' Dr Moon touched William's shoulder. 'We must move him, William.'

Another bullet bounced, rang out and shattered the glass case of a taxidermy fish.

'Alright,' William sighed. Morality, decency, often came at a cost. 'We go now. Quickly.'

'Are you fuckin' mad?'

William heard Queenie's question as he and Dr Moon grabbed the dead man's ankles. Within seconds, they were away from the pockmarked door, leaving the parson in a more dignified resting place: underneath the moth-eaten country tweeds and Queenie's city furs, which hung damp and desultory from coat hooks made from the same Black Country brass as Irwell's ordnance.

'I must talk to Irwell.' As Dr Moon spoke, a bullet hit the sole of the Reverend Andrews' shoe. 'I still have a duty of care.'

'He'll kill you.' William ushered Dr Moon and Queenie into the refuge of the corridor, where they became unlikely, and temporary, comrades with Sammy and the cowering Arthur. 'If you go out there, he'll kill you because he wants to, and because he doesn't like you. Then he'll claim to his big brother that it was an accident.'

'I heard that.'

'You were meant to.' William inched towards Sammy. 'How much ammunition did you give him to play with?'

'Three rounds. He'll be out of bullets soon, but there's more on the boat.'

'What boat?' Queenie asked.

'We came along the canal on the *Little Marvel*.'

There was a note of apology in Arthur's blustering reply, and then came a pause in the gunfire. Queenie used it to give the Judas three sharp slaps across his left cheek. 'My home. My boat. You thief.' She said nothing more, and Arthur, still squatting, took his punishment with the passive hatred of the frequently belted.

William nodded to Sammy, who then ran towards the open door. He was intelligent enough not to go outside but hunkered down, back flat against the wall closest to the entrance way. 'Cut it out, Vincent,' he called. 'Stop shooting or you'll kill us all.'

There came no reply, but also no machine-gun fire. Sammy used the lull to dash out onto the driveway. Arthur escaped Queenie, following hard at his new boss's heels, and William took Sammy's place, squatting down by the open door. He took a brief look outside, into the dark.

Irwell stood decorously away from the swimming flood-water on the refectory table, which now served as a makeshift stage. Tommy gun in one hand, and hunk of cake in the other, he looked down on his brother with a frustrated deference. To William, both men seemed ghostly, gesticulating behind a wall of sleeting rain, the outlines of their bodies frayed and fading into the enveloping night. Arthur Stokes was deep in the shadows, maintaining the hovering, diplomatic distance of a hopeful lieutenant.

Suddenly, Sammy pulled at the barrel of the Tommy gun with such force, his brother nearly fell from his perch and into the water he had so fastidiously avoided. Irwell had a boy's grace, however. Rebalancing himself, he shook his head at Sammy's orders and offered him a fierce grin. Then, sodden, muscular and frantic, he called out like some romantic hero, 'Persephone, come down from your tower.' He punctuated his proposal with a short burst of machine-gun fire. 'Speak to Mr Irwell, Persephone.'

But Irwell was no Romeo, and the tower proffered blank indifference to his violent courtship.

'It's famously impenetrable.' Dr Moon, now at William's side, watched the brothers' continued, and increasingly frantic, argument with interest. 'There's only one way into the tower and no exit. All the windows are barred and on the second floor. Cromwell's men couldn't breach it during the Civil War.'

'This is not a folk tale, Dr Moon,' said William. 'Irwell has a submachine gun, and even Sammy knows how to use a ladder.'

'Persephone, come on down.' Irwell showed his displeasure by peppering Red Hollow Hall once more with gunfire. 'Do you want me to climb up and get you? Persephone, can't you hear me?'

In response, the tower remained deathly quiet; neither candlelight nor shadow flickered in its black windows.

However, Irwell was the kind of man who demanded a girl's attention and so brandished his Tommy gun until the bullets stopped flying. Then he shook the gun, as if a decent jolt would get it going again. It didn't. He took a bite of fruitcake and chewed, meditatively, his eyes focused on the tower. Cake finished, Irwell pulled a box of bullets from his pocket and began to reload the magazine, his wet, inexperienced fingers fumbling with the machinery.

This lull was William's chance. He must capture the Tommy gun with enough violent bluster to persuade the brothers he meant business. Arthur, no doubt, would crumble at another cross word from Queenie. His muscles tautened, poised to run and fight, but it had been over a decade since William had disarmed more than one man, and those men had been fellow boys, sleepless, homesick and punchy with war. He shuddered in the breathtaking cold of the night air. It had taken him a minute to reason it through, to decide to take the gamble, but it was a minute too late. Irwell had reloaded the machine gun. This was the difference between being thirty-six and eighteen. You thought instead of acted, and your chances passed. He sat back down on his haunches in a cold sweat, racking his drug-addled brain for a new plan, and knowing Irwell was right about one thing: William wasn't as quick as he once was; he had eaten too much cake.

Despite the reloading, Irwell did not shoot. Sammy clambered onto the refectory table, and grabbing his brother by the shoulders, he pulled him in close, whispering. Sammy stepped back, looked into Irwell's eyes, and then spoke some more. Irwell nodded in response, grinning. Sammy had not taken charge but had agreed to accommodate his brother's requirements, so at least there would be no more gunfire for the time being.

'You in the tower and in the house. Get down here now.' Sammy's voice called out deep, and with purpose, over the patter of the storm. 'There will be no exceptions, your ladyship. Someone has stolen my property, and I aim to retrieve it. Now, it would be silly to make me send my brother up to fetch you. It ain't worth you and your loved ones getting a beating or worse, is it? Just for a few rocks.' Sammy was met with nothing but the sound of rain. 'This ain't the olden times. The Tommy gun will shoot through a wooden door, no problem.' He tapped his brother's shoulder, who, throbbing with a wicked excitement, swivelled and aimed his submachine gun at the ancient door to the tower. 'Those of you in the house. Just come down, for Christ's sake. It'll save my shoe leather, and I'll look kindly on you.'

The tower now stood resolute against Sammy's rhetoric, as it had done against the vulgarity of modern ordnance. It was too old to be shaken by callow threats.

Sammy twitched in response, shrugged, and then beckoned to Arthur. He trotted towards the brothers, ears pricked, and ready to be a good dog. Sammy mouthed instructions. Arthur glanced towards Red Hollow Hall and nodded, but Irwell shook his head, pointing with the barrel of the machine gun at the floodwater. Sammy gave further orders, and with more force, so Irwell, wrinkling his nose, finally jumped down from his perch. Both men sprinted towards the open door.

William leapt to his feet, thinking that shutting the door might buy him time, but he was too late. Within seconds, the cold, heavy screw of Arthur Stokes's pistol dug hard into William's left temple, and he became enveloped in the man's wet embrace, inhaling his cologne-masked stale sweat. 'Don't you move a fuckin' muscle, Billy Garrett. You know I can't stand you.' Arthur's breath was sour with the thick, fruity smell of cheap brandy. 'Fuck me about, and I'll shoot. Then, I'll make Queenie clean your blood and brains up off the floor.'

Irwell sped past and grabbed Queenie by the hair with an unrestrained glee. She thrashed her arms and legs in outrage, screaming in fury and pain as Irwell dragged her, heels scraping along the flagstones, until they reached the front steps. Bump, bump, bump, down she went on her arse, mouth open, stupefied with wrath and humiliation. William's heart broke at the indignity of the spectacle.

'Oh good God, Mr Irwell, leave her alone.' Dr Moon stepped forward, but Arthur shifted William in front of the doctor, shielding Irwell from any move Dr Moon wanted to make.

William struggled into an ungainly dive towards Queenie, but Arthur held him back. 'You treacherous fucker. After all she's done for you and yours.' William took one more desperate lunge. 'Can't you see the little pervert is getting off on this?' Arthur responded by twisting the pistol to William's wadded cheek with enough force to make him yelp in pain.

Queenie kicked herself to her feet, making Irwell loosen his grip, and elbowed him in the solar plexus. Irwell cried out, but the shock of pain only served to increase his violence. Two swift right hooks and Queenie was on the ground. Once more, he had her by the hair. Down, but not out, she raised her pale hands and held her dark curls near the scalp to mitigate the damage of Irwell's fierce hold.

Arthur Stokes shunted him outside. William was sick with shock and shame at the brutal night and his own inadequacies, but nonetheless managed to spit a deep-felt curse Arthur's way. The bigoted bastard had known William's Romani mother, and he was as gullible as he was prejudiced. Halting, for a second, Arthur twitched in fear. 'You hear me, Arthur? In two weeks' time, they'll find you floating down the Grand Union. Belly so bloated they can hardly bear the stink of you at the mortuary.' Arthur cuffed him on the temple with the butt of his pistol in response. William, high on swimming pain, laughed.

Dr Moon followed without the need for duress. He called out to Irwell and Arthur, begging the men to stop. An innocent, futile pacifism in the face of abject greed and cruelty, pleading with them to see sense and choose brotherhood.

Now all surrounded Irwell's makeshift stage. He leapt up like a cat scared of the water, and for a second, a free Queenie looked poised to bolt. However, Irwell was simply a delivery boy, and Queenie, the package, was now in Sammy's arms.

'Come down. Or we'll kill the woman,' Sammy called, his left elbow crooked tight about Queenie's throat, his right hand holding the muzzle of Dr Moon's Webley to her head. 'We'll kill one person every fifteen minutes until you decide to come down. And remember to bring my necklace.'

The church clock chimed the three-quarter hour as an eerie response to Sammy's ultimatum.

Irwell grinned, and shouted, 'Listen! God is keeping time.'

An icy chill soaked through William's jacket, flattened his hair against his forehead, seeped into his shoes once more. He and Queenie were facing the house, downstage from Irwell. William shuddered at the thin-lipped ferocity on Queenie's face; she had declared war, and her enemy was too drunk on guns and muscle to know it.

Suddenly a window opened, but not from the tower, and a white sheet, twisting into a wet bundle in the wind, flopped from Phyll's room. William did not see her face, but heard her clear, calm voice call out. 'I want to come down, but my brother is in a bad way. We don't have your necklace. I don't know who you are. My brother is harmless but ill. He is hiding and very frightened. I can't get him to come down.'

William shifted his neck slightly away from Arthur's tight hold and glanced at Sammy. The man was resolute, not moving an inch despite Queenie's squirming fury. And although he didn't seem the type to kill for fun, because that was his little brother's perversion, William was certain Sammy would commit murder out of necessity. 'Freddy,' William called, his voice muffled by Arthur's choking grip. 'Come down or they'll kill Queenie. Do you hear me, Freddy? You must come down. I promise I'll take care of you. Nothing will happen to you or Phyll. I promise I'll protect you. Please, Freddy. They will kill her.'

William counted a full five seconds before Freddy's answer came as a terrified tremor in the night. 'Do you promise, Billy? Do you promise me everything will be alright?'

William shifted his head towards Irwell. Up on his perch, the man salivated at his brother's violence. Without the necklace, and as a foot soldier in Queenie's future war, it would be a difficult promise for him to keep, and yet William meant what he said. 'Yes, I promise, Freddy. I'll look after you.'

In response, William heard nothing but a fresh barrage of rain, and Arthur Stokes's deep, rattling breaths.

Finally, Phyll called out, 'We're coming down, Billy, and I hope to God you know what you're doing.'

With that, the solid oak door to the tower opened, and out came Lady Sabrina Pike and Persephone. Rubber boots on their feet, oilskin coats draped over tartan wool dressing gowns, the two Pike women padded across the flooded driveway towards the grinning Mr Irwell and his invading force.

32

Ushered into the house by Sammy and his men, the captives, sodden with rain and shivering in shock, drifted into aimless clumps of friendship and allegiance. Phyll, Freddy and Queenie stood behind William; Dr Moon placed himself diplomatically a foot away, but not quite with Lady Pike and Persephone. Arthur Stokes shut and barred the oak door behind them, and the entrance hall became dim with shadow.

Irwell carried Queenie's lamp, and Sammy now had the doctor's electric torch, and they used the scant light to assess the group. The younger brother grinned at them all, blinking and trembling, then sidled over to Persephone, moving in close so he and the girl were hip to hip. She edged towards her mother. He pursued. Lady Pike maintained a haughty silence, but placed a protective arm about her daughter's shoulder. Irwell, uncowed, leant into the girl's ear and uttered, in a hissing whisper, 'I ate all your birthday cake.'

'Where's my fuckin' necklace?' Sammy's voice came as a pompous, tiresome refrain, like an orator at Speakers' Corner. He waited for a reply, but his prisoners only shivered. Sammy twitched, distracted, and moving to the wall, he stared into the doleful eyes of a shield-mounted stag's head. He reached up and rubbed the creature's dun fur between his thumb and forefinger. Now it was Sammy's turn to shudder. 'This is real.'

His voice was astonished, outraged. 'I'm an animal lover, ain't I, Vincent?' He motioned to the mute swan, now free of its glass prison thanks to Irwell's bullets. 'What is wrong with you people? These are noble creatures. They belong to the King.'

'Sammy won't even have dog-fighting on his manor,' said Irwell.

'Won't have it.' Sammy shook his head, sagely moral. 'Cruel. I don't like my Violet to wear furs either, but she does insist.'

William wondered what Sammy would make of the hideous monkey peeping out between the spines of a cactus in Dr Moon's conservatory.

'Sammy is a vegetarian.' Irwell spoke with pride.

'I ain't ashamed of it. It's more healthful. Besides, what kind of monster looks at a baby lamb and thinks about mint sauce? It ain't natural. They're little innocents.' He patted his temple as if to indicate omnivores were all touched in the head, and looked about the room once more, twitching at the crumpled mass of dead clergyman tucked beneath the coat rack. 'I don't like it here, Vincent. It's a house of horrors. Take me somewhere comfy.'

Irwell, lamp aloft, Tommy gun bouncing against his hip, led them through Red Hollow Hall's web of corridors, single file. Sammy, with Arthur hovering at his elbows, brought up the rear. It took William a few seconds before he realised this dark, sorry traipse had finished at the door to the patients' sitting room. There, the prisoners waited in watchful silence.

'Nowhere for me to hide in there, Billy.' Freddy moved from Phyll's side and breathed in William's ear. His drug-induced loquaciousness gone, Freddy spoke in whispered fragments. 'No cover. Quite exposed. Rather frightening.'

'That might be just the thing we need, old pal.' William shuddered at his own, loosely forming plan. 'When we get in there, just keep out of their way, and do exactly as they tell you. Sammy won't be interested in you once you've been searched, I promise.'

'Shut up, conspirators. Two-faced schemers.' Irwell rattled at the doorknob, violently. 'Why is it all locked up?' He spoke to Dr Moon, and it was more of an accusation than a question. 'I've got my good gramophone records in there.'

'I'm sure we'll be much more comfortable in the library, Mr Irwell,' said the doctor. 'There's been an accident, and the conservatory is out of use.'

'I'm not leaving my American jazz in this shithole.' Irwell pleaded with his brother, a wheedling, childish attempt at manipulation. 'Sammy, I've left all my Duke Ellington records in there. Louis Armstrong, Bix Beiderbecke, loads. I brought them all with me.'

'Unlock it for the kid,' said Sammy. 'He'll take his gramophone records with him when he leaves. Vincent is an aficionado.'

'Of what?'

Only Dr Moon heard William, and he shot him a desperate glance.

'I really don't think the sitting room is quite suitable for the ladies,' said the doctor.

'The ladies are the managing kind,' said William.

'Persephone is a child.'

'Unlock it, Dr Moon. I bet Sammy's getting interested about what's in there.' It was a gamble, confronting the brothers with Tom's emasculated corpse, but one William was willing to take.

'I hope for all your sakes it's my fucking necklace.'

Dr Moon, nervous of his audience, took the key chain from his pocket and fumbled with it for what seemed like minutes.

With Sammy's attention elsewhere, William took the opportunity to put his arm about the hunched and shaking Freddy. Giving his friend a quick squeeze, he then looked at Phyll. Poised and alert, she had strength enough for them both. Phyll was stalwart, a classic coper. He felt a sad empathy, but he dared not hug her. Dignified resilience was an exhausting, lonely business, William knew.

'We're in the presence of a terrible evil, and the mermaid is close at hand.' Wide-eyed, Freddy convulsed with cold and sleeplessness. 'She'll be with us soon. Can you smell her?'

'He's been talking this way since the gunfire started – haven't you, darling?' said Phyll.

'Do you think I'm mad?'

'No,' said William. 'I think you've been speaking sense since the first time I met you. Treasure seekers, that's what you said about Brooke. And that's what he was doing, looking for treasure. Just like these bad bastards.'

At last, the sitting-room door opened. William followed Dr Moon and the brothers across the threshold, leading his small troupe – Freddy, Queenie, Phyll and the Pikes – into a roaring darkness. The wind sang, and moist air danced in softly from the black opening to the conservatory. William moved towards the fire, now dwindled to the merest embers, and watched Sammy wave torchlight in a haphazard surveying of the room, but the light didn't linger over the bundle of blankets on the sofa. Irwell placed the oil lamp next to the gramophone and began the business of sorting through his records. William heard Arthur Stokes close the door behind him, and now everyone was together, corralled in one room, for better or worse.

'Christ almighty, I'm freezing my bollocks off.' William heard the shiver in Sammy's voice. 'I've never been so bleeding wet.'

'The door to the glasshouse is open.' Dr Moon was now at William's side. 'It's letting in the night air.'

'Well, close it then,' said Sammy.

The doctor did as he was told.

'I can't see a fuckin' thing, and it ain't getting any warmer.' The glare of Sammy's torch hit William full square on the face. 'You, fancy man, put a shovel of coal on the fire.'

'There should be candles in the corner cupboard,' said Lady Pike. 'We always kept them there in case the generator went.'

'Get them and light them.'

Lady Pike obliged. William crouched before the scant warmth of the embers, lit a spill and passed it to Persephone. Then he built up the fire, and watched the flames lick and spark, as all around him became illuminated. It was a sickly light, but enough to see Sammy, a bulwark of tense muscle, take in the Gothic horror of the room: the startling crack in the plasterwork ceiling; the huge fireplace, with its stone colonnade and mantel sagging ornamentally forward; the wide, undulating floorboards, and the oak wainscoting, blackened, and as old as England. Sammy's captives, William included, seemed to be actors on a ghost-addled stage.

Phyll joined William by the fire, Freddy at her hip, and lit cigarettes for them all. 'I don't even know what they want.' Phyll inhaled, lips fluttering, the smudges of grey beneath her wide blue eyes pronounced. 'Do they? They seem violent, but rather stupid.'

'The necklace we read about, Phyll.' William spat the words quickly and low. 'The necklace stolen from that bank in Stoke. It was hidden here. Irwell murdered the bank clerk. Queenie hid Irwell here as a favour to his brother, and it all got fucked up. She ain't happy, and won't be, until she gets her pretty little hands on twenty grand's worth of rubies and pearls.'

'I blame her for bringing them here.' Phyll's voice held a hard dignity. 'Do let her know that, Billy. She's no friend to Freddy and me.'

'Well, she blames Sammy, and she holds grudges hard.'

Phyll gave him a slow nod of understanding. 'Will Queenie kill them all?'

'Eventually.' William glanced Queenie's way. She stood in a far corner, waiting in the wings. Soon, she'd be the star turn. 'Every single one of them.'

'And you have a plan?'

'Yes.' William's scattered thoughts weren't much of a plan, he knew, but often all it took was being alert to the main chance and acting on it. He nodded towards the pile of blankets on the sofa. 'I'm waiting for Sammy to look under there. It's enough to scare any man to death. Once he sees it, then we make a move. It won't be long.'

Red Hollow was a magical place, and so the words spoken out loud became manifest. Sammy moved towards the sofa and made to shift the heavy covering of blankets.

Dr Moon leapt forward, grabbing Sammy by the arm. 'No, don't remove them.'

Sammy didn't listen but shrugged the doctor off. 'I want to rest my feet,' he said, and uncovered Tom's corpse with a flourish. For a second, the man was quite still, until Lady Pike let out a deep, pained groan. Sammy, startled into action, replaced Tom's shrouds with the blushing, panicked care of someone covering a naked, vulnerable grandparent. Then he bent double and wretched, gagging to the point of tears.

Irwell looked up from a small pile of gramophone records as if irritated by a minor commotion. 'What's the fuss?'

'Jazz records, you daft twat? Is that what you brought me in here for? Christ almighty, Vince. The bloke's been cut up. All in his privates.' Sammy pointed to Tom's corpse but spoke directly to Queenie. 'What kind of place did you dump my brother?'

Queenie took her cue and moved centre stage. Lifting the blankets, she peeked at the body, stepped back and crossed herself. William smiled at the pointlessness of the action. If there was a God, he'd been on a fag break for years. Prayers over, Queenie looked Sammy in the eye, and said, 'That's the handiwork of a monster, ain't it?'

'Is that Tom Sherbourne?' asked Phyll.

'What's left of him, yes,' said William.

Lady Pike, now seated and silent, sat upright in an armchair and crossed her slender ankles, composure regained. Her face hardened, aged now, she was not ready to cry but to fight. Here was an ally, however temporary, icy and clever. Persephone placed her hand on her mother's shoulder in solidarity, her pale, intelligent face solemn and candlelit, like the portraits of her wigged and powdered ancestors.

'The sooner we get the fuck out of here, the better. Search them all.' Sammy looked at Freddy, as if for the first time. Shuddering and smoking, hunched like a man already beaten, he was the perfect scapegoat for Sammy's anger. 'Find my necklace. Start with that crazy bastard by the fireplace.'

Irwell took the responsibility with glee. Freddy acted with the perfect acquiescence of one too used to humiliation and violence. He stood at Irwell's barked orders, cigarette trembling in his puckered mouth, dead eyes fixed on some imagined horizon. William and Dr Moon moved closer, both ready to catch Freddy should he fall. But Freddy wasn't a fainter; he was a bolter. He'd run, probably to the church, and be mowed down by machine-gun fire like the boys he went to school with. There, he'd die in the mud, but twenty years too late. Old wounds.

'Raise your hands higher, crazy Freddy,' spat Irwell.

Freddy, swaying, was too far away to respond, so Irwell slapped him back into the room: two wicked back-handers and done with contempt. Freddy's only response was to tilt back on his heels.

'Leave him alone. Can't you see he hasn't got it?' Phyll ran towards Irwell full pelt, arms windmilling in fury, letting her blows land indiscriminately. However, she was no match for Irwell's practised muscle, and with one exultant arm, he pushed her into the fireplace. William caught her before she hit the flames.

Freddy turned, staring at them as though they were behind glass, and said, 'The wave is black.' Irwell frowned at Freddy's talk, but continued his frisk, patting down his jacket pockets. 'Huge and frightful, it engulfs me with such terrifying speed, I hardly know it's coming until it's arrived. All is cold and black under the wave. It is a place fit only for woe.' Irwell found Freddy's mermaid, as William knew he would, and held the carved roundel flat in the palm of his hand, squinting at her gilded tresses. Freddy groaned, pitifully.

'What do you have there?' Sammy leapt towards his brother in one leggy stride. 'Is it my Violet's necklace?'

'No.' Irwell grinned, and looking Freddy in the eye, gathered phlegm at the back of his throat. 'It's a horrible old piece of firewood.' Then he spat. Mucus landed green and brown on her Marian blue scales. Every inch the sadist, Irwell threw the sullied carving onto the fire and grinned. Sparks licked about the mermaid's bare torso. Gilding flaked and lifted into soot and fell. Freddy cried out, lunging towards the flames, but William held him back.

'Please, Freddy, endure it,' William whispered, holding his friend tight, as if squeezing both the will to live and sanity into the man. 'Irwell has taken mescaline. It was in the cake. He'll see the mermaid soon. Then, it will all be over. Please, Freddy, stay with me.'

It took no more than a few seconds in William's arms for Freddy to become calm, his breathing deepen and steady. William released his grip, and Freddy stood upright. The man straightened to his full height and smiled at Phyll. 'I love you,' he said. 'You are the finest person I know.' Freddy reached out to caress his sister's cheek. She took his hand and kissed the slender fingers. Then Freddy turned his back on Phyll and faced Irwell. 'You are a woman-hating little pervert.' His voice was quiet and measured. 'You are a shameful disgrace to manhood. May the women in this room call upon the mermaid. May she come, teeth sharpened to needles, and drag you down to the stinking depths. May you, Mr Irwell, be the mermaid's eternal bridegroom.'

Irwell convulsed. His face became a grotesque gargoyle as he reached for the nearest candlestick. Still lit, the candle fell, splattering wax as Irwell swung it with a psychopathic confidence at Freddy's skull. Freddy wavered, took three staggering steps away from Phyll, eyes rolling to the back of his head, until his legs buckled, and he dropped to the floor, cracking his temple with a terrifying thud on the cast iron fire dog. William went to him, cradled his limp body, and Phyll let out the pained, primal howl of a grieving woman. She didn't move, not attempting to come to her brother, but emitted a great, raging moan.

'I need to see him.' Dr Moon shifted William out of the way.

'It's too late.' William felt Freddy's death deep in his bones. 'Oh Jesus Christ, I couldn't keep my promise.'

'You're not a doctor, William.' Dr Moon unclasped his bag and began to rummage. 'Keep back and let me work.'

William crawled to Phyll, but Queenie held him back, shaking her dark, solemn head. Still on her knees, Phyll howled with rage in the centre of the room. Queenie knelt before her, clasped Phyll's hands in hers, and swayed to the music of her friend's cries. Phyll did not reject her, but accepted Queenie's scant, strange love, her act of solidarity. Lady Sabrina Pike rose from her chair and joined them, wiping away Phyll's tears with a white handkerchief. Persephone came too, and, kneeling, she moved the sodden hair away from Phyll's forehead with perfect care.

'Shut Burlington Bertie up, why don't you?' said Irwell.

'Try it, you fucker,' said Queenie.

'Freddy has a chance if we can get him to hospital.' Dr Moon's once rugged face was now drawn. A deep grey had appeared in the ridges between his nose and mouth. 'And I mean immediately.'

'No hospital. If the nutter dies, he dies.' Sammy made his declaration like a king.

There came a meaningful silence as Phyll rose to face Irwell. She motioned to the women in one vast sweeping gesture, and they too stood, surrounding Irwell so that he was at the centre of a claustrophobic, feminine circle. 'That was an ancient carving of the mermaid my brother was protecting,' she said. 'And you've just destroyed it with fire. Anathema to a creature of the water. The mermaid won't like that, will she?' Phyll's blue eyes were bluer with wrath and tears. 'Yes, you're in terrible trouble, Irwell. But I don't pity you. I pray for your destruction.'

'Is Mr Irwell a pervert, Mummy?' Persephone's voice was clear and steady.

'He is just as Mr Hall said, a woman-hating little pervert, and more than likely, a murderer.'

'Mr Irwell raped and murdered a bank clerk.' Queenie clicked her tongue and shook her head in sorrow. 'He did it for fun and Sammy let him. Sammy spoils his little brother. Gives him bank clerks to play with. Lets him be alone with young girls and turns a blind eye. They're both bad men.'

'And the other man?' Persephone pointed to Arthur Stokes, who attempted, but failed, to melt into the shadows of the room.

'He's nothing but a stinking traitor,' said Queenie. 'A pathetic liar.'

Freddy and the women knew the plan. The mermaid would save them all.

33

'You're dead right about Arthur, love. He ain't got no backbone.' Sammy reached out and grabbed Irwell by his sleeve. The boy turned, and gazed at his brother, a little slack-jawed and vacant, but stood, once more at Sammy's side, safe away from the women. 'God knows, the National and Provincial job had its ups and downs, but I'm a reasonable man. I only hurt people if they ain't behaving decent to me.' He waved an arm towards the near-lifeless Freddy. 'He weren't a bad fellow, I know. And I'm cross that our Vince hit him so hard, but he said some hurtful things, and deserved a bit of a slap. All I want is my necklace. Then, me and Vince will go.' He squinted at the doctor's black bag; the paper-wrapped dressings; the bottle of iodine; the syringe full of morphine. 'Then someone can try and get him to hospital. If the roads are passable, that is.'

'At least let me move Freddy to a bedroom.' Dr Moon stood and began a vigorous, absent-minded, massage of his bad leg. 'He needs warmth, quiet and cleanliness, at the very least. William and I will carry him upstairs.' Limping towards the brothers, the doctor faced them with dignity. 'Phyll can nurse him. Once Freddy is settled, I'll return to this room. You have my word. We must do all we can, right now, to save the poor fellow.'

'You can do what you want with him, once I have what I came for.' Sammy assessed his audience, grinning like some fickle king taken with sudden beneficence. The great hunk of gold in his gob glimmered in the candlelight, until his hard, assessing eyes became exhausted with disappointment, and all smiles stopped. 'Search them.' He nodded towards the women. Irwell stepped away from his brother's side, grinning with pleasure, but Sammy pulled him back. 'Keep your hands off them, Vincent. Arthur will do it.'

Arthur Stokes obeyed, frisking first Phyll, Lady Pike, and then Persephone with the efficient distaste of a copper searching a gin-soaked shoplifter at the end of his shift. When he'd finished, a sudden gust of wind rushed down the chimney and coughed into the room like a smoky ghost. The candles flickered in the resulting breeze. 'They're all clean,' he said. 'Nothing on them.'

'Where is my necklace?'

'Oh God, stop saying that. You're repeating yourself, and it's getting tedious. For a gangster, you're a terribly boring man. We don't know where the bloody thing is, and what's more, we don't care. Why don't you just fuck off? Fuck off back to the north and leave us all in peace.' Phyll uttered the words with such honest exasperation, William wondered if she knew she had spoken out loud.

'That was very rude of you, Burlington Bertie.' Sammy's voice held a note of self-righteous indignation. 'I've been courteous. That was a lack of respect, that's what that was. What's wrong with you people?' Sammy clenched his fists, near fizzing with fury. 'Alright, Vince, take the kiddie. Do whatever takes your fancy.' It was like letting a greyhound out of the starting gates. Irwell, lithe and fast, grabbed Persephone by the waist before William had time to think. The child's eyes, once more, bulged, rabbit-like, in fear. 'She's my brother's property now. He will take her somewhere private until someone coughs up, do you understand me?'

Irwell twitched, and kissed Persephone's ear, sniffing her hair. 'Welcome to womanhood.' He did not carry the child, but manoeuvred her body, holding her by the neck like a rugby ball with his left arm, right hand proudly hovering over the trigger of his Tommy gun, and marched towards the door. Persephone managed a dragging shuffle behind him.

'The mermaid has your necklace.' Lady Pike's voice was icily polite, as if she were presiding over a difficult meeting of the parish council. She spoke, not to Irwell, but directly to Sammy. 'Mr Brooke had been searching for it since your brother let slip that he'd hidden it somewhere in the house or grounds. Eventually, he found the pearls in the church and gave them to me. I handed them to the mermaid. I can summon her, as can Persephone now she is of age. The mermaid keeps the pearls and rubies. They are hers, now.'

'Oh, I see. Yes, of course,' said Phyll, sagely. 'She must swim in the crypt when it floods. That's where Freddy saw her, and that's where Brooke was doing his magic ritual. Churches are such ancient places; one never knows what haunts them.'

'Stop fucking me about.' Sammy looked around the room for an ally in his disbelief, but Irwell had turned towards Lady Pike in rapt, fearful attention, and Arthur had hidden himself in the room's many shadows. 'Lie to me again, and he takes her to the nearest bedroom.'

'I'm telling you the secret of Red Hollow,' said Lady Pike. 'There never was a murdered girl. The folk tale is for the peasantry, a woman's story for a winter's fire, you understand. The mermaid is an ancient goddess.' She smiled tenderly towards the prone Freddy. 'Dear Mr Hall knew this. An intelligent, sensitive man, responsive to this place. If you do not like the word *goddess*, then think of her as a revenant, as old as time and with great power. The mermaid is a good, nurturing creature. She has guided and protected Pike women for generations, but she is old. Ancient, female creatures do not flinch from meting out punishment; they're too tired of the ways of men to hear the pathetic excuses of the rapist and bully.' Lady Pike's cold, sedgy eyes were fixed on Sammy, but her words were meant for Irwell. 'If your brother hurts a hair on my child's head, I will call her, and she will come. She will take you down to the depths, and your mother will have nothing of you to bury.' She clicked her fingers. 'Gone. Disappeared. It is not my business what she does with men like you. It has been some time, hundreds of years, since she went to war, but I will ask her to polish her scales.' Sabrina Pike took a deep breath, and the storm rattled the windowpanes as if about to break in. Then she swayed, head tilted back, her eyes swimming with power and hatred, like some Pre-Raphaelite Circe. 'It's too late. She's in the rain. She's coming. Persephone has summoned her.'

All this time, Irwell's and Sammy's eyes were transfixed on Lady Pike, but William was watching Irwell, waiting for his moment. It soon came. Beyond the sitting room, a volley of rain landed on the remains of the glasshouse like buckshot. Irwell jumped in fright, loosening his grip on Persephone. William flung himself on the length of the barrel of the Tommy gun, forcing Irwell to the floor, sliding with him towards the glasshouse. Persephone ran to her mother, and William turned his head to see the women surround the child within a shield of feminine flesh. On top of Irwell now, William buried the kid under all his weight – too much cake, you little fucker. His face on Irwell's squirming chest, William's right arm forced the boy's chin upwards as his left hand reached for the gun which was still tight in Irwell's grip. Then William shimmied across Irwell, and behaved like the mermaid, biting the boy's fingers until he yelped and released the submachine gun.

William knew Sammy had hammered him with a flying kick when he heard the man land heavily on the floorboards beside him. He rolled off Irwell's body and lay on his side for a moment, breath held, and in exquisite, mind-bending pain. Blood trickled warm down his damaged face and pooled in the hollow of his ear. William closed his eyes at the sound of the revolver's readying click, and thought of his son; the legacy of violence and pain he would inherit. 'Forgive me,' he muttered.

'If you murder Billy, you must murder us all.' Phyll's voice rang out clear. 'We're all witnesses. The police don't like mass murder in country houses, and they surely have your fingerprints on file. Killing Billy won't get you your necklace, and really, I think you like life too much to risk the gallows.'

The sweet release William expected didn't come. Phyll, a good partner, instinctive and clever, had called a Mexican stand-off. William shook with dizzying nausea as he shuffled on his arse towards the conservatory door. He closed his eyes and rested his hot head against the cold wood. If William ever got to be a cowboy, he'd wear a white hat, like Tom Mix. Behind him, Dr Moon's cacti suffered the relentless weather of an English February, and the monkey, bedraggled, despite all his magic, wished he'd never been born. If Dr Moon was right, the kid had eaten a whole birthday cake full of mescaline. But the young were resilient, not like William. His senses were dulled, reflexes buggered through age, and beer, and neurosis. William closed his eyes, drifting into a dream of warm desert breezes, and pink-flowering peyote growing beneath red sandstone cliffs. Thanks to Phyll, William's plan was working. Nearly. He slapped his good cheek. Stay sharp, Billy. Wait for the inevitable and stay sharp. He prayed that the mermaid would come soon because he couldn't fight anymore. William knew it in his bones. 'I'm a lover, not a fighter,' he said, expecting Tom's ghost. But, this time, it didn't appear.

34

'Sammy, you're in such deep shit. You must know that.' William touched his cheek, tenderly. The stitches had popped, and blood poured. He would be scarred for life, but what was fucking new. William patted his pocket out of instinct, or hope, but knew he'd run out of cigarettes. 'Christ, I need a fag.'

'You need a lot more than a cigarette.' Dr Moon knelt before him. Once more the black bag clicked open with an ominous sound. Numb with grief, William glanced towards Freddy, who, like Tom, lay still under a woollen covering. 'I'll stitch you again. It won't be such a neat job this time. Good God, I've done more actual doctoring tonight than I have done in all the years since the war. Let me give you something for the pain.' He peeked under the dangling dressing and then brandished a syringe like a surgeon in a film.

'Let me feel it, Henry. Sometimes you just gotta feel it.'

'You're a masochist. Whatever you're punishing yourself for, stop it. It does you no good.' The doctor left him for a second and came back with a lit cigarette. William took a deep, steadying drag on his fag. The tobacco hit his lungs, and the morphine hit the spot, and William became pleasantly giddy while Dr Moon once more threaded his needle.

'What did you mean by me being in the shit?' Sammy trudged towards them; loomed over Dr Moon, throwing William into shadow, and blocking the doctor's scant, precious light. 'It looks to me like the other way around.'

'Take another look at that poor bastard and tell me you're not in the shit.' William leant forward and pointed with his fag towards Tom's blanket-covered body. 'And the bloke who killed the vicar has copped it, too. He's up in the attic, swinging from a rafter. Christ, three dead bodies, Sammy, and your brother's dabs are all over the house. Like I said, it puts you and yours right in the shit, pal.'

'Prints wipe clean, and I'm a thorough housewife.' Sammy shrugged, and then winced as the needle penetrated William's cheek. 'Besides, this is a madhouse, ain't it? Any one of you could've gone on the rampage. Probably that half-dead loony by the fireplace.'

'You're not that stupid, Sammy lad. There's only one lunatic in this asylum, and it ain't poor Freddy.'

'The mermaid got Tom.' Irwell may have been mad, but his hearing was sharp. 'Just look at the state of him. That's her doing.'

'Mr Sherbourne was a dear friend,' said Lady Pike. 'The mermaid would never hurt my friends.'

'Shut your stupid face, bitch. Who rattled the posh bitch's cage? Not me.' The storm was impossibly loud, and had the enveloping, heavy drone of static on a poorly tuned wireless. Irwell tapped the side of his head, as if clearing the noise, and raised his voice. '*I suffer not a woman to usurp authority over the man, but to be in silence.* God said that. Know your place.'

'This is my place, Mr Irwell. You are the interloper, and your hysterics are becoming tiresome.' When Lady Pike spoke, the storm quietened, out of respect. 'Who is the other dead man, Mr Garrett?'

'Mr Brooke.'

'Well, the mermaid would never have taken him,' said Lady Pike.

'Another one of your lovers. Whore.' Irwell spat the words like a firebrand preacher. Swaying with righteousness, his eyes rolled to the back of his head. 'Necromancer, whore, I turn my face against you.'

And, quite madly, Mr Irwell did.

'Brooke was her loyal servant.' Queenie, deadly quiet until now, was pointed with her words and glanced at Arthur, who shrank into the shadows by the door to the corridor. 'A good dog.'

'Brooke was her brother,' said William. 'The family portraits along the staircase tell a story. Pike women may have a touch of the Anglo-Saxon warrior princess about them, but the men are pure Norman conquest, short, dark, good-looking, very French.'

'Mr Garrett is quite correct. After my father met Mr Crowley at some vulgar jamboree, he became quite giddy with the maids. Doing as he wanted all over the place. *Do as thou wilt.* What does it even mean? The poor things simply weren't safe in their beds.' Lady Pike brushed her faded, blonde hair away from her face and gave the nonplussed Sammy a challenging look. 'Mr Brooke, I'm afraid, was a failed abortion. Father married the girl off to his valet; a confirmed bachelor and devoted to Father. Wicked degeneracy does somewhat complicate the family tree, and poor Brooke had an abiding passion for the manor. Despite his obvious bastardy, he saw it as his rightful inheritance. The male child, you see. A weak man, and with only a modicum of the Pike depravity, he offered me the necklace by way of payment into the legitimate stream of the family. But all Pike men, even the bastards, die young.' Lady Pike sat in her armchair and beckoned Persephone to her side, and her thin, pale hand appeared almost skeletal as she placed it on her daughter's red-gold hair. William was suddenly reminded of the Hand of Glory. 'The necklace, once broken, reset and sold as smaller pieces, will pay for the restoration of Red Hollow. Keeping the mine owners and land-grabbers away takes money, and not ritual magic. I really should pay Percy's school fees, so that she may return to St Bridget's next term. Think of the jewels as your contribution to history, and to the education of a bright young woman, and as reparation for the damage you have done these past few months.'

'Are you trying to wind me up?' Sammy was stymied with the weight of Lady Pike's icy authority. 'This ain't right. Why do you reckon you can take what ain't yours?'

'And why do you?' asked Lady Pike.

William wondered how it developed, that self-confidence. The woman had all the *noblesse* but limited *oblige*. Brazen in her greed, she had no intention of returning the necklace to the rightful owner or allowing the bank clerk's family to see justice. What was it that Queenie said about the English landed gentry? Lady Pike had gangsterism bred into her. Sammy had, quite literally, been outclassed.

'Do you think I'm going to let you have it?' He stood before the seated Lady Pike like a tenant farmer pleading against increased rents. 'Are you the only one who knows where the necklace is?' Her reply was a thin-lipped smile. 'Then I'll beat it out of you. Dead bodies don't scare me. I've seen enough of them. I don't believe in no mermaids, either.

This is the real world, where only money and power counts, and in this situation, I got power enough to claim the money. Her ladyship's hand ain't as good as she thinks.'

'Beat Lady Pike, and when you leave, we tell the police everything. Including all the terrible things Vincent did,' said Phyll.

'What did Vincent do? Prove it.'

'He murdered and emasculated Tom Sherbourne.' William pointed towards the sofa. 'This time, take a careful look.'

Sammy moved to Tom Sherbourne's body and pulled back the blankets, shining Dr Moon's electric torch along the length of the corpse. Lady Pike averted her eyes, decorously; Persephone gazed at her rubber boots; Phyll kept her vigil near Freddy, all her exhausted concentration focused on her brother; Queenie crossed herself once more, and then whistled through her teeth.

'Oh God, Vincent.' Sammy replaced the covers over Tom, and grimaced, blanching in disgust. 'That ain't a normal murder, pal.'

'Your brother is a liability, Sammy,' said William. 'He hit Tom over the head with a hammer and emasculated him with a knife from Freddy's toolbox.'

'Not a hammer, but some nice lead piping, fat man. Found it in the stable block. Bam! Got Tom first with the element of surprise. Out but not dead.' Irwell mimicked a swinging lob. 'Brooke was scared silly, and fought a bit, so I had to use my hands.' He held his splayed palms before him, as if gripping an invisible vase. 'I was waiting in my bedroom for Sammy, just like he asked, walking off the filthy Veronal Dr Moon gave me. But I saw Brooke coming out of the church with my jewellery case, and I knew I had to get the thieving bastard.

You can't let that kind of behaviour pass, can you? He came creeping about the house like he owned the place, and I followed him, but so did Tom. When I got to the attic, they were arguing about Percy. Tom was calling him a pervert and an idiot, and Brooke said Tom was a common fool. They were so busy with each other, they didn't know I was there until I struck. Bam! In time to the chiming of the church clock.' Irwell paused as if expecting applause.

'And afterwards, you went back to bed.' William attempted to fathom the strange mentality behind such an action. 'All nice and comfy.'

'It's a cold night.' Irwell waved his arm towards the window and the sleeting storm. 'Besides, Sammy told me to wait in my room until he arrived. I always obey Sammy's orders.'

'And the hammer?'

'Lead piping. I told you.' Irwell sighed in irritation. 'I threw it in the flood. No fingerprints, fat man.'

'But they're all over the knife you used to emasculate Tom,' said William.

'I didn't do that.' Irwell shook his head. 'I'm not interested in cock. The mermaid is the cock-happy whore. I'm not one of those types. Filthy types hanging around the public lavatories. No, I'm not interested in cock, not at all.'

'You're protesting too much, Vincent,' said William. 'Telling Sammy all your shameful secrets.'

Irwell glanced at his brother, and twitched with misery. 'I'm not feeling very well, Sammy. I've been feeling sick since I knew the jewellery case was empty. Sick to my stomach for having let you down.' The leather strap of the Tommy gun irritated Irwell's neck; he shifted it about and scratched at an angry red welt. 'I've got a horrible headache, and I'm all upset. That big Brummie bastard has been picking on me ever since he came here. He's been bullying me, Sammy. Will you belt him for me?'

'We have a witness to the murders,' William lied, indicating poor, prone and broken Freddy. 'He told me and Dr Moon all about it. He was hiding in the wardrobe when your brother stunned and sexually mutilated Tom. Vincent did it when Tom was still alive, Sammy. But I reckon he'd done similar stuff to women. Practice makes perfect when you're an evil, mad fucker.'

'Cut up a man's privates when he was still alive?' Sammy's face, a picture of exhausted frustration since he'd arrived at Red Hollow, suddenly became flooded with concern. 'Jesus, Vince. That ain't usual.' He shook his head, hangdog. 'There's something wrong with you, our kid. It's my fault, I suppose. Queenie's right. I spoil you.'

'Sammy, this is the deal.' William saw his chance. 'You leave. We will tell the coppers that Brooke murdered the vicar and Tom in a fit of madness and then committed suicide. You don't get the necklace, but your brother avoids the noose.' Outside, behind William, the storm raged against the ravaged glasshouse, as if in its final throes. 'What option do you have? What option do any of us have? Compromise is good business, Sammy. Cut your losses and fuck off back to Manchester. You should never have come to Red Hollow. The countryside ain't for the likes of you.'

'I didn't do it, Sam.' Irwell rubbed once more at his neck and shifted the Tommy gun from across his body, so that it hung loosely on one shoulder. 'The mermaid killed Tom. She comes and gets men. She killed a man at Christmas. Can't you remember me telling you?'

Outside, the storm moved in muffled waves. Its rhythmic ebb and flow would have been a comfort to some, no doubt, but not to Mr Irwell whose sweat-pricked skin seemed sickly sallow in the scant candlelight.

'She's coming for you, Mr Irwell.' Phyll cupped her hand to her ear, like a child listening for the sea in a shell. 'Can't you hear her tail knock against the windowpanes? If Billy moves away from that door, she'll be in here.'

Irwell's bottom lip trembled. 'Don't move away from the door, Mr Garrett. I'm sorry I called you fat.'

'For fuck's sake, Vincent.'

'You don't understand, Sammy. I did bad things to the bank clerk and other girls. Hurtful things, like Mr Garrett says. I couldn't help it, but I did stuff that made them cry. If the mermaid comes in here, I'm for it.'

William rose judderingly to his feet, head swimming with morphine and grief, the slow panic of shell-shock creeping along his jaw. Using the remains of his scant energy, he flung open the glasshouse door.

The candlelight quivered, and the sitting room became swamped in a watery green light. A fierce, near-horizontal sleet surged into the room. Spots of icy rain hit Irwell's cheek; the boy batted away the drops with strange, frantic arm movements as if beset by some biblical storm of flies.

'There. It's done,' said Persephone. 'She's here.'

Irwell shot Persephone a pained look, but then turned towards the open door, staring into the green shifting light as if compelled. His mouth gaped, and he turned half-away, as if too terrified to face what he saw. Then he let out a harrowing falsetto whimper. Sammy ran to his brother, shook his shoulder violently so the Tommy gun fell, spun on the floorboards and landed at Phyll's feet. She pointed it directly at Irwell, but he did not care; what he saw scared him more than any gun. He twitched violently, and, raising his hand to his ears, he fell to his knees, rocking, and sobbing. 'I cannot bear to hear her sing. She's beckoning to me. She has the pearls, Sammy, and she's bleeding from her ears. The mermaid carries all their wounds, absorbs them into her soft fishy body. All the bruises and the beatings and the hands around their pretty necks. She feels all their pain, and then she bites. Oh God. Oh Jesus Christ.' Then Mr Irwell burst out singing. Hands still covering his ears, tears streaming down his cheeks, the hymn surged from his lungs in the cracking, high tenor of a choirboy well past his prime. '*Rock of ages, cleft for me, let me hide myself in Thee. Let the water and the blood, from Thy wounded side which flowed, be of sin the double cure: save from wrath and make me pure.*' The last notes of the hymn were nothing but a desperate gulping sob. 'She won't leave me alone, and it's the only watery hymn I know. Why won't she fuckin' forgive me? Creature without mercy.'

Dr Moon moved to Irwell's side and placed his hand on the boy's shoulder. 'Mr Irwell, the mermaid isn't here. She belongs to the twilight world of the mind.' The doctor, fascinated but squeamish, regarded Irwell as if he were a specimen under glass, perhaps a mutated tubercular bacterium, or a Spanish Flu virus. Nonetheless, when he spoke, he managed to convey a dispassionate professionalism. 'Come now. I can help you sleep. In the morning, we can find you the care you need.'

Sammy leapt forward and removed Dr Moon's hand from his brother's shuddering shoulder. 'Oh no, you bloody well don't. Vincent don't need your kind of help. Do you, Vince?'

'Go now.' William moved away from the door so that he was face to face with Sammy. 'He'll only get worse if he stays here. Fling the mad bastard over your shoulder and catch up with Arthur Stokes. He fucked off as soon as your brother started with all that *Rock of Ages* shit. Go now. Go.'

Sammy grabbed his brother by the sleeve. 'Come on, our kid, we're off.' Irwell didn't budge, but muttered a muddled, fearful Hail Mary. Sammy looked up from his brother, the tears forming. 'You bunch of bad bastards. Look what you've done to our Vincent. It'll take me ages to get him right.' He bent again, and lifting from his knees, scooped Irwell up onto his shoulder, as a shepherd does a sheep. Sammy made heavily towards the exit, his brother motionless and silent, but with his hands on his ears. However, the man turned and faced them once more, needing the stupid last word. 'I don't know how I'm going to explain all this to my Violet. She told me not to come back unless I had that necklace.'

'If she loves you, pal, she'll understand,' said William.

Phyll, tucking Dr Moon's army greatcoat around Freddy's morphine-stilled body with one hand, and holding the Tommy gun in her right, began to laugh. Great, shoulder-shuddering laughs which soon became heaving sobs. Then she fell fully to the floor, as soft and silent as a dropped hand-kerchief, and letting go of the Tommy gun, she folded her hands beneath her chest, and rocked as if in unbearable pain.

Sammy blinked at them both, uncomprehending, and left the room.

William was unsure how long it took Phyll to cry herself out, but when she did, the storm stopped. The resulting calm seemed eerie, sentient, sensitive to the prevailing sense of grief and pain. So Queenie's voice, as she spoke, became a terrible intrusion, as though she'd sworn during Mass. 'Where did you hide the pearls, Lady Pike?'

'I don't know what you're talking about, Miss Maggs. We've had a rather tragic series of murders at the hall. Mr Brooke was a madman, a deranged psychopath, and he killed the Reverend Andrews and one of Dr Moon's patients in a most brutal manner.' Her eyes were like an English river, dark grey, freezing cold. 'There will be a scandal, but one we can easily withstand. Now.'

'You ain't gonna share. We deserve fair dibs.' Queenie sidled over, and hovered a little too close to her betters. She was no observer of the proprieties of class. 'We endured this shitty night as comrades, pals.'

'There is nothing to share.'

Queenie twitched in anger. 'Fuck me.'

Lady Pike rose from her armchair, glanced at her reflection in the mirror-like window, and adjusting those yellow locks into perfection, said, 'I'd rather not, Miss Maggs.'

Queenie was a bad bastard; Sammy was right about that, but she'd met her equal in Lady Pike. William shuffled over to Phyll and Freddy, looked down at his friend's pale face, half-covered with Dr Moon's bandage, and listened to the unsteady, knocking breaths. Phyll grabbed William's hand and giggled in mad, sad relief that the worst of the night was over.

'Billy knows where you've hidden them. He'll tell me,' said Queenie. 'He's a good dog.'

William closed his eyes. The mermaid – ferocious, fanged, and the shining brown of a fresh conker – rested in a choir stall behind St Peter. When she saw William, she came away from her wooden home and swam towards him. Her tail all muscle, habituated to the water, she was triumphant in her powerful amniotic beauty. The mermaid assessed William for a second, and displayed her pouting lips. Pearls, perfect and precious, shone like teeth, and rubies glimmered bloody in her orifice. William opened his eyes and looked at Queenie. 'I haven't got a fucking clue where those bastard pearls are.' William was a bad dog. 'I'm off to get help. You and Lady Pike can fight it out between yourselves.'

Then he kissed Phyll on the head, squeezed her shoulder, prayed that she and Freddy would hold fast, and left the sitting room with Dr Moon at his heels.

35

William sat on a hard, straight-backed visitors' chair in the hallway. Above him, the taxidermy badger peered down at William in disgust.

'How much do I owe you?' Dr Moon packed away his medical bag; William's cheek had needed another stitch and a fresh dressing.

'Me, nothing. Phyll, a shit ton,' said William.

'Are you sure you won't wait until dawn?'

'No. If I go now, Freddy has a chance, at least.'

'It won't get light until gone seven o'clock,' said Dr Moon. 'Freddy probably won't make it, you know that.'

'*Some are born to endless night.*' William was maudlin, cold, quoting poetry, and about to steal the dead squire's mackintosh. 'If he has a one per cent chance, I'll take it. I've lost too many friends.'

'I'm concerned about you walking through the flood in the dark. Tricky for a local, let alone a stranger with a fear of water. Wait till the sun comes, old fellow. We'll make Freddy comfortable. It's all we can do for him now.'

William glanced at the unflinching dolour of the hallway. The mute swan, her snow-white feathers perfect in death, eyed him beadily; the bulls' heads gazed as solemn as judges from their chipped wooden plaques; the cased trout stared unblinking and critical. All the dead creatures hated him. 'I'd rather risk the flood.'

'I'm looking around for a monkey,' said Dr Moon.

'I'm pretty sure I killed him tonight, so let us be grateful for small mercies. Will Phyll be alright, do you think?'

'No,' said Dr Moon. 'I'm too exhausted to even bother to lie to you. In my professional experience, I believe if Freddy dies, Phyll will be permanently scarred by the night's events.'

'Perhaps she'll learn to gild the cracks.'

'One can only hope. And at least she has good friends.'

'Was it the mescaline, do you think?' asked William. 'And for God's sake don't tell me it's moot.'

'William, he didn't join us for tea and sympathy tonight.' Dr Moon rummaged about the base of the coat stand and found a pair of rubber boots. 'Your size?' William shrugged. 'All that strange ferocity and arrogance was pure Irwell. He killed both men, and emasculated Tom when quite sober. He has a rather unusual psychopathic personality.'

'He went to grammar school. Sammy was strangely proud of that.'

'I imagine some psychopaths do. If I wasn't so traumatised, I'd be very interested in those brothers.' Dr Moon frowned. 'They need a good deal of analysis. I wonder how they feel about their mother.' Dr Moon reached for his pipe. 'What are you going to tell the police?'

'Either I'll lie, or I'll tell them the whole sorry truth. I haven't quite decided yet.' William closed his eyes and remembered the dead. 'The whole sorry truth. Tom and the bank clerk from Stoke deserve nothing less. Christ, even the Reverend Andrews deserves justice. I keep forgetting about that poor bugger.' He opened his eyes and waved his hand towards the sad figure of the dead parson laid out beneath the coats.

'But what is the whole sorry truth?'

'That people are infinitely cruel and strange, and that people are infinitely good and brave.' William placed his feet in the rubber boots. They didn't fit and he wasn't wearing socks. 'You were right about the chain of events. If Phyll hadn't known Queenie, Irwell wouldn't have hidden out here, and Brooke wouldn't have disturbed your patients while looking for the necklace. You wouldn't have suspected an intruder and called in a detective, and Irwell wouldn't have telephoned his brother scared that coppers were sniffing about.' He glanced at the elephant foot umbrella stand, and the unbearable cruelty of the manacled fox tail. 'I'm tired of the gentry. None of this would've happened if they all had proper jobs.'

'Like detecting.'

'Or psychotherapy.'

Dr Moon once more rummaged about the coat stand. Returning with a knitted muffler, he wrapped it around William's neck, pulling the wool up over his cheeks.

'What will the police believe, do you think?'

'The truth as Lady Pike wants it. They'll say Brooke went mad, murdered the Reverend Andrews, killed Tom in some bizarre ritual and then committed suicide. You'll take a lot of the blame, Dr Moon.'

William rose, moving with difficulty over the stone floor in his rubber boots; the ancient mackintosh crackled stiff about his body; the dusty wool irritated his tender cheeks. He was a man ill-prepared for the coming ordeal, he knew, but that seemed to be William's lot in life.

Dr Moon opened the oak door wide, and both men breathed in the wet, early morning air. William squinted out onto the vast expanse of flat black water. Here at Red Hollow, the gloom of night seemed perpetual.

'You seem to have got over your fear of water.'

'Maybe I just know there are worse things to be frightened of.' He paused. 'People, mostly. The outrageous strangeness of human beings never ceases to amaze and terrify me.' He turned to Dr Moon, kicking a sandbag with the toe of his boot, and smiled. 'At least the floodwater didn't get into the house.'

'All down to poor Tom Sherbourne's tenacity and organisational abilities.'

'Will you be alright, Henry?' asked William.

'Yes. There'll be a horrible scandal, of course, but afterwards I shall run away to America. It's a smashing place for a rather ineffectual coward such as me to disappear.'

'You're not a coward, because you are unafraid to be kind. You're not ineffectual, because even in our short, horrific time together, you've taught me a few home truths.'

'Has anyone ever told you that you were good, William?'

'Not many people. Just a woman I once loved.'

'Clara?' asked Dr Moon. 'The woman you spoke about during our peyote session.'

'Yes.'

'Well, Clara was right. You are good. Just try to remember it from time to time.'

'What will you do in America? Farm cacti?'

'Yes, or raise cattle, or run a saloon, or export artistic silver jewellery. The continent is my oyster. Why not come to America with me?'

'You're not the first person to ask me that. But I like the weather here too much to leave.' He turned to the doctor and managed a slight, painful smile. 'Come to Needless Alley before you catch your boat and bring a few cacti. I have just the windowsill for them.'

William stepped across the threshold of Red Hollow Hall and into the dark of night. He did not turn to wave goodbye, but took one heavy step after another, puncturing the stillness of the black water, creating a wake. He slipped on something slimy. Panic punched at him and lasted, bruise-like, step after step, until he felt the hard gravel underfoot. He was tentative, wobbling like a tiny child. His muffler flickered about his face in the breeze; his mackintosh billowed out around him. William felt the cool of the water, and let go, just for a moment, closing his eyes. He was the Ten of Swords; minor arcana; the drowned Phoenician Sailor; but this time, reversed: healing wounds, regeneration, resisting the doom. Sunrise was inevitable, even in the darkest winter, William knew. And soon, he would be home, in Birmingham, with his son. He smiled. 'Forward,' he said.

Epilogue

'God, I'm thirsty.'
'The water at Red Hollow makes everything quick with life. In spring, you can traipse about in all this green and feel that if you were to nap under a tree, you would awaken covered in nettles, bindweed, cleavers.'

Freddy was a Burne-Jones angel. Made from Victorian glass, pale and solemn, and sad.

'The green engulfs you, taking over your flesh, but it wouldn't matter,' said the angel. 'It would simply be the appropriate culmination of life. The dead man would be of use to that vast expanse of brilliant green.'

I know a bank where the wild thyme grows.

'I'm thinking in fragments of poetry,' said William.

'That's perfectly normal,' said the angel. 'I do it almost constantly.'

There was a forest with a fairy-tree. Its twisted limbs, gnarled and aged, had fat mossy holes to put your hand in. Watch, or it might bite your fingers off.

'My dad was a gunmaker,' said William. 'Gunmakers were paid at the Bull. Every Friday, given your pay in a bloody pub. Well, I ask you.'

Near it, a clump of foxgloves, native pink – pink to make the boys wink – and in their spotted hoods, bees hummed. Butterflies, too. Something scurried in the thicket: a flicker of tawny fur.

'I think I need some tea and sympathy,' said William.

'You shall have it, old son. It shall rain down like manna from heaven.'

'Manna is bread. It can't rain bread.'

'Oh, Billy. Why are you such a pedant?' asked the angel. 'Enjoy the beauty of the idiom.'

Rossetti, curled and purring, sat on Dr Moon's lap. The doctor smoked his pipe and fussed the cat's ears. Eyes lowered to slits through the tobacco smoke, Dr Moon smiled like a benign, ancient god, and poured a Tommy's brew from a huge Brown Betty pot.

A few steps beyond the fairy tree, the boys found a pond. Black, and deep enough to bathe in, its mirror-like surface reflected the bordering hart's-tongue ferns and whips of young willow.

Billy sat on a flat rock at the waterside, and felt the stone cool the back of his thighs. The scab on his knee cracked. He glanced at his hands, filthy, nails thick with dirt, threw a stone in the water and called to his best mate, Ronnie Maggs.

'By the time he got to the Gunmakers' Arms, he'd pissed away the rent money,' said William.

'Alcoholism is a disease of the mind, as is all addiction.' Dr Moon's face became huge and golden, like the sunset over the Sierra Nevada.

Food, drink and Veronal, it was just a way of staving off the darkness. That frightful winter black which burrowed deep into your marrow. That creeping, black damp which took over and did no end of harm. What a man needed was warmth and light.

Ronnie dived into the black water. Panic punched at Billy and lasted, bruise-like, until he could see Ronnie's pale body, lithe like a fish in the green, all amongst the weeds. Ronnie rose, glistening, and beckoned to him. Billy stripped down to his drawers, and went in. It was slimy underfoot.

'When I got to about eleven, Mom would ask me to get money off Dad any way I could,' said William. 'I would wait until he was drunk enough to rob, but still had a bit of money left. He'd leave the Bull and head for the Gunmakers' around nine at night. I would wallop him and swipe his pay packet.'

'Father, Father, where are you going? Do not walk so fast,' said the angel. 'I'm speaking mostly in poetry. Do you enjoy Blake?'

'Yes, Freddy. You and William Blake were right all along about everything.'

Once in the water, Ronnie held Billy by both hands, and then moved backwards, pulling Billy along until he was flat on his belly. Ronnie's feet kicked at the red clay beneath him, dispersing it, so it rose as bloody clouds about them both. And then, Ronnie, weightless in the water, turned Billy around, and held him by his underarms.

'One night, he weren't that drunk, and he fought back. It was my first proper fight, the one with my dad. I won. I pushed him in the cut. He didn't surface. I thought I'd killed him.'

'Father, speak to your little boy, or else I shall be lost.' The angel sang William Blake's song. Beautiful, like a robin in a hedgerow. Like a boy soprano. A boy.

'Yes, Freddy. You know. You understand.'

'And did you kill him?' Dr Moon leant over in his seat; teapot poised to pour; Rossetti leapt from his lap at the injustice of the movement. 'Did you murder your father?'

'I need some tea and sympathy, please, Dr Moon.'

Billy lay in Ronnie's arms as they swam. Ronnie's strong legs kicked beneath him, keeping him afloat. The red water went up

Billy's nose, and into his mouth, touched every inch of him. Billy coughed. The water burnt his nostrils, and the back of his mouth, but he did not go under.

He looked up. A man stood at the water's edge, near the stolen crate of jam. The man smiled and waved.

'I told my mom all about it. She hid me in the coal hole. I was there all night. Either way, I hadn't killed the bastard. He came home with the cock-crow, Friday suit all damp and stinking with the canal. He beat me with a shovel, booted me, near killed me. That's when I left. Went off with my best mate Ronnie and his sister Queenie.'

The boys came out of the water, and the man gave them both a cigarette. He sat and smoked with them while they dried off after the swim. He was a rich man, richer than a teacher or a priest, in thick tweeds the colour of Warwickshire clay. The man wore leather-clad binoculars around his red neck. Billy wanted to ask if he could take a peek through them.

'Queenie in the striped pyjamas,' said the angel. 'I thought her quite the dish.'

'The archetypal mother figure.' Dr Moon nodded. 'She keeps a Derringer in her knickers.'

'No, it was her garter belt. What a thrill!' The angel fluttered his great white wings in pleasure. 'Knickers lack the necessary subtlety, Dr Moon.'

'A subtle woman,' said the doctor. 'Would you say dissembling?'

'A mermaid lives in this pool, did you know?' said the rich man. 'I've written a book about it.'

Billy had a book on nature given to him as a Sunday School prize. His only book. Billy knew the name of every tree, and every plant and animal, in the forest. And he knew mermaids didn't exist, whether rich men wrote books about them or not.

William's head swam with visions of symmetry. The scales on a fish. A spider's web. The whirl of a cactus's spines. The sepals of a flower. The excellence of nature. For everything on earth is holy.

'The night was dark, wasn't it, Billy?' said the angel. 'No father was there.'

'No, Freddy. It was a hot August day. Ronnie Maggs was teaching me to swim.'

'You're mad, mister,' said Billy. 'Mermaids don't exist.'

The rich man laughed and shook his head, as if Billy were a stupid boy.

'I'm not a stupid boy, am I, Dr Moon?'

'No, William. You're a very observant fellow, and you can quote Shakespeare.' Dr Moon stirred the tea. One, two, three lumps of sugar spun and dissolved. 'You'll do. You'll do very well indeed.'

'Does your mother know where you are?' asked the rich man.

'Billy's mom is too pissed up to care, fella,' said Ronnie.

Billy flushed in anger, but the rich man nodded, as if he understood the terrible shame of having a pisshead mom.

'The child was wet with dew,' said the angel.

'No, Freddy. We'd dried off by then. It was a hot day, despite the shade of the woods.'

'Would you like to earn a shilling?'

'Each,' Ronnie said, and the man nodded.

Since that day, terror hung heavy and permanent in William's gut, like a tumour.

'The body remembers what the mind cannot face,' said Dr Moon.

Buckthorn, dogwood, blackthorn all to his left. Spines on the whip-like branches, protecting hard purple berries, which gave us kiddies the gut-ache. These were the trees he was used to, trees for the margins. And then there was a touch of warmth, sunlight. Above him was a circling buzzard and to his right a snakeskin. An adder. No, just a slow-worm or a grass snake, probably. Billy had a book on nature given to him as a Sunday School prize.

'The mire was deep, and the child did weep. And away the vapour flew.' Freddy enveloped him in his fragile, glassy wings. 'Gild the cracks, Billy.'

Freddy's eyes swivelled in the back of his head, and then he disappeared.

There was no birdsong. Something made the forest air fizz. Yarrow and self-heal, their heads slumped and broken – necks snapped – the purple and the white withered and rotting. Knowledge was a comfort to Billy.

'I fucking hate the country.'

'You're not in the country anymore,' said Phyll. 'You're home in Needless Alley.'

The windows were wide open, and flimsy curtains quivered in the morning breeze. William blinked at the brutal light. The air in the room was still thick with sleep. Too late in the morning for birdsong, only the rattle of traffic on New Street and the distant hoot of the factory sirens could be heard.

'I had to open a window. It stinks in here.' Phyll was reassuringly city smart: lightweight wool suit in a Windsor check, pale grey; green tie; silver tie pin; a tiny posy of violets in her buttonhole. She smelt of cedarwood and cinnamon.

William sat up in bed. 'You always say that.'

'You're slurring your speech. How many did you take?'

'Veronal?' William glanced at the packet on his bedside table. 'Enough. I'll be alright after coffee. Do you want one?'

'Bathe and dress. In something smart, for God's sake. I'll make the coffee.' Phyll offered him her first smile of the day. 'Shifty has come up trumps, old son. We've got a paying client. She'll be here in an hour.'

William took a deep intake of breath, and then exhaled. 'Forward,' he said.

Acknowledgements

First, I would like to thank The Museum of Witchcraft and Magic, whose wonderful displays inspired much of the magical content of the novel. Secondly, I would like to thank Whitby Museum. I couldn't resist including their remarkable 'Hand of Glory' in my peculiar garret.

As always, I must thank my tireless agent Abi Fellows for all her good work, and the excellent staff of Baskerville, John Murray, for their professionalism and kindness over the past year. Particular thanks must go to Jade Chandler and Zulekhá Afzal for their editorial guidance and help.

Finally, I owe a great deal of gratitude to my husband, Andy: an excellent reader and the cleverest man I know.

About the Author

Natalie Marlow is a historical crime novelist with a fascination for the people and landscapes of the Midlands. Born into a family of storytellers, she takes inspiration from the colourful stories her grandparents told. Her debut novel, *Needless Alley*, starring private detective William Garrett, received glowing reviews from press and readers alike. Natalie holds an MA in Creative Writing from the University of East Anglia and is currently working on the next book in the William Garrett series.